SAGE

ANTHONY MESI

iUniverse LLC
Bloomington

SAGE

iUniverse books may be ordered through booksellers or by contacting:

iUniverse LLC
1663 Liberty Drive
Bloomington, IN 47403
www.iuniverse.com
1-800-Authors (1-800-288-4677)

Because of the dynamic nature of the Internet, any web addresses or links contained in this book may have changed since publication and may no longer be valid. The views expressed in this work are solely those of the author and do not necessarily reflect the views of the publisher, and the publisher hereby disclaims any responsibility for them.

Any people depicted in stock imagery provided by Thinkstock are models, and such images are being used for illustrative purposes only.
Certain stock imagery © Thinkstock.

ISBN: 978-1-4917-1795-0 (sc)
ISBN: 978-1-4917-1797-4 (hc)
ISBN: 978-1-4917-1796-7 (e)

Library of Congress Control Number: 2013922488

Printed in the United States of America.

iUniverse rev. date: 12/17/2013

For Jennifer, Jacob, Emma and Maxwell

CHAPTER 1

Looking back, I have to admit I never saw it coming. Not that it was a complete surprise—I'd been stalked a thousand times before. All I'm saying is it caught me off guard. It always works out like that. Just when I think I've got things figured out, life moves in with a swift uppercut to the jaw and drops me to the mat before I even know what's hit me. Like two years ago when I left quiet little Coventry, Vermont, to start my freshman year of college at Geneseo State.

Geneseo, New York, seemed a thousand miles away from Coventry at first, but the homesickness wore off fast. It didn't take long to figure out that college was a haven. I mean, seriously. Two to three classes each day, beautiful girls everywhere I looked, and no one to answer to other than myself. What wasn't to like about that setup?

My biggest challenge was getting to class on time, and that horrible Monday morning in late October was no exception. After three hits to the snooze button, I sprinted through Erie Hall in yet another last-minute effort to make my eight o'clock class. Something didn't feel right, though.

"What the hell happened to you?" Vince Weegan asked as I flew past, leaving a vapor trail behind.

My stomach had been flip-flopping since I rolled out of bed, but I thought I could keep my inner turmoil hidden from everyone else. Apparently not. I never did have much of a poker face.

I glanced across a busy campus full of heavy-lidded students downing their morning coffee and marching off to class. I tried to convince myself I could will the feeling away and blend in with the crowd. My sweat-drenched forehead suggested otherwise. Then the dreaded voices kicked in—hushed whispers at first. In no time, a multitude of voices swirled around in my head, shouting over each other in a booming chorus of obnoxious noise. I picked up the pace, hoping to outrun them. It didn't work. They only got louder as I made my way up the path toward the College Union.

"Holden," a voice boomed, as if it were right behind me. "Danny Boy!"

I turned to see Rog Dubell flagging me down. What a relief—a voice with a real person attached. "Party at 30 Court Street tonight. You in?" he asked, walking backward in his trademark baggy pants and tilted Yankees cap.

My stomach went sour. "I'll think about it," I said, trying to downplay being seconds away from unloading last night's dinner on anyone or anything that crossed my path.

He rolled his eyes. "What's there to think about? There's gonna be, like, fifty hot girls there, minimum. You don't wanna miss this one."

"All right, all right. I'll let you know."

"It's a no-brainer, dude," he said, taking off toward Newton Hall. I continued on toward the academic buildings when something sharp jabbed the back of my head. A mild burning sensation followed, and within seconds, it was as if someone had twisted a giant corkscrew into the back of my skull and was cranking up the pressure one-quarter turn at a time. I made it to the stairwell leading up to the main quad, but I had to grip the bottom rail for support. My brain was about to split down the middle, and my once churning stomach growled like an angry demon. I dropped onto the bottom steps, holding my head in my hands. What was I going to do? I didn't want to have a total meltdown in front of half the campus, and I sure as hell didn't want to stagger into class in this condition either.

A blurry figure streaked past and disappeared behind Jones Hall. Oh God. My worst fear had come true. *They* were here. The shadow people had followed me all the way to New York. I'd spent eighteen years looking over my shoulder. Now they were on my trail again. I had to get to class—away from them.

I scurried off to Sturgess Hall on sheer willpower and made it to the classroom, only two minutes late. Everyone's eyes were on me as I walked casually toward the back of the room. I knew I looked like crap, my face pale, covered in sweat. But at least the voices were fading away. Eventually, they went silent. I was safe. For now.

That morning was just the beginning. The voices and the head-splitting pain continued for weeks, intensifying with each episode. The throbbing was so excruciating, I begged for death, shutting myself in my room with the shades down, skipping class, and praying for the voices to go away. I'd been down this road before, but it had never been like this. My tormentors had taken things to a whole new level.

Then there was the stalking. The shadow people were everywhere. Things became so bad I couldn't leave my room for more than a few minutes without sensing them, feeling them.

They lurked behind corners and ducked behind trees as I turned to see them. Why wouldn't they just leave me alone and let me live a normal life for once? What was so fascinating about me anyway? I kept wondering... could others read my mind? Could they see the fear in my face? Did they know how completely insane I was becoming? I carried on as best I could, but I wondered how much longer it would be until I reached the breaking point.

The answer arrived one miserable, overcast morning in early November. My morning shower came courtesy of an ominous gray sky that decided to open up and unload while I was on the way to my least favorite class—introduction to psychology. Alison, my foster mom, had always ragged on me for never carrying an umbrella. But c'mon. What kind of guy carries an umbrella? I thought this over as I took my seat near the back of the classroom, drip-drying all over Professor Urban's floor. The old prof droned on and on about the significance of Abraham Maslow's "hierarchy of needs" in his typical dead-man-talking monotone. While the rest of the class clung to his every word, the only sound registering in my brain was that of my own fingertips galloping mindlessly across the desktop.

"Daniel," a soft voice called out from behind me. I turned around and found myself face-to-face with the hottest girl in the class. She stared back with this dumb-struck expression that screamed, *What the hell are you looking at?* Spinning back around, I slithered down in my seat.

"Daniel." There it was again. A horrible high-pitched shriek pierced my eardrums. Professor Urban's lips moved, but I couldn't hear a thing he said. I only heard garbled voices and that horrendous ringing sound bouncing back and forth inside my head like a rubber ball.

I saw something through the window. Someone ducked behind the sagging pine tree in front of Frasier Library. The throbbing returned. Sweat beaded on my forehead as the room spun faster... faster... everything blurring past as if I was looking out the window of a speeding train. My chest heaved like I'd just run a quarter mile at full sprint. People had to be staring at me. I could picture the stunned looks on their faces as they wondered what my next move would be. I wiped my sweaty brow and pushed back dripping hair in a pathetic attempt to be casual. My vision cleared.

Then an intense wave of nausea kicked in. "Ouugh," I blurted out.

Professor Urban's lips stopped moving. Now I had everyone's attention.

I tried to cover up my outburst with a few fake coughs. "Sorry," I apologized. "I'll be all right."

I was pretty damn far from all right, and anyone with a working set of eyeballs could see that. The muscles in my stomach tensed. The last thing I wanted was to lose my breakfast in the middle of psych class, but I didn't know how much longer I could hold back. I was on fire, burning from the inside out.

The voices weren't whispering anymore. They crashed inside my skull with the most God-awful, nails-on-chalkboard screeching sound I'd ever heard. I wanted to scream, cry, bash my head against the desk—anything to make them stop. Then, just like that, they did. The voices were gone. My stomach was still. I could hear again. But for how long?

I couldn't face another day of this torture, but I knew it wouldn't go away on its own. It would only intensify. I had to do something. This had to stop. Everything became crystal clear in my mind at that moment, as if I'd climbed out of a dark tomb and finally saw the light of day. I knew how to put an end to this madness once and for all. Leaving my books on the desk, I walked out of Professor Urban's class and strode down the empty corridor of Sturgess Hall. My college career was over, as far as I was concerned. I stepped outside into the crisp autumn air, strangely empowered. A lifetime of suffering was about to come to an abrupt and decisive end.

CHAPTER 2

The car ride to the Upper Falls parking lot at Letchworth State Park probably took thirty minutes, but it felt more like thirty seconds. The lot was empty when I pulled in, just as I'd hoped. An old trestle bridge towered in the distance, a mountain of iron and steel. I'd visited this scenic spot several times already, even though I'd only been in Geneseo for a couple months. Standing on those elevated train tracks and looking down at the waterfall two hundred feet below liberated me. Everything seemed so perfect up there, as if nothing could hurt me. I'd loved that place from the first moment I saw it.

I stepped out of the car and drank in the natural beauty of the park. It would be the last time. For one brief, beautiful moment, I was at peace.

It didn't last.

The voices returned with another chorus of garbled whispers, soon escalating to unbearable shouting. I pushed my palms against the sides of my head, desperate to relieve the pressure. It was useless. The shouting became an obnoxious clatter, haunting me from within, gauging at my sanity. The ground spun. My stomach churned.

Something rustled nearby. I turned around only to see a pile of dried-out leaves hitching a ride on the latest gust of wind.

The voices fell silent.

It was over—except for the aftershock.

I braced myself against the warm hood of my Honda Civic as a cream cheese bagel made its way up my esophagus and emptied out onto the blacktop. My throat burned from the acid.

No more. I couldn't take another minute of this. I needed to put an end to this torture forever and finish what I'd started.

A stone stairway led up the tall bank of the gorge and ended at the foot of the trestle bridge. I wasted no time. As I ascended, thoughts of my family back in Coventry flashed through my mind. How would Ted and Alison react when they learned what I'd done? They'd been so good to me. No one had forced them to take in a scatterbrained twelve-year-old with a hefty dose of baggage and an endless supply of smart-ass attitude. They already had their hands full with their other foster kids, Kevin and Riley. This was so unfair to them. The Davis clan was the only stable family I had ever known, and this was how I was repaying them. The least I could have done was say good-bye.

I had to let it go. No one would understand. No one *could* understand. They'd forever ask why, but nothing could explain the relentless torture I'd been living with. I had to stop second-guessing myself. It was time to end the suffering.

I stepped out onto the bridge and felt instant peace with my decision. The view of the gorge below looked even more amazing than I remembered from my last trip to the park. Orange- and yellow-leafed trees swayed in the gentle breeze. Tiny streams flowed from the moss-covered cliffs, cascading to the river below.

Meantime, the roar of the waterfall lured me, challenged me to take that ultimate leap.

I ducked under the guardrail and positioned my feet on the edge of the overhanging train tracks. Nothing stood between me and my destiny now. For some strange reason, thoughts of my biological mother raced through my mind. I pulled out the Celtic cross necklace from beneath my shirt. It was the only reminder I had of a mother I'd never even met.

I rubbed the trusty crucifix between my right thumb and forefinger, trying to work up the courage to release my left hand from the rail. The waterfall rumbled its thunderous encouragement. One quick release of the hand and my agony would be over. Freedom was a short step away.

Off to the left, I spotted a huge black crow coming straight toward me. It seemed to focus in on me as it circled around and around just above my head. I locked eyes with it as a strong gust of wind slapped against my back, throwing me off balance. My grip on the bar loosened as the necklace snapped in my other hand, slipping from my grasp. I lurched forward to catch it, but lost my grip on the rail. My arms flailed, but I wasn't ready to fall. Not yet.

Somehow, I'd managed to clamp my hands around the edge of the railroad track as I fell from the ledge. I dangled there, gasping for breath. My entire body went rigid as my fingers slid toward the outer edge of the wooden supports. What had I done? I wasn't ready to die. I'd give anything for another chance. Anything!

Seconds remained before my strength would give out. Straining with all my might, I gouged my fingernails into the wood. My forearms burned. My wrists straightened as I slid toward the edge of the tracks. Pain radiated throughout my arms and shoulders.

The Celtic cross teetered on the edge of the bridge, inches from my hand. It hadn't gone over after all. I fought against the tireless pull of gravity, but I was losing the battle. *This is how it ends*, I thought. I closed my eyes and prepared for the inevitable.

Something tightened around my wrists, and suddenly I was traveling upward with great force. I came down face-first on the railroad tracks, knocked senseless on impact. The stars gradually faded, and my eyesight returned. Something wet flowed from my nostrils, and the bitter taste of blood coated the back of my throat.

What had just happened? I lifted my throbbing head from the cold train tracks and looked around. Not a soul. Rising to my knees, I spotted the cross, still teetering on the edge of the bridge. I scooped it up and clutched it tightly. The black crow reappeared for a moment, circled above me, and flew off again without a sound. I made my way across the bridge to solid ground and never looked back. I was alive. I wasn't sure how or why, but it didn't really matter. I was alive. It felt damn good.

CHAPTER 3

Climbing the steps to the third floor of Erie Hall usually required minimal effort, but not that day. I was winded halfway up the second flight of stairs. It couldn't have been much later than noon, but it may as well have been midnight. The emotional roller coaster of the last few hours had taken its toll.

"Tough morning, Danny Boy?" Chris Tarski asked as we passed in the walkway. "You look like shit."

"Feel like shit. Thanks for noticing, 'ski," I said, continuing on to my floor.

The dorm was practically empty, which was pretty typical for the middle of the day. The lingering smell of microwave popcorn greeted me before I reached my suite. My stomach grumbled, a not-so-gentle reminder that I needed sustenance. I was too spent to even care. After what I'd just been through, all I wanted to do was enter my room and shut out the world. I collapsed onto the bed still wearing my coat.

It wasn't long before I found myself in familiar territory, walking along a well-worn path, winding my way through a barren forest. It was late autumn, and the towering trees stretched their naked limbs toward a darkening sky. A cool wind chilled the back of my neck, reminding me once again of my chronic inability to dress for the weather. The forest seemed familiar, but I couldn't shake the feeling that I'd wandered into something unknown, something unpleasant.

I strained my eyes to see the path ahead. The setting sun was already half-hidden on the horizon, and the trees cast long shadows across a wooded landscape. I wove my way around another bend, and then I stopped in place. The crow from the bridge sat perched on a rotting branch of a dead tree. He stared at me. Through me. His eyes were empty black holes. I couldn't resist their mesmerizing pull. Without warning, he flew off, soaring high above the treetops. I raced across the weeds and shrubs, unable to stop myself from chasing him. I was nearly out of breath when I realized there was no use continuing. I'd lost him completely, and I'd lost my way in this forest. I'd run right off the trail in a mindless pursuit of a stupid bird. Now what?

I searched for the path, but the shadows had taken over; the sun had deserted me. I was lost. Cold.

I was being watched again. My senses sharpened in response. The entire forest came alive, moving and breathing. A loud noise crackled behind me. I caught a passing glimpse of a shadow as it disappeared behind a giant tree. Something drew me toward it, pushing me forward against my judgment. I tried to resist, but my body took over. Whatever drove me toward that tree was way too powerful to fight. I sensed something dark, something dangerous, but my legs wouldn't stop moving forward.

My shallow breathing accelerated as my pulse pounded harder with each step. I was almost there. The butterflies in my stomach morphed into dragonflies, churning mild anxiety into pure adrenalized fear. I was so close to the tree trunk, I could almost touch it. Then I stumbled over a massive root bulging up through the soil and felt the tingling sensation of a thousand spider legs scampering across my clammy skin. No more. I couldn't. I wouldn't… but I *had* to look behind that tree. There was no use trying to hide. The shadow figure sensed me. It heard my rapid breathing and the dry leaves that crunched below my feet. I tried to turn back, but my feet refused to obey. Then I heard a horrible squawk from that hideous crow perched on a limb, two feet above my head. I looked up into those dark, infinite eyes. What I saw froze my veins and sent a shiver through my entire body.

Everything faded to black.

I awoke to the familiar feeling of a moist pillowcase below my sweat-covered head. There was no reason to be so rattled. I'd been through this dream sequence plenty of times before. Still, this was the furthest I'd ever gone. I'd never actually made it all the way to the tree in earlier dreams. This was real progress.

Yeah, right. Progress. My subconscious mind prodded me with haunting dreams while my conscious hours were spent wrestling with paranoia—not exactly what most people would call progress.

CHAPTER 4

College was just a memory now, and the days all blurred together. With no classes or job to go to, life felt meaningless. Since my fateful trip to the bridge a week earlier, I'd done little more than eat and sleep. If I felt up to it, I'd hang out with my floor mates, but most days I didn't feel like doing much of anything. Instead, I retreated more and more into my room. At least the voices had died down. The stalking was still a daily reality, but I had to admit, nowhere near as bad as before. So why did I still feel like crawling into a hole most days?

My prospects for the future looked dimmer by the day. Once the semester grades went out, my living arrangement in the dorm would be a thing of the past. I still hadn't worked up the nerve to break the news to my parents. I could only imagine their reaction. They'd never get over it. The thought of hurting Ted and Alison, the only people who ever gave a damn about me in this world, made me want to hurl.

The calendar on the wall displayed Thursday. My alarm clock reported noon. If it weren't for the grumble in my stomach, I would have pulled the sheet over my head and escaped into dreamland for another six hours. Sleep was the only thing I could get motivated to do. Life had become monotonous—an endless cycle of eat, sleep, shower, and stare out the window. I knew something had to change. I couldn't go on like this. I was flying faster and faster toward a giant black hole, but I had no clue how to change my trajectory.

My stomach grumbled again. I needed food but wasn't up to the whole dining hall scene, and I didn't feel much like making a run uptown to Wegmans for groceries either. A quick walk up to the sandwich shop on Main Street sounded like a good compromise. Showering would have to wait, but the severe case of bedhead had to be dealt with now. I threw on a baseball cap and made it out of the dorm unnoticed.

About halfway across campus, Dan Domino and Chris Daley from Erie Hall rounded the corner of the Bailey Science Building. I guessed they'd just finished class and were heading uptown to grab some grub themselves. I glanced around quickly for a place to hide and found a good spot behind a fence. I couldn't face them. I couldn't face anyone.

I wiped the sweat off my upper lip with the collar of my shirt. How had I gotten to this point? I had been the big scholarship winner in my high school with the killer SAT scores and the golden future at his fingertips. Now I was dropping out of college, hanging from bridges, and hiding from my friends. Impressive.

Dan and Chris strolled past me, deep in conversation. I let out a sigh and decided to go through the KFC drive-through instead—there was less chance of running into anyone there. I left my post behind the fence and walked toward the parking lot and my car. A yellow flyer fluttered on the light pole in front of it. I drew in for a closer look.

Looking to turn your life around? Waiting for that perfect opportunity to fall into your lap? Look no more—Full-Time Opportunity: GENERAL CONTRACTOR'S ASSISTANT— No prior experience necessary. Contact Jo @ 243-4386.

I rubbed my eyes, sure I was seeing things. Could this be real? It was like a sign from above. Considering my current academic and employment status, it was definitely worth looking into. I wasn't even sure what a contractor's assistant did, but I had to give this a shot, if for no other reason than it gave me a reason to get up in the morning.

I plopped down into the driver's seat and wasted no time punching the number into my cell phone. It couldn't have been more than forty degrees outside, but the air inside the car was stale and stuffy. I opened the windows. The phone rang at least twenty times, but there was no voice message. I was about to hang up when a deep baritone voice greeted me.

"Hello."

For some reason, that one word sent shivers down my spine. I felt nervous, unsure of myself. That voice sounded like it came from a guy who had his shit together. There wasn't a chance in hell he'd want to hire a clown like me, who couldn't even get through one semester of college.

"Uh, hi… this is, uh, Dan… or Daniel, I mean. I'm calling about the assistant contractor general… I mean, the general contractor's assistant posting… flyer?" Great. I was already making a complete jackass out of myself.

"Do you have transportation?" the voice asked in an impossibly deep, penetrating tone.

"I have a car, yes." I crossed my fingers and waited for a response. The pause seemed to endure for minutes.

"You can stop by for an interview at six tonight—2242 Reservoir Road." Click. Dial tone.

Okay, so this Jo apparently wasn't the most talkative guy in town. I could deal with the quiet type. I could deal with just about any type right now, since my dorm arrangement had almost run its course and I desperately needed a job if I was ever going to be able to afford an apartment. I'd already made up my mind that I wasn't going back home to Coventry with my tail between my legs. I needed to stay put for the time being and at least try to stand on my own two feet.

When five thirty rolled around, I figured I should print off the MapQuest directions and head out early. With my track record of getting lost, leaving early and bringing directions was pretty much standard protocol. As I pulled out onto Route 20A, I looked down at the passenger seat and realized I'd left my cell phone back at the dorm.

"Figures," I muttered. "I'd forget my head if it wasn't attached." At least I had the directions and more than enough time. About five minutes down the road, I noticed a strange sputtering coming from under the hood. It got louder with each passing second. I glanced at the dashboard. Shit. The engine light was on.

"No! Not now. Can't you wait until after the interview to crap out on me?"

The Civic answered with a steady flow of black smoke belching out from under its hood. "I don't friggin' believe this! Of all the luck."

I pulled over to the side of the road and propped open the hood. I wasn't sure what I thought I'd find, since I didn't know the first thing about cars. Sure enough, I didn't have a clue what was wrong with the old clunker.

This couldn't be happening. My one chance to turn my life around—sabotaged by my own car. Part of me wanted to forget the whole thing and just walk back to Erie Hall. No. That wasn't an option. I wasn't going to spend the rest of my life hiding in a room with the shades down and the sheets pulled up over my head. It was now or never, and I was determined to get my sorry ass over to that interview, even if I had to crawl there on my hands and knees.

I'd have to put it in high gear, though, if I was going to show up anywhere near six o'clock. With no cell phone, I couldn't call Jo to tell him I'd be late. I'd just have to wing it and hope he'd understand. Then I'd have to beg him for a ride home—nothing like making a good first impression.

The road ahead was a straight shot uphill as far as I could see. After that, the directions showed a crossroad and a right turn onto Reservoir Road. At this rate, though, I'd be lucky if I made it by nine o'clock. I kicked the front bumper of the Civic in frustration, nearly breaking my big toe. Then I noticed a small figure coming toward me from the top of the hill. As he trudged closer, I could swear he was at least ninety years old. He was all bent over with spotted, wrinkled leather for skin. I had to give the old-timer credit though—no walker, no cane, and still cruising the back roads all by himself.

"Excuse me, sir." I approached, waving my MapQuest directions. "I'm trying to get to 2242 Reservoir Road, and my directions show a crossroad coming up. Can you tell me if I'm going the right way?"

"Twenty-two, forty-two." He took the paper from me and nodded, holding the directions an arm's length away. "Twenty-two, forty-two," he repeated, continuing to nod. "Sure, I know it—know right where it is. If you don't mind my asking, what business would you have at that place?" He looked me up and down.

"I've got a job interview."

"A job interview, huh?" The wrinkled grooves across his forehead converged into an accordion of suspicion. "If you say so. You're not going to walk there, are you?"

"Actually, my car just died, so, yeah, I'm going to have to hoof it."

He gave me another strange look, as if he wasn't quite sure what to make of me or my story. "Any idea how much farther I've got to go?" I asked.

The old man nodded again, staring off toward a wooded area set back from the road. "That depends on whether you take the shortcut or not. You stay on these roads here, and you won't get there for another hour or so." He pointed toward the trees, straining his tired eyes on the not-so-distant horizon. "Go through these woods here, and you can make it in twenty minutes—long as you stay on the path."

"And where would I find this path?" I searched for a break in the tree line.

"Just to the left of that big oak tree there." I followed the trajectory of his crooked index finger. "Stay on that path there, and you'll run right into it. Can't miss it. It's the only home in those woods, far as I know."

"Guess I'd better get moving," I said, already moving toward the trees. "Thanks for your help."

"Don't mention it," he said, still eyeing me with uncertainty. "Just hope you know what you're getting yourself into."

CHAPTER 5

"Twenty minutes," I said between huffs. "Twenty minutes gets me there on time." The oak tree wasn't as close as it looked from the road. After a few minutes of nonstop running, I had to stop in the tall grass to catch my breath. When I finally made it to the big tree, I was completely winded. A narrow walking path was visible between the overgrown crabgrass and tall weeds, right where the old man had said. Peering over my shoulder, I checked to see how much sunlight was left before committing to the unknown. It was late November. The days were much shorter now, and it was already getting dim. The horizon was lit up in an awesome display of pink and orange brushstrokes. It made for a picture-perfect sunset.

"Better keep moving," I said. The gray autumn landscape formed a bold contrast against the colorful evening skyline. Barren or not, these woods had a timeless quality that seemed to cast a spell over me. There was something familiar here. It was as if I knew what was around each twist and turn of the path before I even got there.

After crossing a shallow creek, the trail climbed upward toward higher ground, revealing another stretch of seemingly endless trees. I darted along the path and was making pretty good time. But then I heard a rustling noise in the trees above, and I stopped to glance upward. There in front of me sat a giant black crow, perched on the rotting leftovers of a decrepit old tree. All sense of confidence vanished. The creature glared back, his eyes even darker than I remembered from my dreams. If I wasn't such a skeptic, I'd swear this was the same crow I had seen up on that trestle bridge.

"Coincidence," I muttered to myself as a chill crept up my back. The mysterious bird flew off, soaring high over the naked forest. Then I was chasing after him at full sprint. No matter how fast I ran, he put more distance between us. I continued to chase him anyway, until a face full of low-hanging tree branches stopped me in my tracks.

It was useless. He was out of sight in twenty seconds flat. What I couldn't figure out was why I felt the need to chase this stupid bird in the first place.

And now I'd lost the main path. I stood smack in the middle of nowhere. The dying rays of the setting sun had no chance of penetrating this deeply into the forest. I was cloaked in darkness, no exit strategy in sight.

"Now what am I supposed to do?"

A crackle sounded behind me. I whirled around, my heart pounding in my chest. Something blurred by and disappeared behind a tree with branches so massive, they challenged the trunk for dominance. Thick, veiny roots bulged up through the ground.

I approached the tree. Even with heightened senses, I barely avoided taking a major digger when my foot snagged on something in the soil. I glanced up, expecting my old feathered friend to meet me with that horrible squawk. The crow was nowhere to be found. The only sounds penetrating the eerie stillness were my half-muffled breathing and the crunch of dry leaves beneath my feet.

As I approached the tree trunk, that old, familiar souring in my stomach returned. Something was behind that tree. I couldn't see it, couldn't hear it, but I could feel it. My legs moved forward even as my mind screamed, "Turn back!" I felt trapped in my own nightmare, unable to stop this momentum. My face was just inches from the twisted, knotted bark, but still I couldn't hear a sound. I knew I had to find out what lurked behind that tree, even though fear threatened to suffocate me. Pushing forward with all the courage I could manage, I peered around the other side of the trunk. Nothing.

"Nothing?" I asked in disbelief.

A deep voice pierced the quiet evening air. "What is it you seek?"

I reeled back and came face-to-face with a hooded figure. Every hair on my body stood straight up.

"I... didn't... see you there," I squeaked.

The dark figure moved closer. "What is it you seek?"

"I'm, uh, lost, I guess. I went off the trail, and now I can't find…"

"Your destination?" he interrupted.

"I'm supposed to meet someone named Jo on Reservoir Road. I was cutting through these woods. My car broke down."

"You're in luck." The figure lowered his hood and held out his hand. His piercing hazel eyes practically glowed in the dim twilight. His face was capped with a tight beard that completed the just-got-back-from-Hades look. "I'm Josiah—Jo, for short. You must be Daniel, here for the interview."

I shook his hand. "I am." This was definitely the same penetrating voice I had heard on the phone earlier.

He nodded toward a path. "Follow me."

We walked in silence until I felt the need to say something, anything, to break the ice. "So I assume you haven't found your contractor's assistant yet?" I cringed immediately at this pathetic attempt at small talk.

"And why do you assume that?" he asked.

"I guess I figured… Hey, wait a minute." I changed course. "Why would you be here in the woods if you're expecting to meet me at your house? How'd you know I'd be here?"

He stopped walking and focused his insanely bright eyes on mine. For a brief moment, I felt as if I'd just come face-to-face with a startled mountain lion. My knees nearly buckled. Those eyes were unsettling. They had a wild intensity that made me wonder if he wasn't a secret serial killer, leading me off to certain death. After a few more uncomfortable seconds, he cracked a partial smile.

"I followed my intuition." He started down the path again, and I hurried to keep up with him.

We continued along in silence until we finally approached a clearing. In the fading twilight, I saw what looked like a log cabin through the trees. Why a person would build a home in the middle of nowhere was anyone's guess.

He pointed toward a faint light in the distance. "Straight ahead."

A porch light guided us along as we left the woods and made our way toward the side yard. We were about fifty yards from the house when an explosive howl pierced the evening air, sending me back on my heels. Josiah didn't flinch. A giant wolf sprinted toward us, growling and gnashing its teeth. I prepared to head for the nearest tree. Josiah raised his hand above his head, and the creature slowed to a trot. It stared me down with distrusting eyes, still growling suspiciously as it approached.

"Easy, Randall," Josiah said to the beast. "This is Daniel. He's with us now." The beast wagged its massive tail and rose up on its hind legs to lick Josiah's face. Oh my God, was this thing gigantic. It was at least a foot taller than its master when standing in this position, and Josiah was well over least six feet tall.

"Is this your, uh… dog?" I asked.

"My one and only." He leaned forward and scratched the massive creature's back.

"This is the biggest dog I've ever seen! What breed is it?"

"Irish wolfhound," he said. "One of the biggest in the world."

"*One* of the biggest? He looks more like a small horse."

"Eats like one too." Josiah smiled again with fatherly pride.

"Great watchdog. There's none better." Randall returned to his guard position on the front porch, and Josiah led me into the house.

"You can have a seat at the table. I'll be right back." He disappeared into a side room.

I looked around the small but comfortable home. An amazing display of history surrounded me. The walls were covered with the most interesting collection of items I'd ever seen, outside of a museum. An old stacked-stone fireplace took up most of the center wall across from me. Ancient swords, helmets, shields, battle-axes, and other weapons were mounted around its mantle. Another wall held a series of shelves displaying dozens of pewter and silver-plated drinking glasses, along with revolvers, muskets, muzzle-loaders, and other collectibles. The opposite wall looked like a shrine to ancient Egypt: four-foot statues of Egyptian gods, partially displayed scrolls written in hieroglyphics, and something that looked like a golden staff with a cobra head for a handle.

Josiah emerged from the side room with a small wooden chest in his hands and set it down on the table next to me. He offered me a drink, which, after all that running, I was glad to accept. I gulped it down like a thirsty horse while looking him over. Seeing Josiah in normal lighting only highlighted the intensity of his appearance. Again, I couldn't help but notice the eyes. I'd been told on more than one occasion that I had the deepest hazel eyes anyone had ever seen. The people who said this had clearly never met Josiah. They were the same deep hazel color as mine, but there was something about them that seemed almost alien. It was like looking into a kaleidoscope of mesmerizing shapes and colors. I tried making eye contact at one point, but looking directly into those eyes was as difficult as staring into the sun. After a few seconds, you just *had* to look away.

"So, Daniel, tell me why you're here." He casually lifted his own glass for a sip. I thought this was a weird way to start off an interview, but, then again, so much about this guy was weird.

"I believe I'm here to interview for a job," I said, trying not to sound insulting.

"I suppose that's one way of putting it." He looked me up and down. "Your mission will be similar to a job—an all-consuming, never-ending job."

Well, that cleared things up. I almost laughed.

"My mission? I'm not sure I understand. Aren't you looking for an assistant?"

"I am, but you'll be much more than an assistant."

"How can you know what I'll be when you don't know anything about me yet?" I asked.

"I know everything about you, Daniel Holden." He leaned back.

"Wait a minute. How do you know my last name? I never told you my last name on the phone."

"You're Daniel James Holden. Born in Buffalo, New York, on May 16, eighteen and a half years ago, give or take. Your mother was Heather Holden. She died shortly after your birth."

He'd been researching me. This was getting creepy. "What are you, CIA or something?"

"Calm down, Daniel. I'm not with the CIA," he said in a calm, almost soothing voice. "I've been watching over you since you were born. Before you were born, if you must know the truth. I watched over your mother as well, leading up to your birth."

"What the hell is going on here?" I asked, rising from my seat. "I don't believe a word of this. Why would anyone want to follow my mother or me? I'm a nobody." I'd had just about enough by now, and I probably would have walked right out the door if I hadn't been smack in the middle of nowhere, with no clue how to get home.

Josiah slammed his drink down on the table and stared right through me with his mystical eyes. "That is most certainly not the case." The power in his voice and the intensity in his eyes sent me back to my chair like a frightened little schoolboy at the principal's office.

He softened his tone. "You're very much a *somebody...* somebody whose arrival has been highly anticipated for a very long time."

"The more you speak, the less sense you make." I gripped the bottom of the smooth wooden chair, trying to summon up enough courage to continue. "I want to know who you are and why you lured me here."

Josiah nodded slowly, as if he had been expecting me to ask this. He removed a necklace from around his neck and laid it out on the table. "*This* is why you're here."

My body went still. Staring back at me was an exact replica of the Celtic cross I'd worn around my own neck for most of my life. I took off my cross and placed it next to his. A perfect match.

CHAPTER 6

Who was this guy anyway? And where did he come off talking about my mother?

"This is some kind of trick," I said, trying my best to keep the old temper in check. "You went through my room when I was out. How else would you know all these things about me?"

"Is that how you think I acquired this?" he asked, picking up the cross from the table. "Do you normally keep a spare lying around?"

He had a point. "Well, then how *did* you get it?" I asked, softening my tone. All I wanted was answers. For once in my life, I wanted someone to shine a light through the perpetual fog that clouded my past.

"You want the truth?" he asked.

I rolled my eyes in frustration. "Of course."

Josiah picked up my cross from the table, examining it in his outstretched hand. "I doubt that you're ready to hear it, but I'll tell you the God's honest truth. I made both of these crosses many years ago, long before you or your mother were born. They were the only two cast from that mold." He continued staring at the cross, examining its every detail. Something about the way his eyes glimmered told me he was drifting off into the deep recesses of a distant memory.

He continued. "I held on to them until I was informed of your mother's pregnancy. For several months I watched over her, waiting for the right time to approach. She was quite young, probably seventeen or so, and on her own. One warm evening in April, she took a long walk by herself. Daylight was fading fast, so I had to keep a closer watch than usual. She must have been about eight months pregnant at the time." He traced the outer edge of the cross with his index finger. "Then she wandered up the steps of St. Bonaventure Church and walked in. When I entered, I found her alone, staring at the crucified savior high above the altar. I tried to approach quietly, but every footstep echoed off the walls. I startled her. The poor girl was trembling."

"Maybe she thought you were stalking her," I said, trying not to sound too insulting.

Josiah shook his head. "It wasn't me she feared. She was just a kid. A teenager, really. Not ready to be a mother." He shut his eyes. "I handed her the cross and told her to keep it close at all times. She tried to decline, of course, but I insisted." He opened his eyes again and settled them in on me. "I could tell from her aura she didn't have much time left."

"Hold on," I interrupted. "What was that? What do you mean, you could tell from her aura?"

He leaned in close, like he was ready to share a secret. "Every person has an aura, Daniel. The aura surrounds your physical body, a perfect reflection of your spirit and a reliable indicator of your emotional and physical health. Very few can see auras, but I've been able to for most of my life."

"Can you see my aura right now?" I asked.

"Couldn't miss it if I tried," he said. "It's easily the most unique aura I've ever seen."

This was a lot to digest, but as crazy as it sounded, something told me Josiah was telling the truth. "What about my mother's aura?"

"Heather's had faded considerably for one so young." He made brief eye contact before looking down at the table. "It was obvious even then. Her time was running out."

I felt a lump in my throat as my eyes welled up with tears. I'd never met my mother, but I always felt a deep sense of loss when I thought of what could have been... what should have been. She was the one person in this world who'd never let me down. Maybe she just never got the chance. It didn't matter to me. For whatever reason, I missed her.

"Why didn't you warn her?" I asked.

Josiah shook his head. "I couldn't read that far into it. I didn't know the time, the place, or the means of her passing... only that it would occur in the not-so-distant future. Besides, I didn't see the point in warning her about something she'd have no ability to understand and no power to correct. My job was to ensure *your* safe passage into the world."

"I still don't understand," I said. "What could possibly be so important about me? I'm a college dropout who can't even hold down a part-time job at a—"

"Pizzeria?" He finished my sentence.

I squirmed, completely creeped out. I had tried to earn some extra money delivering pizza back in October, but it hadn't worked out. The nervous breakdown made it impossible to show up for my shift most of the time. Who could blame them for giving me the boot?

"You know about that too. Is there anything you *don't* know about me?" I asked.

Josiah stared back, expressionless.

"Look, I'm impressed by your investigative skills. You know an awful lot about me, but something doesn't make sense here. I don't know who you are or what kind of game you're playing, but you sure as hell aren't a general contractor looking for an assistant. So unless you're planning on using one of those battle-axes on me, I'd appreciate it if you would take me home. I've had enough for one night."

"I'll take you back to Erie Hall," he said, with a confident look on his face. "But first, there's something we need to do." Josiah cracked open the lid to the small wooden chest sitting on the table beside us. "I was hoping we wouldn't have to resort to this, but it appears there's no other way."

He had my full attention. I wasn't sure if I might have to make a break for the door. Who knew what was in that little treasure chest of his? Maybe he really was a serial killer and was about to introduce me to his torture tools. How would I meet my end? A knife? A gun? Strangulation cord? Considering how strange this evening had already been, I wasn't taking any chances.

Josiah reached inside the chest and pulled out a cast iron plate with fancy patterns carved into the outer rim. Next, he withdrew a plain ceramic cork-topped vase. He opened it, tipped it on to the plate, and poured out a black powdery substance. I watched, puzzled, as he reached back into the chest and pulled out a small glass vial containing bright blue liquid. He removed the stopper and tilted the vial slightly, so that only three or four drops fell into the black powder. After a few seconds, the powder on the plate reacted with the liquid, hissing as tiny bubbles appeared on its surface. Wispy pillars of thick green smoke rose from the surface.

"So we're gonna have a séance now?" I asked, trying to figure out what he was up to. Ignoring me, he placed two tall candles strategically on either side of the plate and lit them. He was so careful and precise with his movements, you'd think he was dismantling a bomb.

"Okay, we *are* going to have a séance now," I said, hoping that was all he had in mind. I glanced over at the door to make sure it wasn't bolted shut. If I needed to make a break for it, I didn't want anything slowing me down. I'd never be able to overpower this guy, but I might be able to outrun him.

"Behind you is a light switch. Flip it off," he said. "Daniel, I want you to place your hands on either side of the plate and apply light pressure. Focus your eyes on the smoke."

I hesitated. Following orders from some whacked out, hazel-eyed hermit I'd met in the forest didn't sound like the greatest idea in the world to me. Not to mention I had no clue what kind of weird black magic this guy might be into.

Josiah placed his hand on my shoulder and stared into my eyes. His entire body went still. "Daniel, you need to trust me. Do as I say."

I made the mistake of looking directly into his eyes. His pupils dilated bigger and faster than any eyes I'd ever seen before. It was as if his entire eyeballs turned black. I was hypnotized in seconds. Disoriented, I found my hands cradling the silver plate, with no memory of ever having placed them there. I became aware of a strange tingling sensation traveling up my left arm, through my chest, and back down my right arm. A continuous circuit of static energy glued me to the plate. I tried pulling back but couldn't. I literally *couldn't* let go. Some invisible force held me to this plate like a powerful magnet.

"Don't resist… and try to relax," he whispered. "It's tuning in to your vibrational patterns now. We'll get a much better reading if you remain calm."

The fog above the surface rotated, accelerating into a miniature twister, gaining speed with each passing second. My skin tingled as an invisible current coursed through me. Then, just as the whirlwind seemed to reach its peak, the funnel unraveled and settled into complete stillness.

"Focus on the surface," he whispered.

As I stared at the powder, my eyes clouded up and I felt hot and dizzy. Maybe Josiah had slipped something into the drink I'd guzzled.

Something was happening just above the surface of the powder. A beautiful young girl materialized like a holographic image, only much more real. Pregnant and rubbing her belly, she looked to be about my age, maybe younger. Her eyes were downcast; her lower lip quivered.

This was crazy. It couldn't be. I shut my eyes and opened them again. I wasn't hallucinating. The image was so real, so lifelike, I felt as if I could reach out and touch her. Then I noticed something that just about dropped me to the floor. The young girl wore a Celtic cross necklace exactly like mine. Even though I'd never seen a picture of her, I knew this was Heather Holden, my birth mother. She looked just as I'd always imagined she would.

A thumping echoed in the background. I couldn't quite make it out at first, but it reminded me of a heartbeat. Lub-dub, lub-dub, lub-dub. As the noise rang louder, a muffled voice mumbled. The heartbeat drowned out most of it, but it was definitely a female voice, and it sounded familiar.

The scene changed. I saw Heather again, only this time she was writhing in pain on her back. The heartbeat grew louder, faster, but then a chorus of distressed voices blocked out all other sound. A dull pressure, a squeezing sensation, compressed my head, shoulders, and ribs. I began to have trouble breathing. The voices grew louder. Blood stained the white sheets, as doctors and nurses scurried around Heather, their faces pale, their movements practiced. Something was terribly wrong. The pain in my sides shifted to my legs and eventually faded, along with the scene.

Another image materialized, of a baby in a car seat. The woman caressing the baby also looked familiar. She turned her head for a brief second, and I recognized her from an old picture I had in my top dresser drawer. She was Dianne Miller, my first foster mother. She looked so happy, kissing and caressing me in the backseat.

The scene faded out. A new scene emerged. A two- or three-year-old boy was being handed over to a lady in a blue dress. The lady took the boy by the hand and led him down a long hallway. The loud, rhythmic clicking of her heels against the hard ceramic floor was soon replaced with soothing words about a big playroom and meeting new friends. I recognized the hallway. How could I not? I'd traveled down that lonely corridor countless times as a young boy, always hoping and waiting for another family to come along and take me home with them.

Fade out. A new scene. I saw my second foster mother, Judy Vogel, laughing and playing with me at the park playground behind our house. And there I was, little Daniel, sitting at the top of the metal slide I loved to go down, trying to muster up the courage to let go of the handrails. Mommy was waiting at the bottom to catch me, but I was still too scared to let go.

The vision got cloudy, and then a new scene came into focus. It was a few years later, and I was in tears looking down at the photo Judy had given me to remember her by. I still had that photo in my dresser drawer—the two of us standing in front of the elephants at the Buffalo Zoo, smiling into the camera. After she handed it to me, she turned and waved, and then walked out the door of the children's home... and out of my life forever. I felt the sting of this desertion all over again. It was every bit as painful as the first time. Tears streamed down my face.

Fade out. Fade in. I was chasing Kevin and Riley through the woods. We were playing our favorite game, cowboys and Indians. The old teepee we had built from fallen tree branches stood off in the distance.

Fade out. Fade in. I was walking across the stage at my high school graduation. There I was, shaking Mr. Prindeville's hand and accepting my diploma. Looking out into the crowd I could see the Davis family, my family. Ted, Alison, Kevin, Riley, and Grandma and Grandpa Davis—they were all clapping away. I felt the pride well up in me all over again as the cheers faded and fell silent.

Another scene materialized, and I recognized the landscape right away. I was back in Josiah's woods. Daylight had faded, and I was honing in on that old, familiar tree. My heart pounded as I approached the massive tree trunk. There was a rustling behind me. I spun around to look—everything went dark.

Then, in an instant, the fog above the powder disappeared. It was as if someone had pulled a plug and cut off the power to Josiah's magic plate. Josiah rubbed his eyes, got up from the table, and flipped the lights back on.

"I hope this wasn't too much." He looked me up and down. "You're going to need some time to process all this. I'd better get you home."

I sat in stunned silence, staring like a mindless zombie at an empty spot on the wall across from me.

"There's much I need to share with you, Daniel," he said. "But we don't want to rush this. You have plenty of time to learn who you are. Tonight was the beginning of your *revelation*. Tomorrow, you'll learn what that means."

CHAPTER 7

I woke up in my dorm room Wednesday morning with a splitting headache and a wicked case of dry mouth. I sat on the edge of the bed with my head between my palms, staring down at the floor. Images from the night before came alive in my mind like a highlight reel from my own personal history. Somehow, I'd relived my entire eighteen years in a matter of minutes with someone I didn't even know—someone who knew everything about me. Maybe I'd finally gone completely out of my skull. The gurgling in my stomach reminded me of a more immediate concern. I was starving.

I trudged through the student parking lot on the way to the dining hall. My meal card was still active, so I figured I might as well milk whatever money was left on it before on-campus privileges were a thing of the past.

I made it about twenty steps across the parking lot before something caught my eye. The old Civic was parked in its usual spot, right under the light post. The last time I'd seen my car, smoke had been pouring out from under the hood. Not to mention I'd brought my car keys home with me when Josiah dropped me off. How was this even possible? I needed to get to the bottom of it ASAP. Racing into the dorm, I nearly bowled over Bruce Hanson on the stairwell.

"Holden, what the hell?" Bruce jumped out of the way as I took the stairs, three at a time.

"Sorry, Bruce. In a bit of a hurry here," I said, continuing up to the third floor. I was back in the parking lot three minutes later, car keys in hand. One turn of the wrist, and the old clunker revved up like a Formula One race car. Not only that, but the gas tank was full.

After a quick pit stop at McD's, I hopped onto Reservoir Road and found my way to Josiah's unmarked driveway like I could do it in my sleep. Normally, I'd get lost going around the block, but today it was as if I had a GPS device installed in my brain. Randall barked like the hound from hell as I cruised up the stone driveway. When I stepped out of the car, the ferocious beast charged at me in full attack mode. I held my hand out in a brave show of courage, secretly praying he wouldn't tear out my throat.

"Heel!" A deep voice boomed from the porch. Randall eased up and lowered himself to the ground.

"Thanks," I said to Josiah. "You just saved me from becoming a midmorning snack."

"Perfect timing." He hopped off the porch. "I was just about to take Randall for a walk. Why don't you join us?"

"Why not?" I shrugged, placing my foot on the Civic's front bumper. "By the way, you wouldn't happen to know anyone who fixes cars, would you?"

"Why?" The corners of his mouth turned up slightly. "Need a tune-up?"

Despite his intimidating eyes, Josiah had a pretty decent sense of humor. I guessed he was warming up to me.

"I wanted to say thanks, that's all. But I still can't figure out how you found my car, fixed it, and parked it back in my favorite spot. And all in the last twelve hours. Don't you sleep?"

"Not much. There'll be plenty of time for rest in the next life. This life is meant to be lived."

"Right. Well, anyway, that was awfully nice of you, but I don't know how long it will be before I can pay you back."

"You owe me nothing." He slapped his hand down on my shoulder. "It's I that owe you."

"What could *you* possibly owe *me*?" I asked.

He stared at the Celtic cross around my neck. "Revelation of your true identity for starters. Then there's the matter of your education."

"Education?" I repeated. "Look, no offense, but I'm not interested in going back to school, if that's what you're suggesting."

"Not exactly," he said, with another half grin.

"Look, Josiah, I already went down that road. I left college for a reason."

"Care to elaborate?"

I stared down at the crushed-stone driveway. "Some sort of breakdown, I guess." I'd never opened up with anyone about my real reason for quitting school. Trying to explain it to someone I had just met would have made prying a T-bone steak from Randall's hungry jaws seem easy.

Josiah pointed toward a trail leading into the woods. "This way." He began walking, and I followed behind. "Any insight as to what caused this breakdown?"

This was the exact same question I'd been trying to answer since I took my fateful trip to the trestle bridge. "It just felt like I wasn't following my true calling, whatever that means. It's hard to explain. I wasn't on the right track. The courses I was taking, the people I hung out with. Nothing felt right."

We headed into the woods with Randall trotting slightly ahead. Everything in the forest was silent and still. No birds chirping. No wind whistling through the trees. Only the sound of our footsteps crackling down on the occasional pile of dried-out twigs. Something about the quiet stillness welcomed me, relieved me. The weight of my recent troubles lightened with every step.

"There was something else, though," I continued. "My mind… it felt like my mind was playing tricks on me. Voices calling out to me at all hours, and someone, or something, always watching me, stalking me. It's hard to explain."

Josiah looked straight ahead with no expression. "It's unfortunate that suffering always precedes the revelation."

I stopped walking and stared at him. "You understand? How? Unless… Wait a minute. Did you go through this?"

He nodded briefly, eyes closed. "We all did, Daniel. We develop amnesia when we enter this world, but the soul never forgets. Those voices you heard were your own soul reaching through the subconscious, trying to reveal your true identity."

Great. More riddles. I was about to question him further when he reached down, grabbed a stick, and tossed it into a shallow stream about twenty yards ahead. Randall bolted after the stick, but didn't return with it. Instead, he sloshed around in the water, occasionally dipping down for a gulp or two. A broad smile spread across Josiah's face. "He loves the water. This is his favorite place."

"Josiah, what are we talking about here? What do you mean, *we* all went through this? Who's *we?*"

"It's time for you to understand who you really are, my friend." He motioned toward a fallen tree just off the edge of the stream. "Have a seat."

He grabbed a broken tree branch and scratched at the moist soil between his feet. He drew three interconnected ovals that overlapped in the center. I recognized his sketch as the triquetra symbol I'd read about. It had spiritual significance.

"You belong to a special order of human beings. You're not like everyone else. You're also the last of our kind."

"I'm not following," I said, watching his expression.

He continued, stone-faced. "There have only been eleven others like us in all of human history. That's right. I happen to be one of them." He tossed the stick to the ground and looked me square in the eyes. "Daniel, you are a Sage."

All sound and movement stopped. It was as if someone had hit the pause button and the whole world was frozen still. I looked down at the intersecting ovals, still digesting what he'd said. I should have laughed out loud at such a ridiculous statement, but there was nothing in his voice or expression to suggest he was joking.

"A Sage?" I asked. "You mean, like one of those hermits who lives forever and hides out in the hills?"

He chuckled. "Folklore, my friend, mere folklore. We're mortal, not hermits, and we don't hide out in the hills. The biggest distinction between our kind and the rest of the human race is our longevity. There's a few other little differences as well."

I stared at Josiah. There had to be a punch line.

"We heal quickly," he continued. "We're also more or less immune to sickness and disease. You'll learn the rest when the time is right."

That explained why I'd never had so much as a sniffle my entire life, never missed a day of school, never had to take medicine of any kind… ever. And yet this was the craziest thing I'd ever heard. A Sage? Me? Still, there was something in those piercing hazel eyes that assured me he spoke the truth. Plus, I couldn't explain away the flashbacks he'd brought to life right in front of my face the previous night.

Josiah continued. "It's believed that a Sage can live as long as five thousand years. That's supposedly our upper limit, but it's never really been tested. Although Atum, our Master, is approaching that age."

"Five thousand years old?"

"Close to it." He glanced at Randall frolicking in the stream. "Atum is the first of our kind and the greatest of all Sages, a true father figure to us all."

"So there are others besides us and this Atum?"

Josiah nodded. "Ten remain, including you and me."

"I thought you said there were eleven others like us."

"I did." He looked out across the water again. "We've suffered three tragic losses throughout the ages. Jian, Cyrus, and Marius all fell prey to the ignorance and violence that plagues the hearts and minds of humankind. The impact of their absence on the forward progress of civilization cannot be overstated. The loss of Marius was especially difficult for me. He was my charge. I revealed him. Mentored him. Delighted in his development as if he were my son." He shook his head, still struggling to accept his own words. "Such a loss."

"I'm sorry to hear that. Did he die recently?"

"Relatively speaking. We lost Marius in Ipswich, Massachusetts, back in 1692." He turned away from me, but not before I noticed the tears forming in his eyes.

"I shouldn't have asked. I didn't mean to upset you."

"Not a problem, Daniel." His voice hardened. "You can't know where you're going until you know where you've been. It's important that you understand our history."

"In that case, I hope you don't mind my asking another question."

This brought a smile to Josiah's face. "That's exactly what you should be doing. Ask as many questions as you can. Never stop seeking. The foundation of your knowledge is built one question at a time."

"You said this Marcus was your *charge*. What did you mean by that?"

"Marius," he corrected. "His name was Marius, and he was my second charge. Atum has foreseen the coming of each Sage, you and me included. When my revelation was complete, Atum introduced me to my *sphere of influence*, or mission as some call it. My mission is the oversight of all religious and spiritual matters for the entire human race. No small task, mind you." He paused for a moment and looked down at his sketch in the dirt. "I was the third Sage to be revealed by the Master. Asha, the first, was born in Africa. Sumati, the second charge, was from modern-day Pakistan. Atum revealed the three of us within a few years of each other. We were responsible for the oversight of all humanity... with Atum's supervision, of course. We would ultimately become the Master Guides to all future Sages."

"This is incredible," I said.

Josiah continued, "We carried on like this, the three of us, for a couple centuries before Atum called us to Council. Our spheres had become far too vast to manage. We were in desperate need of assistance." He laughed to himself. "Atum merely confirmed the obvious. It was about this time that he foretold the coming of future Sages. We learned that three Sages would be provided for each of us... in due time, of course. Atum would inform us whenever his spirit guides revealed the details to him. Our role was to watch over these future Sages and keep them safe until the time of their own revelations." He let out a loud whistle and waved Randall in.

"This is so amazing. When will I know how I fit in to all of this?" I asked.

"In time, young man." He patted me on the back. "In time. There's so much for you to learn, but we mustn't get ahead of ourselves. All I can share with you now is that you'll assist me with the spiritual oversight of the human race. Beyond that, I can't elaborate. The true nature of your work has to be revealed by the Master himself. In the meantime, we need to focus on your education. We'll start with the fundamentals."

"Fundamentals?"

"You need to learn the *Code*, which is what we call our alphabet. It will be unlike anything you've ever seen, but it's essential to your future development. You must master this before we can move forward. Once you've mastered the Code, you'll be ready to read through the *Chronicles*. It's there that you'll learn our true history and understand your role in the grand design." He motioned for me to follow him back the way we had come.

For the first time in months, I felt motivated and hopeful. I actually had a purpose.

"When do we start?"

He laughed at my enthusiasm. "Your course of study will begin in three weeks. But first, we'll need to get you moved in. Then I can begin your program."

Three weeks. This would allow me to tie up loose ends at Geneseo and spend some time with my foster family back in Coventry. I wasn't so sure about the living situation, though. I'd literally just met the guy within the last twenty-four hours. Now I was supposed to pack up my life and move in with him? Truth was, I knew almost nothing about him—other than the fact that he claimed to be nearly immortal. That's always a good sign.

CHAPTER 8

I was really looking forward to seeing the family again. Being on my own was all well and good, but part of me missed my old life. It had been a while since I'd tasted Alison's cooking, hung out with Kevin and Riley, and seen some of my old friends from high school. This break in the action was just what I needed.

The ride back to Coventry seemed to take forever, but the minute I climbed up the front steps, it felt like I'd never left. Hugs, kisses, and high-fives came raining down as soon as I walked through the front door, but I knew the mood wouldn't last. I managed to make it all the way to dinner before they started asking questions about school.

Alison gave me a quick once-over with her eyes. I knew that look. She sensed something was wrong. The woman had to be psychic. She offered me a dinner roll. "So tell us about your classes."

I took a roll from the plate and dipped it in gravy. "I was hoping to wait until after dinner to talk to you about this."

"Here we go." Ted put his fork down. My foster father was a man of few words, but when he did speak, I usually wished he hadn't.

I looked down at my plate. I couldn't bring myself to make eye contact. The last thing I wanted was to see that look of disappointment I'd caused so many times before. "I kind of quit school, I guess."

"You guess?" they both said in perfect unison.

"What do you mean, you guess?" Ted asked.

Kevin and Riley squirmed in their seats.

"Let him talk, Ted." Alison placed her hand on my arm. "What's going on, sweetie?"

I rose from the table. "Not now. I can't do this now." I bolted to my room and shut the door.

That night, Alison came to my room and I admitted that my heart just wasn't into college. I didn't dare tell her how bad things had gotten, but I did mention my new job. That seemed to comfort her a little, but over the next two days, she must have tried to talk me out of it a hundred times. Ted, on the other hand, didn't bother me. In fact, he barely spoke to me for the rest of the time I was home. He had a close relationship with Kevin and Riley, but the two of us never seemed to click. I always had the feeling that adopting me was Alison's idea. Ted just went along for the ride.

The rest of my visit was pretty uneventful. I managed to spend time with Kevin and Riley, but not much. They had their own social lives now and, more often than not, didn't have time for me. This was depressing. What had happened to the pesky little brother and the needy little sister who fought for my attention and worshipped the ground I walked on? I'd only been away for a few months, but it might as well have been years. They were growing up right in front of my eyes, and there was nothing I could do about it.

One afternoon I decided to go for a walk through the fields behind the house. I moved along the old, familiar trail I'd followed so many times as a kid with my brother and sister. I could almost see us climbing trees together, staging sword fights with broken sticks, playing hide-and-seek around the tall trees. I missed those days.

The woods were unchanged. Unchanged. Just like my new boss. Josiah had been kicking around for almost four thousand years, yet he looked all of about thirty-five. In the years to come, how would I explain why I never seemed to get any older? Fifty years down the road, Ted and Alison would be wrinkled and gray. Kevin and Riley would probably be grandparents. How weird would it be if I were sitting next to them looking like I was barely old enough to get into a bar?

Someday, all these people I'd known and loved would be dead. I pictured myself placing flowers next to their headstones, year after year, always looking the same, never changing. I saw a troubled soul, a lonely soul, struggling to come to terms with precious memories that wouldn't fade. For the first time, being a Sage seemed more like a curse than a blessing.

My two weeks in Coventry came to an end on a Monday morning. Alison hustled around the house, preoccupied with my laundry and the care package she'd been working on. Kev and Riley were too caught up in their own pre-school routines to have time for anything more than a quick hug before they scooted out the door. I sat across from Ted at the kitchen table feeling dejected. They wouldn't see me again for weeks, maybe months, yet they went about their daily routines like it was just another day. I took one last bite of a cheese Danish and got up from the table. Ted hid behind the sports section of the morning newspaper.

"Well, I guess I'll be on my way now," I said, watching for a reaction from Ted. Nada. I grabbed the bag of clean laundry and started for the door.

"Alison," Ted shouted, "Daniel's leaving now."

Alison came rushing down the stairs. "You're leaving already?"

"Mom, I've got a long drive ahead of me. I'd like to get there sometime this week."

"Did you get some breakfast?"

I nodded.

"What about the care package?" Her eyes darted around the kitchen, scanning for anything I might have forgotten.

"Got it. Already packed and in the trunk."

"But you don't have the apples. There's a whole bag of apples in the fridge." She walked over and opened the fridge. "Look, the green kind. Granny Smith. You like this kind."

At least someone gave a damn. "Mom. Really. I don't need to bring a huge bag of apples with me."

"Nonsense. Take them. You might get hungry on the way." She piled the apples on top of my laundry bag. "Besides, you could use more fruit in your diet."

I laughed. "Okay, okay. I'll take the apples. I really need to get going, though."

"Call me when you get in." She hugged me and cleared her throat.

On command, Ted crawled out from behind his newspaper and held out his hand like he was meeting me for the first time. "Good luck, son. Stay out of trouble. Okay?"

I faked a laugh. "I'll try."

After a boring seven-hour drive, I was back in Geneseo. My favorite parking spot under the light was available, and, sure enough, another flyer had been taped to the pole.

"Call me when you get in. Jo"

I laughed as I tore it down. How did he know I'd see this? Not that it mattered. Josiah was an enigma, and it would probably be at least another hundred years before I figured him out. I made a quick call to Alison on my way across the Erie Hall parking lot. Then I called Josiah when I reached my dorm room. As usual, the phone rang forever before he picked up.

"Daniel," his deep voice greeted me. "I was wondering when you'd return. I have something to show you." His words tumbled out fast. He seemed excited.

"It's good to be back, Josiah, but I just rolled into town. Should I come over right now?" I asked.

"No rush." He laughed. "But you might want to make it sooner, rather than later."

I could tell something was up, something major. "I'm just going to put a few things away, grab a bite, and then I'll be right over."

"I'll be here."

I started unpacking, but I couldn't stop wondering what Josiah had in store for me. Unpacking would have to wait. I flew down the hallway toward the stairs.

"Nice to see you, Holden," Dennis Dugan hollered from his favorite roost on the main floor couch. "Why don't you stick around and hang out for a change?"

"Sorry, Doogs, gotta go. I'll catch up with you later," I shouted, making a beeline for the stairs.

As I drove up the long driveway to Josiah's house, I was once again treated to a terrifying howl from my dear friend Randall.

"Notice anything new?" Josiah called from the porch. A huge structure that hadn't existed three weeks earlier was visible, behind and to the left of Josiah's house. It looked like a smaller version of the main house. I moved to get a better look.

"What in the...?"

"It's yours, my friend." Josiah gleamed. "Built it while you were away. You'll need your own space while you study, so I thought we'd get you a place of your own."

"I don't know what to say. When did you...? How did you...?"

Josiah chuckled. "I've built a few of these shacks over the years. It's not much, but it should suit your needs for now."

"It looks amazing." I raced up the steps of my very own porch and opened the door to get a look inside. Josiah's so-called *shack* was a beautiful log cabin home decked out with hardwood floors, a peaked ceiling, stacked-stone fireplace, and modern kitchen. Floor space was pretty tight, but it was more than enough room for me. In addition to the kitchen and common area, there were two small bedrooms and a small bathroom.

"How in the world did you do all this in three weeks?" I looked all around, marveling at the craftsmanship.

He shrugged. "It's not that difficult if you know what you're doing... and if you've got good help."

"You had help?" I tried not to sound too surprised. I guess I had always seen Josiah as a loner, a true hermit living a solitary life of his own choosing. The possibility of his having social contacts had never really occurred to me.

"Aydin was in town, and he brought a few friends. Between the five of us, we put it together in record time."

"I'm sorry... Aydin?" I asked.

"Aydin, that's right. You'll meet him when you go before Council. Aydin is one of Sumati's charges, and he's one of the most innovative Sages you'll ever meet. He has a great sense of humor too. You'll like him."

"Hang on a second. What's this about a Council?"

He paused. "Eventually, everyone goes before Council. Once you've mastered the Code and read through the Chronicles, you'll be ready for your induction ceremony. It's an age-old tradition, and it's nothing to worry about. In fact, it'll be a great experience for you. You'll get to meet the entire family, even Atum."

Those last two words sent a shiver through me. I could see myself standing there like a tongue-tied idiot before this Council. Why would these enlightened souls—who had shaped human history for hundreds, even thousands, of years—have any interest in a college dropout who couldn't even hold down a part-time job? It gave me a major case of heartburn just thinking about it. "Then I'd better get to work," I said in all seriousness.

Josiah let out a cackle that would have sounded almost demonic to anyone who didn't know him. But to me, it made him seem more normal, more human.

"We start tomorrow. But first, you'd better get moved in. Need help gathering your things?"

I waved him off. "Wouldn't think of it. You've done more than enough for me already. Besides, I don't have much. I can get it all over here in a couple carloads anyway."

"Well, let me know if you change your mind. You know where to find me."

Josiah headed back to his house, Randall in tow, and I headed back to my dorm room to pack up what few possessions I had. None of my floor mates were around, which made the move that much less dramatic. I managed to slip in and out of Erie Hall unnoticed. I'd already broken the news of my dropping out to most of the guys on the floor, but I got the impression they only half-believed it. Maybe they thought I'd change my mind or something. Nothing could be further from the truth.

The move took less than four hours. I seemed to be running on a crazy new level of energy lately, firing on all eight cylinders for the first time in a long time. I felt empowered, hopeful, even invulnerable. The world was about to experience a new Daniel Holden—one who wasn't afraid to take life by the horns. I was a Sage. What did I have to be afraid of anyway?

CHAPTER 9

Training would begin the following morning. I couldn't think about anything else. What would he have me do? What if I didn't live up to his expectations? I tried to read an old paperback Ted had given me over the summer, but I couldn't get through more than a few sentences without drifting back to the training session.

It was close to midnight, and I still wasn't tired. Peeking out the window for the umpteenth time, I noticed a dull, flickering light in Josiah's kitchen window. He was still awake. I wondered if he'd mind some company at this late hour. There was only one way to find out.

I kept an eye out for Randall as I crept up Josiah's front steps. I peeked into one of the living room windows to see if anyone was up, but the curtains were closed. The kitchen window was unblocked, but there was no porch to stand on. I walked back to the front door and knocked. Nothing. I considered heading back and forgetting the whole thing, but my gut told me to stay.

On a whim, I tried the doorknob. It turned freely in my hand. This felt like a total invasion of privacy, but I couldn't stop myself. The door opened with a slow, annoying creak that should have alerted Josiah. Maybe he was sleeping. Scanning the room, I spotted Randall snoozing by the fireplace. Next to him was Josiah, seated on a bearskin rug, facing the fire. Neither of them flinched. Josiah sat cross-legged, gazing at the fire.

"Josiah," I called out in a hushed voice. No response. I rapped my knuckles on the half-opened door. "Excuse me, Josiah? All right if I come in?"

Still, no response. Randall wasn't flinching either, and that dog could hear the footsteps of a caterpillar from a mile away.

My heart rate accelerated. Something was wrong. "Ahem." I cleared my throat. "Uh, Josiah?" I entered all the way, shutting the door behind me. Moving forward cautiously, I stood in front him. I gasped. His eyes were open, gazing into the fire. His chest rose and fell in a slow, steady rhythm. He didn't blink.

I wasn't sure what to do next, but I was pretty sure I shouldn't interrupt. I held my breath and took a step backward, intent on leaving. But then I noticed something; Josiah appeared almost out of focus. I rubbed my eyes and moved in for a better look. Still blurry. The man hadn't moved a muscle since I entered the room, and yet, somehow, he seemed to be vibrating.

I looked over at Randall again. Still comatose. I was definitely in the wrong place at the wrong time. I needed to go back to my place and get some sleep. I'd ask Josiah about all this weirdness in the morning.

I tossed and turned forever before finally dozing off. What happened next can only be described as chaotic. Vivid images sprang to life in my slumbering mind with amazing detail. I was painting a picture on a cave wall by a roaring fire. I smelled the blood of a recent kill on my fingertip as I retraced the outline of my painting over and over again. The members of my clan, dressed in animal skins, were too busy devouring the freshly cooked meat to pay any attention.

I found myself in a desert, chopping away with hammer and chisel at a huge block of stone in the hot sand. Sweat beaded down my forehead and into my eyes. My throat ached for water. There was no time for that. I had to keep working.

In another vision, I was walking with a handful of people toward a walled-off village in the late evening. The flame from my torch was our main source of light. I sensed these were close friends—fellow villagers, maybe. Two hooded riders appeared on a hilltop behind our group. In the fading twilight, I could only see their outline. They trotted toward us carrying a flag and a long pole with a large crucifix attached. Then the ground shook. Dozens of armored knights appeared from behind the hooded riders, waving swords and spears as they galloped over the hill. They descended upon us as we ran for our lives. I strained with all my might to get to the village gate but felt something cut into me from behind. I tasted blood and fell to my knees. Darkness.

The last vision was the most memorable of all. I opened my eyes to find myself face-first in the dry, dusty soil. Pain radiated throughout my entire body as the blistering heat of the midday sun beat down on my weary head. A crowd of thousands packed a massive coliseum all around me. Cheering and laughter filled the air as bloodthirsty spectators took great delight in the pitiful sight of my broken body, writhing in pain on the ground in front of them.

My side was slashed open, and my right arm was practically in pieces. The soil below me was moist with the continuous flow of blood from my open wounds. I wasn't sure what had happened to me, but the four lions devouring another unfortunate soul in the distance were a pretty good indicator. Blood filled my lungs. I was drowning in my own fluid. I felt nauseous, light-headed, and desperate for a quick death. Anything to bring an end to this slow and brutal torment.

Someone's hands wrapped around my legs and torso, and I was hoisted onto a gurney. I was being carried toward an exit. The crowd shouted insults at me in Latin. Toga-wearing men, women, even children jeered and spit on me as I was carried out of the large arena. What kind of madness was this?

Two centurions brought me into a dark chamber, where they dumped my broken body onto the stone floor to die. Surrounding me were the dead and those who prayed for death. Flies swarmed and rats scurried as the stench of rotting corpses filled my nostrils to the point of choking. A creeping chill blanketed my body.

A dazzling flash of light appeared. It was so bright I had to close my eyes. When I opened them again, a beautiful woman peered down at me. She caressed my face with the tenderness of an angel. Dark shoulder-length hair cascaded down her cheeks in perfect little ringlets. Sparkling hazel eyes drew me in with their mysterious power, replacing my pain with pure fascination. The gentle stroke of her silky-soft hands infused me with peace and tranquility. When she spoke, her Latin dialect came out a gentle whisper, and somehow I understood every word of it. She assured me I'd soon be pulled away from this misery into a perfect place of love and acceptance.

The light behind the angel grew brighter, further highlighting her beauty and burning an image into my soul that I knew would carry me into the next life. The angel faded into the expanding brilliance of the light. Her glowing hazel eyes were the last image I saw before a massive tunnel appeared. I opened my eyes to see the outer rim of the light fixture on my bedroom ceiling. As painful as this experience had been, I'd have given anything to go back to it. Anything to be with that angel again. Who was she? And why did I yearn so badly to be with her?

CHAPTER 10

Morning arrived, and I couldn't wait to see Josiah. I was dying to share my dream with the one person who might know how to make sense of it. I knocked on his door and was caught off guard by Randall's bark.

"Well, good morning to you too." I petted his head, stuffing my heart back into my chest.

Josiah appeared in the doorway dressed and looking like he'd been up for hours. "Nice of you to join us. I thought you might sleep all day."

"I thought it was only, like, eight o'clock. What time did you get up?" Did the man *ever* sleep?

He looked up toward the treetops. "Before the birds, before the sun, but not before our friend Randall here." Josiah squatted down and scratched his trusty companion on the back of the neck. Randall licked his master in a return volley of affection, while an appetizing aroma wafted out onto the porch.

"I'm not interrupting your breakfast or anything, am I?"

"Breakfast?" He flashed his eyes in mock confusion. "It's almost time for lunch according to my watch. I think that's Randall's leftover stew you're smelling."

That dog ate better than most people, which helped explain why it weighed over two hundred pounds... and every bit of it muscle.

Josiah motioned for me to come inside. "So how was your first night in the new spread?"

I followed him in. "Ah, that's kind of what I wanted to talk to you about."

"How's that?"

My stomach muscles tensed as I tried to come up with a casual way of admitting that I'd invaded his privacy the night before. I chickened out. "Let's just say I had an interesting evening all around."

Josiah stopped for a second, suddenly interested. "Okay. Care to elaborate?"

"There's plenty to talk about. I'm not sure how you're going to react to some of it, though." I glanced around the room and focused on one of the swords mounted over the fireplace. It was really just a pathetic excuse to avoid eye contact.

"Daniel, if there's one thing you need to know, it's that you can come to me with anything. *Anything.* It's critical to your future development that you learn to trust me." He paused and looked me directly in the eyes. "You can trust me with your life."

His words rang in my ears. I'd always been suspicious of anyone who said, you can trust me. More than once I'd been burned by those words, and I was about to dismiss Josiah as just another con artist who was trying to pull one over on me. Something stopped me, though. One look into his eyes was all it took to *know* he spoke the truth. It was difficult to explain and even more difficult to ignore. It was something that had to be felt to be understood. He was right—I could trust him with my life. I was absolutely certain of this.

"It's just that I've only known you for such a short time. I guess I'm not really sure what this is all about. What you're all about."

"That's perfectly normal. You can tell me when you're ready."

I straightened up in my seat. I had to come clean. "Guess I'm as ready as I'm ever going to be. Look, I don't want you to think I'm some sort of Peeping Tom or something, but I couldn't wind down last night." I hesitated for a second. "I came over to talk."

Josiah took a seat in his antique rocking chair and stroked his beard. Swallowing hard, I continued. "I tried knocking, but no one answered. The door was unlocked, so I popped my head in. You were sitting in front of the fire, and Randall was out on the floor over there." I pointed to his spot near the fireplace. "I tried calling out, but you were in some sort of trance or something. Your eyes were wide open, but you couldn't see me, couldn't hear me."

Josiah nodded, unfazed.

"There was something else, though," I added. "You were vibrating, I think. I wasn't sure what to do, but I didn't want to interrupt you. So I left."

Josiah's poker face remained. He stopped stroking his chin and rose to his feet. "Not interfering was a wise decision. What you saw last night was an advanced form of meditation. Normal humans cannot achieve this level of attunement, only our kind."

"Will I be able to do it?"

He walked over to the window. "More than likely, but I've never known a Sage to attain this ability in less than a hundred years' time. I don't even think Atum was able to attune right away." He turned around, and his eyes pierced mine. I hated when he did this. It sent a shiver through me every time. As comfortable as I felt around him, those eyes were still unnerving.

"What else is bothering you, my friend?" he asked.

I stared off into the corner, avoiding his gaze. "My dreams. They seemed so real last night. Only they didn't feel like dreams at all. It was more like I was remembering something that actually happened to me, even though it never did." I knew I wasn't making sense. "It's hard to explain."

Josiah's eyes darted back and forth like he was searching for something. "Now that *is* unusual."

"Unusual?" I didn't like the sound of that. "What's unusual?"

His brow wrinkled as he peered out the window again. "Unusual that one so green would already be having the memories." The poker face was gone now, replaced with a look of deep concern. "You *are* the last Sage. Atum did predict you'd have a certain... certain precociousness. I suppose I shouldn't expect your development to follow standard protocol. The Chronicles didn't provide much detail when it came to your program."

"My program?" I repeated. "You mean my education?"

Josiah returned to the rocker. Tilting way back, he scanned me with those laser eyes again, as if trying to read my innermost thoughts. "That's part of it," he said. "Your program encompasses many learning experiences. Understanding the Code and familiarizing yourself with the Chronicles are just the beginning. A perfect foundation, mind you, but only the beginning. Most of what you'll ultimately learn will be through your own trial and error. I can only prepare you with the fundamentals." He leaned forward. "The rest will be up to you."

CHAPTER 11

The die had been cast, and the time had come to start my program. Learning the Code would be my focus for the immediate future. We wasted no time getting down to business. The big kickoff started with an old-fashioned egg and bacon breakfast cooked up by the Master Guide himself. After some small talk, Josiah shifted gears and excused himself from the table. I was busy cleaning up when he returned with a long cylindrical container, covered from top to bottom with strange carvings. I watched as he carefully removed a large cork and wadded-up cloth from the container's opening. Then he spread the cloth on the table and eased out what looked like a long piece of paper.

He spread out the paper, which turned out to be a set of papyrus rolls, each containing the same odd etchings that decorated the container. Just as he'd suggested, the writing was nothing I'd ever seen before. It looked like some sort of alien alphabet.

"This ancient writing," he said, "is unique to our kind." His eyes came alive with excitement. "These are the original documents. Some date back four millennia, just a few years before I was born. The Master created this alphabet in order to preserve our history and provide us with a tool to train future charges. In his great wisdom, Atum crafted a language that would never fall prey to the whims and faulty interpretations of man." He paused, admiring the ancient etchings as if they were the Holy Grail.

"Asha was the first to learn the Code, followed by Sumati, and then myself. All the other Sages have studied from these very scrolls. Treat them with great care, and keep them in their casing at all times when they're not in use. They must be protected from sunlight, humidity, and extreme temperatures."

"Where do we start?" I rubbed my hands together.

"We'll start with the basics. These documents contain our entire alphabet, all two hundred eighty-six characters. First, you need to commit the characters to memory. Then I'll teach you how to apply them. You must learn to write and decipher Code effortlessly, flawlessly."

Josiah explained that reading the Code involved scanning a line of symbols straight down the page, unlike most languages, which are read across the page. You started along the left column and worked your way from top to bottom. Once you reached the bottom of a column, you shifted to the right and read the next column from the bottom up, followed by the next column from top to bottom, and so on. This was a much more efficient method of reading, he explained, since your eyes could scan from one column to the next without having to move across the entire page to get to the next line.

For the next few weeks, I remained glued to my chair. I barely knew what day of the week it was, let alone the time of day. I became so lost in these symbols that I didn't realize Christmas was just a few days away until Josiah brought it up. He encouraged me to go back and spend the holiday in Coventry with my family, but I decided against it. I couldn't pull myself away from the

Code—mostly for fear that I'd lose the discipline and momentum I'd gained in the previous three weeks. Eventually, I had to make the dreaded call home. Kevin answered on the first ring.

"Hello." He sounded out of breath.

"K-man."

"Daniel? Holy crap, is it really you?"

I laughed. "I haven't been gone that long, you doofus. Of course it's me. Anyway, why are you so out of breath?"

"Just came back into the house to grab my water bottle. It's the weirdest thing. I was just thinking about you, and then you called."

"What's the water bottle for? I though football season was over."

His voice got louder, full of excitement. "Coach picked out a few of us to do after-school sessions in the weight room. He told me I could play first string next year if I keep at it. Imagine that, a sophomore playing first string on the line."

I couldn't get over his excitement. He sounded like a kid on Christmas morning. Oh yeah, about Christmas. "Hey, that's great, Kev. Can't wait to come back up and see you play." I hesitated for a second. "Look, bro, I've got some bad news. I hope you won't be too disappointed."

There was a long silence on the other end. He finally spoke up. "Let me guess. You're not coming home for Christmas."

"I hate to miss it, but there's this thing I have to do for my job. I can't get out of it."

Another long pause. "Well, it won't be the same without you, that's for sure. What am I supposed to do with the present I bought you?"

"Hang on to it. I'll be back sometime after the holidays. I promise. We can exchange gifts then."

"Crap!" he shouted.

"Kev? You still there?" I asked.

"Yeah. Sorry, Danny, but my ride just pulled in. Gotta go. Here, talk to Dad."

I couldn't wait.

"Hello," a gruff voice answered.

"Hey, Dad. I'm afraid I've got some—"

"I already know. I overheard you talking to Kevin." Ted had a nasty habit of listening in on other people's conversations from the upstairs phone. I wasn't sure if he'd really overheard or if he was up to his old tricks again.

I continued my sales pitch. "It really can't be avoided. I hope everyone understands."

"I understand," he said in a dry, emotionless tone. "Sounds like your brother is taking it well. Good luck with your mother and sister, though."

"Can I talk to them?"

"Afraid not. They're out shopping. Probably buying Christmas presents for you." Nothing like a little salt in the wound.

"Will you give them the message for me?" I knew this was a long shot.

"I think you'd better do that yourself. I'll have your mother call you when she gets in. Anything else?"

He was so warm and inviting.

"No. I guess that's enough for now. Talk to you later, Dad."

"Okay, then." Click. Dial tone.

The conversation with Alison was even worse. She grilled me for fifteen minutes, trying to understand what could possibly be more important than enjoying Christmas with the family. I talked in circles until I was dizzy, and she finally gave up, frustrated. Riley wasn't too pleased with me either. The whole thing had me swimming in a deep pool of guilt.

Christmas Eve was spent like most other nights, sitting at my desk poring through Code. Josiah challenged me with scripted assignments, but I'd improved to the point where I could read and interpret most of it without much coaching. My writing was coming along, too. It was much harder to master than reading, but I could scribe basic symbols now with ease. The light at the end of the tunnel grew brighter each day.

The following morning started off with a wicked neck cramp. After lifting my head off the desktop, I rubbed sleep from my eyes, stood up, stretched, and wandered across the room. Staring out the window of my new home, I was greeted with a dazzling snow-covered landscape. Christmas Day had arrived in all its glory. The world outside looked so beautiful, so surreal, I wondered if I was still dreaming. My cell phone jolted me. Josiah's deep voice was on the other end.

"Merry Christmas, young man."

"Merry Christmas to you too," I said, through a yawn.

"I'm sure you were about to call home and talk to your family, so don't let me keep you. When you're done wishing good tidings, though, why don't you stop over? I have a little something for you."

That was the last thing I wanted to hear. I hadn't bought Josiah anything for Christmas, yet he had a gift for me. Now what? "Josiah," I began, "I asked you not to buy me presents. I didn't get you anything."

"I didn't buy you a thing, Daniel. Sages don't subscribe to all that phony commercialism. We do know how to celebrate, though. Stop worrying, and come on over when you're ready."

I was still leery. Josiah was up to something. But what? "Let me call home first, and I'll be over in a few."

"Take your time. I'll be here."

The minute I stepped inside Josiah's house, he held up a hand and said, "Stay right here. I need to get something." He disappeared around the corner and returned with a wrapped present.

I winced. "I thought you said you didn't buy me anything. I feel terrible now."

"I *did* say that, and it still holds true. Now have a seat over here."

I sat on the couch feeling like a total schmuck. Why hadn't I gotten him something? After all he'd done for me, and I couldn't even buy him a small gift? I was a hopeless case.

Josiah handed the gift to me. The box felt like it was full of bowling balls. I almost dropped it on my lap.

I followed his order, removing the paper first, and then I opened the cardboard box. Inside was another box, only this was the several-hundred-year-old wooden variety. Propping open the lid, I was amazed to see a polished leather book about ten inches thick. The Code on the cover spelled out, *Chronicles*. I stared in awe, afraid to even touch it. I'd spent the last several weeks of my life preparing for this, and here it was, my own Holy Grail.

"Go ahead." His face lit up. "Take it out."

I remembered seeing that same look on Alison's face years ago when Kevin, Riley, and I ripped into our presents on Christmas morning. It was the look of sheer enjoyment that comes from seeing pure happiness in another person. I pulled the ancient book out of the box and cradled it in my lap. I knew as soon as I turned that first page I'd be consumed by it.

"This is the best Christmas present I've ever gotten." I swallowed hard, pushing down the budding lump in my throat.

Josiah stood over me and placed his hand on my shoulder. "You've certainly earned it, young Sage."

CHAPTER 12

The day after Christmas had always been a letdown for me as a kid. With all my gifts already opened, played with, and scattered across the family room floor, there was nothing left to look forward to. This year would be different. Finally, I'd get to crack open the Chronicles and learn about this mysterious clan I was born into.

For as much as I'd been looking forward to it, I should have been tearing the cover off the book. Instead, I kept stalling. I was scared to start down this path for fear there'd be no turning back. Up to this point, I was technically still the same Daniel Holden I'd always been. Was that who I really wanted to be? A paranoid loner with no roots or direction? Definitely not.

It was time to take the next step. I settled down at the kitchen table, spread Josiah's cloth out in front of me, and opened the book. I worked my way down the first page of scripted Code, completely absorbed.

The epic history of the Sages began with a preface describing how humans had walked the earth in darkness, stagnating for thousands of years in the physical, mental, and spiritual realms. Atum described how humanity matured through thousands of years according to their own evolutionary pace. The time had come, however, for the hand of God to reach down and pull these lost souls out of the darkness. The Almighty, one of Atum's preferred names for God, threw civilization a lifeline by appointing spiritual mentors to work directly with the humans.

Once I read past the preface, Atum's writing style became much more personal. He had a way of using Code that made you feel as if you weren't reading about his life; you were living it. And so he continued.

The year was 2953 BC, a year that would prove eventful both for myself and for all humanity. I was merely nineteen, yet already serving as chief architect to the Pharaoh Den, ruler of Egypt. Our country was still in its youth, yet strong and confident—more than ready to establish itself as the premier civilization throughout the world. Pharaoh insisted that the city of Abydos, crown jewel of the empire, be a showcase for all civilization, a true testament to the power of the Den dynasty. It was my duty to construct massive step pyramids, or mastabas, to demonstrate that power.

The day that would forever change my life started off like any other. I stood atop our newest mastaba with a small team of architects and draftsmen, discussing finishing touches and our upcoming presentation to the pharaoh. The sun was exceptionally hot for so early in the morning. Soon, the world was spinning, and my knees buckled beneath my tunic in the sweltering heat. Straining to regain my dignity, I looked up at the mighty sun, and the world turned dark. I fell into a void. The void wrapped me in its tight embrace as I moved through it with amazing speed. I raced toward a light that grew brighter as I approached.

Stillness followed. I was surrounded by a warm, welcoming light. A brilliant figure, composed of the same light, stood next to me. No introduction was necessary. My spiritual memory came flooding back as I basked in the light of Rei, my spirit guide. He was as familiar to me as my own earthly father.

Rei took me to a great chamber where I witnessed a living, breathing display of all humanity. I experienced the full evolution of all things in mere seconds, from the primordial swamps to the palaces of Egypt. I was shown my own life from birth to adulthood, with achievements and flaws, everything exposed. Before I had time to reflect, Rei transported me to a massive domed hall. I stood in a circular room, bursting with light that reflected off silver columns and golden walls. The ceiling sparkled with diamonds, dissecting and projecting more light into a prism of every color imaginable. The entire structure pulsated with life and love.

A smooth semicircular table materialized before me with three spiritual masters seated behind it. I recognized these masters as the *Elders*—elevated souls appointed to assist and instruct me through my earthly and heavenly missions. The Elders informed me that I would return to earth with a new mission. I had been appointed protector and guide to all humanity. It would be my responsibility to oversee the physical, mental, and spiritual development of the entire human race while protecting them from the dark forces set upon their destruction.

The Chronicles went on to detail century after century of Atum's earthly ministry and the many lands he visited. In 2007 BC, while still living in Mesopotamia, he discovered his own ability to tap into a higher vibrational frequency while he was meditating before a body of still water. In this advanced state of meditation, Atum's soul left his body and reentered the spiritual plane for the second time.

Rei, there to greet him again, wasted no time leading the great Sage to his Council of Elders. The Elders informed him that three new Sages would be born and placed under his command. He was given the times and places of their births, along with a directive to watch over them until the time of their revelation. He was also instructed to create a written language and chronology to pass on to his future charges. When Atum returned to his physical body, he watched over the birth, childhood, and teen years of Asha, Sumati, and Josiah, revealing and mentoring each Sage as they came of age.

It took me all day to read the rest of Atum's story. By nightfall, I was mentally fried. The history was fascinating, to say the least. This book would be my focus for the immediate future, but I needed to read through it at a realistic pace. Just as I'd suspected, the book had pulled me in, consumed me. It was already nine o'clock in the evening. I hadn't left the kitchen table since morning. After devouring Christmas dinner leftovers, I collapsed into bed.

CHAPTER 13

Something jabbed me in the ribs, pulling me out of a deep and restful sleep. Steely blue eyes peered down at me. Morning was nearly here, and the cold of night had worked its way deep into my bones. The campfire must have died out during the night. All that remained were the remnants of charred logs emanating steady streams of white smoke into the darkness.

A Viking warrior nudged me again with his boot. He rattled off his sharp Norse dialect in hurried whispers. I understood him perfectly. My memory returned. The Viking was my clansman, Vidar, second in command, answering only to Hakon, our leader. Vidar had been with the clan since the age of fourteen and was well respected by all the men. Now in his midtwenties, he had the weathered look of a man many years his senior. I'd been with the clan for only three years, but my bravery and valor had won me the respect of both Vidar and Hakon.

"Gunnar. Gunnar," the gruff voice repeated as I absorbed another boot to the ribs. "Get up. No time to waste. We're sailing early… going to catch them by surprise."

Vidar grunted, his eyes shifting back and forth, gleaming with excitement.

I struggled to my feet. I was only twenty-one, but my body had already been through more punishment than most men twice my age. Ours was a hard life, but it was all I'd ever dreamed of since I was a young boy in Denmark. Vidar crossed his arms and tapped his boot impatiently against a moss-covered rock, peeking out through the soil.

"It's still dark," I complained, yawning and stretching my arms toward the sky.

"Best time to sail. Now grab your weapons, and help me ready the men." His breath trailed off into the cold morning air. "If we sail now, we'll arrive just before sunup. They'll never see us coming."

The year was AD 841, and we'd camped on a small uninhabited island off the coast of Ireland. We had sailed, forty ships strong, from Denmark and reached the small Irish island during the night. Now it was time hit the mainland. I grabbed my essentials: helmet, shield, seax, and sword. We roused the others.

The scene shifted. We were paddling in unison in the ice-cold water. This was what I lived for, the time I felt most alive. With every stroke of the paddle across the calm morning sea, anticipation built up inside me. As day broke across the horizon, we sailed ashore and swarmed inland on foot. My heart felt like it would explode under the heavy battle garb as we approached. We could barely see the village resting peacefully in a thick nest of morning fog. In just a few short minutes, we'd surround the place like the river Gjöll, unleashing our fury on the natives.

But we were spotted. Shouts and screams spread like an early morning wildfire. Women and children fled their homes. A band of about fifty men stood at the ready with swords and spears. The clash of steel rang out as the groans of the fallen soon filled the air. The Irish put up their best resistance, but we rolled right over them. They never stood a chance.

The spirit of Odin dwelled within me. My sword plunged deep into the broad belly of a huge bearded Irishman brandishing a spear. With another strike to the neck, blood spewed forth as his body collapsed, lifeless before me. A sword crashed down on me from the left, but I was ready with the shield, barely escaping a deadly blow. The attacker met with the tip of my sword as I buried it deep within him. Two more thrusts, and he was writhing in agony, his eyes staring straight ahead as his mouth hung open. The smell of blood was everywhere. It was a stench I'd grown fond of in recent years. I was thirsty for more. I knew of no greater pleasure than that of seeing our enemies lying still and defeated before us. The spoils were ours for the taking.

We worked our way through the village, taking anything and everything of value. We left the remaining children and older women alone. Most had gone into hiding or were running for the hills. The younger maidens didn't fare so well. Now and then, screams pierced the morning air.

I entered an abandoned home and scoured for valuables. It was empty of anything worth taking. I was about to leave when a strange shape caught my eye. A filthy blanket had been spread out over the top of something on the floor. Perhaps, something promising. I moved toward it, like a hungry beast on the prowl. I yanked back the blanket to find a feeble old man, shivering in fear. I raised my weapon, but someone grasped my right arm. I turned, ready to strike, only to be stunned into submission by a beautiful young maiden staring back at me with the most bewitching hazel eyes I'd ever seen. She was absolutely perfect in every way. Was I staring back at the goddess Sjöfn herself? Numb and vulnerable, I was defenseless in the presence of this stunning beauty.

She reached out and touched my cheek with a soft, delicate hand. "No more," she whispered in my native tongue.

An immediate sense of calm overtook me. My weapon fell to the floor. It was if she'd tapped into my very soul... calming me, taming me. All my anger faded away. I felt only love for this woman, love for all people.

Something else welled up inside me. Something unpleasant. I was drowning in an ocean of guilt. All the pain and sorrow I'd wrought upon others coursed through me. Every man I'd killed. Every maiden I'd had my way with. I felt the shock of a thousand blades slice through me. My insides burned as I witnessed countless burials, all due to my hand. Children without fathers. Wives without husbands. It was horrible. I was horrible. What had I become?

Things would never be the same. I would never be the same. I'd lost my will to fight, plunder, and kill. This woman was the only thing that mattered now. I'd charge the gates of Helheim itself if she asked it of me. I'd do anything for the chance to bask in the soothing light that radiated from her. Cleansing me. Healing me. I was one with all living things. Everything flowed together. There was perfect unity, perfect love.

Everything went black.

I awoke soaked in sweat. That was the most incredibly lifelike dream I'd ever had. Not only did I feel every sensation, but my sense of who I was and where I came from was crystal clear. I wasn't just seeing the world through the eyes of that Viking... I *was* that Viking. What I couldn't understand, though, was why I experienced this violent life of rape and pillage in the first place.

What did it have to do with me now? What did any of these dreams have to do with me? There was one common theme, though: the woman with the hazel eyes. She was the angel from my ordeal in the coliseum.

I knew of only one person who could make sense of this dream, and he just happened to be my next-door neighbor. It was time for a visit.

CHAPTER 14

The smell of fresh roasted coffee wafted out onto the porch from Josiah's kitchen. Bright-eyed as usual, he waved me in, while Randall practically knocked me over with a good morning welcome.

Josiah held out a coffee mug. "Let me guess. You've come to tell me you're done with the Chronicles already?"

"Yeah, right. I'm barely out of Egypt. Haven't even started your story yet."

"That's the best part of the book, you know." He looked at me out of the corner of his eye.

I grinned. "We'll see." I sat down at the table and motioned for Randall to join me. He rested his massive head on my leg.

Josiah got quiet, a sure sign he was about to go into mentor mode. "Did you have any questions about what you read last night? Were you able to decipher Atum's script?" he asked.

I shrugged. "It was easier to read than I expected. The images really flowed together."

"Atum is a great writer, the best." He took a sip of his coffee. "Are you sure you didn't come across anything that needs clarification?"

I scratched Randall behind the ears, thinking of the best way to bring up the dream. "Actually, I do have something I'm a little confused about, but it's got nothing to do with the Chronicles. I had the dreams again last night. This time, they were even more vivid than before."

Josiah set his coffee down on the table and walked over toward the living room window. He braced himself against the window frame with outstretched arms and stared out into the yard. "Tell me about it, Daniel. I want to hear all about this dream."

"You sure about that?" I asked. "Because I don't want to bore you with every little detail."

"No, no, no." He turned to face me. "It's important you tell me everything, no matter how small the detail." His mood had changed. All of a sudden, he was intense and completely focused.

I described everything I could remember from the Viking memory. Josiah continued staring out the window, nodding occasionally. I came to the part with the beautiful woman. Josiah's shoulders stiffened. He spun around, strode back to the table, and took a seat directly across from me.

"Describe what she looked like again." He kept a steady gaze on me.

"To be honest with you, she was the most gorgeous woman I've ever seen. You had to see her. She had these incredible hazel eyes. Her lips were full, her features perfect… but those eyes…" I paused for a second as her image formed in my mind. "They had to be seen to be believed. I know she was the same woman from my dream in the coliseum. I'm positive. I swear I could fall in love with her."

Josiah's eyes dilated. The color drained from his face. He stared off into the distance, frowning and scanning the floor like he was trying to find the answer to his question in the floor tiles. "It doesn't make any sense," he murmured. "It can't be."

"What can't be?"

He stroked his beard. "I think it's time for us to take a little ride."

"Okay. If you say so."

I followed Josiah out onto the porch.

"We'll take my car," he said. His back was turned to me. Josiah never turned his back when he was talking.

"Is everything all right?" I asked.

He kept his back to me. "You should get a coat. It's cold where we're going."

I walked back to my cabin, grabbed a coat, and returned. Josiah was nowhere in sight. I heard the car revving in the garage and jogged over. Josiah threw the car in reverse and almost flattened me as I rounded the corner of the garage.

I opened the passenger door slowly and looked in. "You almost ran me over, you know."

He looked straight ahead. "Didn't see you coming. Get in."

I dropped down into the seat and looked at Josiah out of the corner of my eye. He turned the car around and headed down the driveway like nothing had happened.

We hit the open road in his black 1985 Cutlass Supreme. The car was nothing fancy or flashy, but it was in perfect condition.

"So are you going to tell me where we're heading?" I asked, breaking the unbearable silence.

"Letchworth State Park." He stared straight ahead, expressionless.

I turned and looked directly at him, hoping to detect something in his face that would help me understand what the hell he was up to. Did he know my history with that park? Or was this just a coincidence?

We pulled into the park and cruised along the winding road that hugged the gorge to our left. It was Wednesday morning, not a very busy time of the week. We passed one car the entire fifteen-mile trip through the park. A fresh canopy of snow blanketed the ground, creating an otherworldly glow. It felt as if we were driving through one of those porcelain Christmas villages you see on display in Hallmark stores. Everything glistened under the brilliance of the morning sun.

Eventually, we arrived at the Upper Falls parking lot.

Josiah pulled into a spot and shut off the engine. "This is my favorite spot in the whole park. You're not afraid of heights, are you, Daniel?" He turned his back to me, staring up at the trestle bridge. The same one I almost fell from months ago.

I looked over at him to gauge his expression. Blank, as usual. "Why? What did you have in mind?"

He handed me a cylindrical object.

"What's this?"

"It's called a monocular. I picked it up from a merchant in Massachusetts in the early 1700's. It was brand new at the time. It's yours now."

"Thanks. But what is it?"

"You've heard of binoculars?" he asked.

"Of course."

"This is the predecessor to the binoculars. Not as powerful, but useful nonetheless. You can try it out up there." He pointed to the trestle bridge. "Best view in the park. Care to join me?"

He was toying with me—that much I was sure of. If he knew of my history with this place, why had he brought me back here? I was a completely different person than the one who had hung from that bridge months ago. I shrugged it off and followed him up the steps. We walked out to the middle of the bridge together.

I took in the view of the frozen landscape below and said, "It was you all along, wasn't it? All those years I spent looking over my shoulder, watching for *shadow* people. The only shadow was you."

Josiah remained silent.

"And it was you that pulled me off these tracks a couple months ago." I glanced down at the icy tracks below my feet. "Right here in this spot."

Josiah nodded. "Just doing my duty. Someone has to protect you from yourself." He continued staring out at the snow-covered scenery. "I knew you'd figure it out sooner or later."

"Would've been a whole lot easier if I could have figured it out about fifteen years ago," I said. "Maybe then, I wouldn't have thought someone was trying to kill me. Wouldn't have thought I was losing my mind."

"Daniel." He put his hand on my shoulder. "There's something I need to tell you. I thought this was as good a place as any."

Something about the way his hair blew back in the cold, steady wind changed his appearance. His hazel eyes appeared darker, more penetrating. For the first time since we'd met, I felt uneasy around him, almost fearful. Maybe it was because the look he gave would scare the hell out of most people. Maybe it was because he'd lured me out onto a two-hundred-foot bridge in the dead of winter. Or maybe it was because he claimed to be a four-thousand-year-old man who hadn't aged past thirty-five. The situation didn't feel right.

"These dreams you're having… they're concerning to me on many levels," he continued. "What you're describing are past-life memories, not dreams. They come to life in the subconscious mind, but they're not to be confused with typical dreams. I'm sure you can attest to that."

"I'm not following you. Past-life memories? Are you saying I've lived before?"

He looked down at the space between the train tracks. "We've all lived before, Daniel. Many times before."

I let this soak in for a minute. It did help explain the crazy lifelike quality of my dreams, but something deep within me was rejecting this concept altogether. Josiah had just challenged everything I understood about religion and its promise of an afterlife.

"I don't know," I finally said. "Sounds a little out there to me. Are you saying this is one of those things where you earn your way into heaven by returning to earth over and over again?"

He put his foot up on the guardrail. "I realize this goes against your current system of beliefs. It's not something most westerners accept, but hear me out. First off, there's no such thing as earning your way into heaven. One must be pure to enter the heavenly realm. Humans are sinful creatures by nature and cannot achieve purity on their own—no matter how many lives they may have lived."

"Okay, so why would we have to come back again if there's no need to earn our way into heaven?" I asked.

"We don't *have* to come back. We don't *have* to do anything. Free will is as much a part of our spiritual life as it is here in the flesh. We're given the *opportunity* to return."

I laughed. "Opportunity? Leaving paradise to come back to this cold, miserable place is an opportunity?"

He paused, biting his lower lip. "Remember what I told you, Daniel. The path to spiritual growth is often filled with suffering. It's every soul's desire to be as close to the light as possible. Total alignment with the Creator can never be achieved, mind you, but the pursuit of it is an end unto itself."

Could that be true? I glanced down at the semifrozen waterfall below us. "I don't know," I muttered.

"Think of it like this." He grabbed the guardrail with both hands and looked out over the gorge. "Our Creator is like a great, eternal bonfire. We're just the tiny sparks cast from the flames. Once those sparks travel out into the darkness, they're forever separated from their source. It's like that with us. Rebirth provides an opportunity for the soul to grow through new experiences, new perspectives, and even through suffering."

I shook my head. "I still don't understand all this talk about growing. Why can't we just live one life and be done with it?"

"Who knows?" He released his hand from the guardrail and turned toward me. "But as the body and mind develop in this life, so, too, does the spirit. It has nothing to do with salvation, my friend. That bridge has already been built. Whether or not we choose to cross it is up to us."

I wished to return to a simpler time when everything was black and white to me. Josiah's reasoning made perfect sense, but it wasn't easy to accept. Still, I couldn't ignore my dreams. They were too real, too lifelike to even be considered dreams. They were memories, plain and simple.

"Why did you say my memories concerned you?" I asked.

Josiah stepped away from the guardrail. "They've never occurred to one so young before. Past-life memories don't typically begin until a Sage has reached at least a hundred years of age, and when they do, they start out as mere flashes. Images. These first flashes signal the Master Guide that the Sage has reached the level of vibrational attunement necessary to begin advanced meditation. It's then that we guide them through the process of past-life reflection."

I stewed on this for a second. "Is there something wrong with me, then?"

"No," he assured me. "It's just odd that your development isn't following the normal cycle. How do I know you'll be able to understand all this new information you're being exposed to? You haven't even finished reading the Chronicles yet."

"So what do you think this means?"

"It could mean that Atum's prophecies will be upon us sooner than we expected. Or perhaps you'll develop faster than the rest of us. I'm sure it's nothing to worry about."

"You said this bothered you on a number of levels. What did you mean by that?" I asked.

"You mentioned a girl with hazel eyes." He turned away from me. "You said you could fall in love with her."

"So? What's the big deal? Is there something strange about a guy being attracted to a beautiful woman?" I challenged.

His face hardened. "There *is* a problem with being so drawn to a particular woman. We mustn't allow ourselves to become entangled in romantic relationships… not with regular humans, not with Sages, not with *anyone*."

"That's insane," I shot back. "I'm not supposed to go out with girls now? I can't get married and have kids? What is this, a vow of celibacy?"

Josiah hesitated, closing his eyes and pursing his lips. His shoulders hunched, as if ready to release a heavy burden. "I'm sorry I didn't mention this earlier, but I didn't want to hit you with too much all at once. You've had a lot to adjust to in the last couple months."

My heart rate accelerated as a rush of anger kicked in. I tried to stare Josiah straight in the face, but he wouldn't make eye contact with me. "Look, I didn't sign up for this. Maybe it's time I thought about a different path."

His face was full of pity as he finally returned my stare. "I'm sorry to tell you this, my friend, but you can't simply walk away from who you are. We didn't choose this path. It chose us. You will follow it. You must."

I looked away as another cauldron of heated emotion bubbled up inside me. "It's not fair."

"Nothing about this life is fair, Daniel," he reminded me. "We can't get involved. There's a certain... understanding we have with Atum. He's made his stance very clear."

"Did he say so in the Chronicles?" I asked.

He shook his head. "Not exactly. Look, Atum respects free will, and he trusts in our good judgment. No relationship is worth jeopardizing your mission or your life. It's dangerous to become involved with others. There's simply too much at stake. We've already lost Jian to this madness. We can't afford to lose another."

I stared out into the distance, speechless. My new life didn't seem so exciting anymore. Not only would I have to watch my loved ones die off in the years to come, but now I'd have to bear the additional burden of marching through century after century alone, never knowing the love of a woman or the joy of raising a family. My stomach turned sour from the thought of it.

"It's not as bad as it sounds," Josiah said. "You'll get used to it. Like everything else, it just takes time, and time is something you have plenty of."

"I think we should head back now," I whispered, deflated. We made our way back down the icy steps. The ride home was dead silent.

CHAPTER 15

The Chronicles sat on my shelf for two days, untouched. My conversation with Josiah on the bridge had sucked the motivation right out of me. Who said I *had* to follow this stupid path that was supposedly laid out for me before I was even born? Maybe I'd run away and never look back. What were they going to do, send out a search party?

As much as I tried to ignore it, the Chronicles kept haunting me. I couldn't even walk past that book without it staring back, nagging me to get off my lazy ass and get to work. This was, after all, my job now, and I was totally blowing it off. Nothing, it seemed, could get me back into the mind-set I'd need to tackle this massive volume of scripted Code. I was too caught up in my own misery and self-pity.

A knock sounded at the front door. I pulled myself off the couch, walked over to the door, and peered through the peephole. Waiting on the other side of the door were Josiah and Randall.

"Daniel. You in there?"

I opened the door and held my hand out for Randall. He wasted no time slobbering all over it. *"Mi casa es su casa,"* I said, putting on my game face. If he knew I'd blown off my duties for the last couple days, he'd be disappointed in me. Josiah had become much more than a mentor to me. He'd become my friend. The last thing I wanted to do was let him down.

"So what can I do for you, sir?" I asked, knowing how formal and phony I sounded.

Josiah shut the door behind him. He put his hands in his pockets. "We've been called."

"*Called?*" I asked. "What do you mean, *called?*"

"Called by the Master." He stood perfectly still, staring at the ground.

"Is something wrong?"

Josiah shook his head. "No, nothing like that; just standard protocol. Atum says it's time for you to meet the rest of the family. We've been called to Council."

"But I've barely made a dent in the Chronicles," I reminded him. "Don't I need to finish reading it first?"

"You do, and that's why I'm here. I had no idea Atum would want to see you this soon. Usually, he provides us with much more time. Everything seems to be in fast-forward these days." His eyes moved back and forth rapidly, like he was trying to work something out in his mind. "We only have one week before we head to Stonehaven. I'll arrange the flights. You just make sure you get through the rest of that book."

A jolt of panic shot through me. "Not to sound completely naïve here, but which state is Stonehaven in?"

Josiah chuckled. "None of them. Atum lives in Stonehaven, Scotland."

"Scotland," I repeated. "I've never even been out of the States before."

"I think you'll like his place," he suggested, "although it is a bit different from what we're accustomed to. We don't have many castles around here."

"Atum lives in a castle?"

"One of the oldest in Scotland. Mind if I have a seat?" he asked, pointing to my couch.

"Sure. I mean, no, I don't mind. Can I get you anything?"

He waved me off and plopped down on the couch. He wore a frown on his face, and he kept staring down at the floor. Randall pranced across the living room to be by his master's side.

"Can I ask you something?"

"Any time," he said.

I cut right to the chase. "What's going on? You look stressed."

He reached down and scratched Randall's head. "It's none of your concern. You've got other things to focus on."

I sat down next to him. "I can handle it. Tell me what's bothering you."

He stopped scratching Randall and looked up at me. "You're going to make a really good Sage. I can already tell." He let out a big sigh. "Let's just say I've got a lot riding on this trip to Scotland. It's got nothing to do with you. I just need to prove myself as a mentor."

"Prove?" I asked. "To whom?"

He got up from the couch, walked to the window, and looked out. "To everyone. Especially Atum. It's a long story." He turned and faced me. "But that's my problem, not yours. You just focus on your reading. In the meantime, let me know if you need anything. No need wasting time on anything I can take care of."

"Thanks, Josiah. Will do."

Josiah walked out the door with Randall trailing behind. I watched them move across the yard and disappear around the corner of his porch. I wasn't sure why he needed to prove himself, but I could tell he was under a lot of pressure. I owed it to him to make a good showing in Scotland. I still wasn't thrilled with some of the expectations of my new job, but I needed to get over it. Like Josiah had said, this path was chosen for me. There was no use fighting it. The kick in the ass I was looking for had just arrived.

I woke up early the next morning to find our world covered in at least two feet of snow, and it was still coming down. The weatherman on Channel 9 said the windchill factor was twentybelow in some sections of the southern tier. The only thing I had on my agenda for the day was making a serious dent in the Chronicles, so the forecast gave me all the more reason to stay in and bear down. And so I began.

The rest of the Chronicles was organized with a section for each of the three Master Guides, covering their life histories and the stories of all their charges. These Sages had written the pages of history itself, and their lives were so fascinating I had to force myself away from the book from time to time. I'd hated history back in school, but this was different. The fact that I was reading about people I would soon meet in person made all the difference—not to mention that these people were members of my new family. Day or night, morning or evening—time became irrelevant as I devoured chapter after chapter of written Code.

The last page of the Chronicles was earmarked for me. Atum had written that the last member of the Sage family was born in Buffalo, New York, but no year was provided. He didn't refer to me by name or mention anything about the circumstances of my birth, either. This entry may have been scribed many years, if not decades, before I was even born. The only other detail he provided had to do with my future mission. *Communion.*

This was the last word captured in the Chronicles. I had now completed the entire Sage history in just under five days, and I should have been ecstatic. I closed the book and stared off into the distance, numb. Exhausted as I was, my mind wouldn't rest. Communion was to be my mission, the primary focus for the rest of my life, yet I didn't have a clue what it meant. What would happen if I couldn't achieve it? What would happen to Josiah if I looked like a complete idiot in front of the Council? There were too many questions and not enough answers.

It was time to prepare for the journey of a lifetime.

CHAPTER 16

We touched down at Aberdeen Airport about twenty minutes ahead of schedule. Scotland looked about as I had expected: gray skies and a steady drizzle of rain coming down. We picked up our bags in baggage claim and walked outside. I waited by the curb with our luggage while Josiah made phone calls inside the terminal. A few minutes later he was standing next to me, waving to an approaching black sedan with tinted windows.

The car pulled up slowly and popped the trunk before I could even grab the handle of my luggage. A gray-haired mountain of a man with a black overcoat hopped out of the driver's seat and greeted Josiah with a hug. Josiah introduced him as Malcolm, and we all climbed into the sedan. Josiah and Malcom sat in front, and I hopped in the back.

Malcolm talked with an accent so thick, I could hardly understand what he was saying. I'd never heard anyone talk like that outside of TV or the movies, but this was the real deal. Even though I'd never met Malcolm, he seemed terribly familiar to me. Judging by his appearance he had to be somewhere between forty and fifty, but I wouldn't want to mess with him.

"So how've you been, old friend?" Josiah asked.

Malcolm chuckled. "Ye know me. The older I get, the prettier I get."

"Still chasing the ladies, I presume?"

"Still chasin' 'em, but they always seem to get away." Malcolm looked at me in the rearview mirror. "Isn't that the way of it?"

I nodded back. "Always."

Josiah patted Malcolm on the stomach. "You might catch a few more if you didn't have this getting in the way."

"Aye. But I'd have to stop swillin' the lager… and that's not going to happen." They both laughed.

We traveled about thirty miles before Malcolm slowed the car and put on his blinker. Nestled back in the trees, about a hundred yards ahead, stood an entranceway. As we approached, all talking stopped. Malcolm waved to the gate attendant to let us through.

We continued climbing the steep, twisting driveway until the top of the castle came into view. It was everything I had imagined a castle to be. Floodlights lit up the front, casting an eerie glow against the dark backdrop of the evening sky. Ivy draped the left side of the building from top to bottom. The rest of the castle, with its cone-roofed turrets and stone walls, looked like something right out of the Middle Ages. Malcolm led us toward the front entrance. A menacing guard stood on each side of massive wooden doors. The place looked more like a fortress than a home.

Josiah introduced me to the guards, who were mirror images of each other. Kaiden and Argylle were identical twins, who looked like the Grenadier Guards in England on steroids. Each stood about six foot five and had to have weighed at least three hundred pounds. With their matching shaved heads and dark goatees, the only way you could tell them apart was the long scar across Argylle's right eyebrow.

We followed Malcolm inside the castle and down a long corridor. Wall-mounted candles lit up a dark, musty hallway. I felt as if I'd traveled back to the time of King Arthur.

"Atum commissioned this castle to be built in the twelfth century," Malcolm said. "He's been the owner ever since, but others have been 'ere on and off… with his permission, o' course."

"It's very homey," I blurted out.

Malcolm let out a grunt that I took to be a laugh. "Takes some gettin' used to, lad, but it'll grow on ye over time."

Josiah motioned ahead as we approached the end of the hallway. "I think you'll like the Gathering Room, just up ahead."

The Gathering Room was the inside of the main castle turret. As with Josiah's living room, ancient artifacts of every kind were on display. In addition to four standing knights in full armor, the walls were covered with swords, daggers, shields, battle-axes, war hammers, quarterstaffs, and bows. The place looked like a museum of medieval weaponry.

Across the circular room hung three life-sized portraits. I walked over to read the inscriptions below the paintings: Sir Duncan MacInnes (c. 1298), Sir Thomas Douglas (c. 1373), and Richard Lockhart (1527). The portraits stared back at me as if their souls were trapped within.

"Previous tenants," Malcolm barked.

I jumped.

"Nerves got the best o' ye, lad? What were ye expectin' to see?"

"I guess I was hoping to find Atum in one of these portraits. Wishful thinking, huh?"

Josiah chimed in, "Atum has never allowed himself to be painted… or even photographed, for that matter. He avoids recorded images like the plague. It's wise to follow his example."

I wasn't sure what Josiah meant. Was he suggesting I keep a low profile from now on? I pondered this as I gazed around the room. Everything was hundreds of years old, yet maintained in perfect condition. Each item had its own history, every piece more interesting than the next. Even the floor below us was impossible to ignore, with its smooth, interconnected stones all fitting perfectly together like a massive jigsaw puzzle. Malcolm motioned us toward another hallway.

"Let's make our way over to yer quarters for the evenin'," he said.

We followed Malcolm down a much shorter hallway with small arched openings carved throughout the length of it. Cool air wafted through barred windows, which livened up the tomblike walkway. Malcolm led us up a winding stone staircase to another long hallway lined with doors. We walked to the end, stopping in front of the last two doors.

"These 'ere are reserved for the two of ye," Malcolm informed us.

I tried the doorknob while the two old friends continued chatting. The door was locked.

"Ye might try usin' this." Malcolm held out an old-fashioned skeleton key that was bigger than my hand. I worked at opening the door while listening in on Josiah and Malcolm's hushed conversation.

"What time do you think he'll arrive?" Josiah asked.

"Have 'em ready to go by nine," Malcolm answered. "He's set to arrive by ten. Don't wanna cut it too close."

"We'll be ready," Josiah assured him.

Malcolm said good-night to us and made his way down the hall.

"So I take it we won't be meeting with Atum or any of the other Sages tonight?" I asked, still struggling to open my door.

"You have to push in a little while you turn the knob," Josiah said, demonstrating. "And no, we won't be meeting anyone tonight. Atum isn't expected to return until tomorrow. The others will be arriving throughout the day."

"Okay. So what are we doing tomorrow morning?"

Josiah stepped out of the way as I carried two overstuffed suitcases into the room. "Did you pack your whole closet in there?" he asked.

I rolled my eyes. "You never told me how long we were staying. Or anything else, for that matter."

"You never asked. Ask and you shall receive, young Sage."

"Right. Well, now I'm asking. And when do I get to meet some of these people I've spent the last couple months of my life reading about?"

Josiah laughed. "Have a seat, Daniel."

I sat down on a huge four-post bed that felt as hard as the floor. The walls and ceiling were covered with smooth cement, but the underlying brick showed through in spots. The lone window extended almost to the floor. A small wooden desk held two candlesticks and a large box of matches. There was no light switch on the wall, so apparently there was no electricity.

"Takes a little getting used to, but you'll learn to love it," Josiah assured him. "I've stayed here many times over the years. Looks the same today as the first time I visited."

"When was that?" I asked.

"Not too long after Atum moved in. Sometime in the early forties."

"1140s?" I asked.

"Very impressive." A big grin spread across his face. "I can see someone's been paying attention. Now back to your original question. We're leaving with Malcolm tomorrow morning. He's taking us on a tour. Or rather, taking *you* on a tour. I'll be with you, but I'd hardly call it a tour from my vantage point."

"Why's that?" I asked.

"Our friend Malcolm's got a pretty good sense of history, but he hasn't lived through it, and he gets things wrong from time to time. It's not his fault. He's reciting what's been handed down to him from so many generations before. Not all the legends of yesteryear are based on fact. I usually just let it go. The old Scot's got a lot of pride, and I don't have the heart to burst his bubble."

I thought about Josiah's unique perspective on history. I'd always taken everything I'd been told about history as fact. Josiah was the only person I'd ever known who could actually validate some of those facts.

"So what time will we return to the castle tomorrow?" I asked.

"Once we receive the call from Atum. He usually starts the *initiation* after sundown. At this time of year, I'd expect a call sometime around six or seven."

"Initiation?"

Josiah patted my shoulder. "Don't worry, Daniel. You'll do fine. There's not much else I can tell you right now, but you will meet everyone tomorrow night. I should warn you, though, this ceremony is a rite of passage all the Sage charges have gone through. We take it pretty seriously, so treat it with due respect. For now, get yourself some sleep. See you in the morning."

I lit the candles on my desk and walked over to the window. The thick wall of clouds from earlier in the day was gone, and the moon bathed the courtyard below in soft light. There wasn't much else to see in this dim light, other than trees and hedgerows off in the distance. Even so, watching the trees sway in the wind was enough to put my mind at ease. The peaceful scene washed over me, cleansing my body of all its pent-up anxiety. Before long, my eyelids became heavy. It was time to call it a night

"Daniel. You awake?" Josiah's muffled voice startled me out of a perfectly sound sleep with his urgent, desperate tone. I bolted out of bed to answer the door.

"What's going on? Is something wrong?" I rubbed my eyes, trying to focus. "I just drifted off to sleep."

Josiah laughed. "It's six forty-five in the morning, sport. You've been asleep for hours." He craned his neck to look down the hallway. His demeanor changed, and his tempo accelerated with a new sense of urgency. "There's been a slight change of plans. Atum just called. He's returning on an earlier flight. We need to clear out of here in fifteen minutes if we want to be out by seven."

"Seven?" I asked. "I thought Malcolm said we had to be out by nine."

Josiah's forehead wrinkled as his eyebrows arched. "Listening in on our conversation, were you?"

I threw my hands up. "You got me. It's not my fault the two of you don't know how to whisper, though."

"If you say so," he said, with a raised brow. "Regardless, we still need to be out of here by seven, so put on some clothes and let's get moving."

"Why?" I asked. "What happens if we're not out by seven? Am I going to turn into a pumpkin?"

Josiah didn't flinch. "Atum insists on meeting new Sages during the formal ceremony. He's kept this tradition for over two thousand years. He'll not be pleased if he sees you before the appointed time."

"Another tradition." I yawned. "I'm beginning to feel like a bride on her wedding day. Can I at least wash up before we leave?"

"There won't be time for that. Malcolm's readying the car as we speak. We need to clear out right away." Josiah was talking twice as fast now. He was also fidgeting with his room key as he talked. I'd never seen him so nervous. This Atum, I thought, must have one hell of a presence to be able to rattle someone as rock solid as my mentor.

CHAPTER 17

Josiah, Malcolm, and I spent the morning and early afternoon touring castles and historic sites all along the shores of the North Sea. Malcolm took great pride in his knowledge of Scottish history, but every so often I'd catch a sideward glance from Josiah, a sure sign that our guide wasn't quite on target. It was our little secret.

After a quick bite to eat at the local harbor, we were off again. A few minutes later we pulled into a small home in a rough-looking neighborhood. Malcolm knocked on the door, and we waited. Nothing. Josiah laid down a few heavy thuds, and that seemed to get things moving, judging by the sudden noise inside. The door flew open, and a young woman with jet-black hair, heavy black eyeliner, and cutoff shorts over fishnet stockings stood before us with a sneer. Her tank top barely covered the heaving ink-covered chest beneath. Sleeves of tattoos ran up and down both arms: skulls, swords, snakes—all the feminine essentials.

It didn't take long before our lovely hostess recognized Malcolm. "Ah, it's just Malcolm." Her face lit up. "Who're yer mates?"

"Ye've met Josiah, haven't ye?" Malcolm asked.

"I would've remembered this one," she carried on in her crazy Scottish accent. Her eyes went up one side of Josiah and down the other, like a predator sizing up its prey. Soon, her attention shifted to me. She practically licked her chops as she gave me the once-over. "You brought us a youngster, I see… a beauty too."

"Behave yerself." Malcolm pointed at her in a mock warning. "This is Daniel, our fresh recruit. Daniel, this is Fiona—Argylle's lassie."

"Bite yer tongue; I'm no one's lassie." She gave him a playful punch on the shoulder. "Argylle! We've got comp'ny!"

Argylle and Kaiden stomped across the front room like a pack of wild elephants. Kaiden waved us in. "We've been expectin' ye."

"We spent a bit more time on the tour than usual," Josiah said. "Still have some time to kill before the ceremony."

They nodded their heads, apparently aware of the upcoming events.

"Yer not workin' tonight again, are ye?" Fiona sneered at Argylle.

"Clam up, wifie," he shot back. "Goin' get these muckers a drink." Fiona showed Argylle her middle finger and led us toward the basement. Kaiden punched his brother in the arm and laughed.

We marched down the steps into a dark basement, decked out like a punk paradise. It had black walls and red lighting, with posters of Scottish punk bands I'd never heard of posted throughout. The place definitely had a nightclub feel, with its stocked bar, pool table, and big-screen TVs. The real attraction, though, was the giant snake slithering up the floor-to-ceiling terrarium in the far corner, next to the couch. I headed over immediately to get a closer look.

"Pretty, ain't he?" A friendly voice startled me. I jumped back, practically banging heads with another punk goddess, who had an incredible resemblance to Fiona. This one was dressed a little tamer, but she had her own set of tattoos climbing up her neck and enough face piercings to stock a jewelry store. If she stood any closer to me, she'd have been on top of me—definitely not the shy type.

"I don't think we've met. I'm Daniel."

She reached out her hand. "Lola." She rolled her eyes. "And to answer yer question, I'm Fiona's twin sister."

"Yeah, I kind of thought… or ah… you live here too?" I fumbled.

"We all live here. I'm with Kaiden," she said matter-of-factly, as if twin brothers living with twin sisters was nothing unusual. Lola went on to tell me all about her python, Aleister, and I did my best to try to figure out what the hell she was saying. She seemed like a really nice person, once you got past the dark appearance.

I spent the next couple hours shooting pool with the sisters and their menacing husbands. Malcolm just sat at the bar tipping them back and occasionally chatting it up with Josiah. I didn't see him speak to the brothers, his employees, the entire time we were down there. I got the impression their relationship wasn't exactly on the best of terms. As if reading my mind, Josiah took me aside and filled me in.

"The twins are pretty strong-willed," he whispered, scanning the room to make sure no one was listening. "They don't like taking orders from anyone but Atum… and especially not from Malcolm. They're fiercely loyal to the Master, though, and that's why he keeps them around. He's like a father to them. I don't think they ever knew their own. If it was up to Malcolm, they'd have been let go a long time ago."

Josiah's phone rang, and he answered it. This was *the* call. Josiah looked over at Malcolm and seemed to communicate something with his eyes.

"Yes, Master," he said, nodding his head repeatedly. He ended the call and motioned to Malcolm. "It's time."

With that, the music stopped, the pool sticks were put back in their places, and everyone headed upstairs. This was it. Everything I'd done in the last few months was preparation for this night. My stomach was tied up like a pretzel twist. I wanted to hurl.

CHAPTER 18

The ride to Atum's probably took less than ten minutes in real time, but the minutes dragged on like hours. I rode over with Malcolm and Josiah. The twins trailed behind in their Hummer. No one spoke in our car. As we turned up the long winding path to the castle, my stomach tightened up again. In minutes I'd go before the Sage legends, and they'd test my knowledge. What if my mind went blank? What if I made Josiah look bad?

As we got out of the car, Josiah told me to wait outside the front door while the others went inside.

About five minutes later, Kaiden and Argylle reappeared and took their positions on either side of the massive double doors. Argylle fidgeted with a handgun, drawing an intense glare from his brother. The brothers fell into position at their stations like robots, perfectly still, eyes staring straight ahead into the distance. Neither spoke a word, which made standing between them all the more awkward. At least ten more minutes passed before Josiah returned, wearing a maroon hooded cloak.

"Everything all right out here?" he whispered, shifting his eyes to the twin towers beside me.

"Couldn't be better. We should do this more often," I joked. No one laughed.

"Here." Josiah handed me a white hooded cloak. "Put this on. I'll take your coat inside for you."

"Any idea how much longer?"

"Should be anytime now," he said. "I'll come get you when we're ready." He ducked back inside.

I couldn't wait to get this ceremony over with. Minutes later, Josiah reappeared. His hood all but concealed his face. He motioned for me to put my hood up. The floodlights over the front entrance suddenly went dark, a definite signal that something was about to begin.

Josiah responded by banging his fist on the door in three heavy thuds. The doors opened, revealing another hooded figure. His hood masked his identity, but I knew who it was as soon as he spoke.

"Are ye ready to present to the Master?" the voice that could only be Malcolm's asked.

"We're ready," Josiah answered, placing his hand on my shoulder.

"Let's get on with it then." Malcolm motioned ahead, and we marched down the torch-lit corridor behind him. We walked about forty feet before stopping in front of a door nestled into the stone wall. Malcolm pounded twice, and the door opened. Josiah led us into the room, while Malcolm stayed in the corridor, closing the door behind us.

The massive hood blocked most of my vision, but I was able to see a circular candlelit room with several other hooded figures seated along the perimeter. We stopped in the center of the room, and Josiah stepped to the side, positioning himself behind me. A rash of goose bumps covered my body as three sets of piercing hazel eyes stared back at me from behind a semicircular marble table. The figure seated directly in front of me wore a dark purple cloak. Two figures in lavender cloaks flanked his right, and another seat sat empty to his left.

No one said a word. I wasn't sure if I was supposed to speak or not. Was I supposed to introduce myself? Had Josiah ever mentioned proper protocol to me? Why wasn't anyone saying anything? My heart pounded harder with each awkward, drawn-out second. Somebody say something, damn it, anything!

Josiah rescued me with a simple whispered command. "Kneel."

I lowered myself to the ground as instructed, all too aware that my pounding heart and sudden dizziness might reduce me to an unconscious heap on the floor at any moment. I had no idea how many people were in this room, but I knew every set of eyes was focused directly on me.

"Josiah." A quiet but authoritative voice pierced the air.

"Yes, Master," he answered.

The hooded figure sat perfectly still. "Whom do you present to us this evening?"

Josiah paused for a brief second. "Brothers and sisters, I present to you, Daniel Holden. Born in Buffalo, New York, in the United States of America."

"Show yourself, Daniel," the voice instructed.

I hesitated. What did he mean? Was I supposed to stand? Expose myself? What did he want me to do?

"Remove your hood," Josiah whispered in my ear, saving me again. I lowered my hood and wondered whether anyone could see my lower lip quivering. I felt dizzy, weak.

"Do you know who I am?" the voice questioned. The person attached to it lowered his hood.

There, for the first time, I looked into the face of the Master of all Sages. Much older and frailer than I'd expected, he was completely bald and might have been mistaken for a meek old man if not for one dominating feature: his eyes. Deep, penetrating pupils burned like bright hazel torches in the darkness, hypnotizing me. Atum's power was clearly not based on size or physical strength. He needed neither of those qualities. The great Master radiated a high-intensity dose of pure alpha charisma. This was power personified. This was for real.

"You are Atum, leader of the Sages." My voice trembled.

Silence followed.

Atum rose to his feet, and the others stood in unison.

He raised his right hand. "Rise, young Sage. It's time to meet your brethren."

Rising as commanded, I stood at attention. Atum and the other two hooded figures moved to stand in front of me. Josiah took his place next to the Master.

Atum looked to the person on his right, and the first robed figure removed her hood. A woman with smooth, dark skin gazed back at me and smiled. Her soft hazel eyes shone much like Atum's, and her hair sparkled in the dim candlelight. She looked to be about the same age as Josiah. She was gorgeous.

"Do you know who stands before you now?" Atum asked.

I answered without hesitating. "This is Asha, the first of the Master Guides, born in southern Nubia and revealed in 1978 BC. Her sphere of influence includes the physical development of all humanity." I paused, unsure if I needed to continue, but Atum pointed to the figure on his right.

The woman lowered her hood. I was positive this was Sumati. Strangely enough, she looked exactly as I'd imagined when I read her story in the Chronicles. Like Asha, she was also elegant, radiating a warmth that put me at ease. She came across as a wise old soul, who just happened to have the body of a beautiful young woman, no more than thirty, thirty-five, at most.

"And who stands before you now?" Atum asked again.

"This is Sumati, second of the Master Guides, born in modern-day Pakistan and revealed in 1976 BC. Overseer of the mental sphere of human development." Atum and Sumati nodded together in agreement.

He glanced at Josiah and then back at me. It was pretty obvious I knew who Josiah was, but I got the impression that our leader was a stickler for protocol. I went along with it. "This is Josiah, the third Master Guide, born in Assyria and revealed in 1973 BC. Overseer of the spiritual sphere of human development."

Atum nodded his acceptance.

With this, the three Master Guides took their seats at the table. Atum paced the perimeter of the room, quizzing me on each figure that lowered his or her dark green hood. I'd never seen these people before and had to rely only on intuition to identify them. My instincts were right on the money every time. I recognized Balaam, Josiah's other living charge, as if we'd known each other for years. Aydin and Nuha, Sumati's charges, perfectly reflected their spheres of influence mentioned in the Chronicles. Asha's charge, Darya, also looked exactly as I'd imagined her.

Finally, I came to the last living Sage, who, by process of elimination, had to be Lucina. She lowered her hood, and our eyes met. A jolt of recognition passed through me like an electric shock. Staring back at me was the same angel who had caressed my face in the coliseum, the same hypnotic stare that had appeared to me in the Viking memory. As beautiful as the others were, this particular Sage had a special quality that had my heart pounding like it was ready to burst through my rib cage. Her eyes shone like emeralds. Her skin glistened, an immaculate canvas of golden perfection. I couldn't breathe or even move in her presence. She was, without a doubt, the most unbelievably beautiful woman I'd ever seen.

I stood there like a statue, unable to speak or look away. Lucina must have sensed my struggle, as she finally looked down, freeing me from her spell and enabling me to breathe again.

"Daniel," Atum repeated. "Do you know who stands before you now?"

"Lucina," I croaked out in a whisper. "This is Lucina. Born in Rimini, Italy, and revealed in 52 BC. Guide to souls traveling into and out of the physical body."

Lucina continued looking down. She had the elegance and poise of a sophisticated woman, but there was something about her that suggested a gentle shyness. I was already smitten beyond saving.

Atum snapped me out of my trance as he motioned me toward three empty seats along the wall. I recited the names, missions, and dates of passing for the departed Sages: Jian, Cyrus, and Marius. The Master patted me on the shoulder and called for a moment of silence to respect the fallen Sages. Afterward, everyone returned to their respective seats while Josiah kneeled in the center of the room. I followed his lead.

Sumati came forward and handed Atum a rectangular wooden box. Inside were twelve empty slots and a sparkling green ring. Josiah removed the ring from its slot and passed it to Atum, who placed it on my finger. Carved into the top of the ring was the same triquetra symbol I'd seen Josiah etch into the moist soil at my revelation. This, I assumed, marked me as a member of Josiah's sphere.

105

"Daniel Holden," Atum announced, "with this initiation, our lineage is complete. You are now officially part of the Sage family. Stand and be recognized."

The room erupted with clapping and cheering, releasing the floodgate of emotions I'd been storing up for days. The word *family* triggered something deep within me. All the pain and loneliness of my youth dissolved with that one word. I hugged Josiah. This was much more than a rite of passage. This was a life-changing event. Suddenly, all those years of looking over my shoulder and feeling disconnected from the rest of the human race made sense.

As the clapping died down, a familiar feeling came over me, one of being watched. I glanced to the right and saw Lucina staring back. She turned away. I didn't. I couldn't. When she looked my way again, it was me doing the staring. She flashed her brilliant smile, and every receptor in my body fired at once.

The watched feeling struck again. I turned to the left and saw Josiah directing an angry glare at Lucina. Her radiant glow seemed to disappear at once, and she returned to her seat. Josiah's frown eventually faded as he walked over to talk with Atum.

I had no idea what that was all about, but I had a feeling I'd find out sooner or later.

CHAPTER 19

The formal initiation was officially over, but any real celebration would have to wait. Atum returned to his seat, and everyone else followed his lead. I took my seat next to Balaam. Atum rose slowly to his feet, and the room fell silent. If it weren't for the sea of glowing eyes staring back at me in the dim candlelight, the room would have appeared to be filled with seated statues.

The Master began his address. "Today is a momentous day in our history, my children. For this day marks the completion of a lineage that spans nearly five millennia. Our newest member emboldens us with a new sense of vigor and purpose. Daniel will pursue a mission that builds upon the very foundation that all of us have labored so diligently to put into place over these many centuries. This mission can be summed up in one word. *Communion*."

He stood next to me. "The Spiritual Elders have spoken. Sadly, the dark souls are rising in strength, and their influence on humankind is greater than ever. Their corruption will continue to spread like the plague that it is, spilling over into the social and political realms, pitting father against son, mother against daughter, and nation against nation. A great war will then be upon us, the likes of which the world has never known. It falls upon each and every one of us to rally the forces of light against these forces of darkness—a communion of righteous souls, bound by love and united in purpose. This will be our only chance to save the world from falling into an eternity of misery. Daniel has been chosen to lead the cause in forging this communion."

My heart skipped a beat. Atum was describing what sounded like the war to end all wars, and he wanted *me* to recruit and gather the troops? I wondered if he had any idea that he was pinning the fate of all humanity on an unemployed college dropout.

"We know neither the time nor the details of these events, but we must move forward with a sense of urgency and determination," Atum continued mesmerizing his captivated audience. "The task at hand is formidable, my friends, but we've faced these challenges before. I have no doubt that our newest member will receive your full cooperation as we collectively seek the culmination of our life's work."

Atum nodded and returned to his seat.

After a long, uncomfortable silence, Josiah rose and addressed the group. "For our next order of business, we'll need to discuss Daniel's training, specifically his mentorship." He glanced over at me but quickly looked away. "Before we proceed, however, we'll break and return at the top of the hour."

What? One minute we're talking Armageddon, and the next we're taking a ten-minute break? I would have laughed if I'd thought it was a joke. Apparently, this was how Sages rolled.

No one moved at first. Dimly lit faces stared straight ahead as if in a drug-induced stupor. Eventually, everyone emptied silently into the hallway except Atum, Josiah, and me. Atum motioned for me to join him at the dais, so I knew the ten-minute break didn't apply to us.

Atum placed his hand on my shoulder. "Until you've completed your mentorship, my son, you won't be able to participate in these discussions. This is in no way reflective of your value to this group, mind you. It's really just a matter of readiness and a few thousand years of tradition." He smiled.

"Understood." I glanced at Josiah. The truth was, I felt relieved for the chance to go off on my own and chill out. My head was still spinning from the excitement of the initiation, but that was nothing compared to the jolt of Atum's speech. Me? Organizing an army of people around the world to fight this battle for the soul of humanity? What were they smoking? Did they really think I had a snowball's chance in hell at pulling this off? It didn't make sense.

Atum shook my hand and offered his congratulations again. As if following an unspoken order, Josiah steered me out the door of the meeting room and led me down the hallway.

He pointed to my hand. "So how do you like the ring?"

"Looks great," I said, taking another look at my new prized possession. "Love the color. Speaking of color, I was wondering about something. What's with the green cloaks? All the charges were wearing green cloaks except me."

"Sure," Josiah said, as if expecting the question. "The color scheme was established by Atum as far back as I can remember. He says it mirrors the different color patterns souls project in the spirit world. Deep, dark colors are reflective of spirits who've attained a higher level of enlightenment."

"So that explains why I'm wearing white."

"Exactly. But not to worry. Once you've completed your mentorship, you'll wear green with the rest of them. It's really just a symbolic representation of your place within the group at formal meetings. The ring, on the other hand, stays green. Ring color links you to your Master Guide."

"And the symbol?" I asked.

He placed his outstretched hand over his chest. "That's my symbol. Picked it out myself many moons ago. The triquetra identifies you as a partner in the spiritual sphere. Our symbols stay with us for life, so get used to that ring." He gave me a playful slap on the back. "You're going to be wearing it for a very long time, my friend."

"If you say so."

We headed through the foyer and down the next corridor. "So what did you think of the ceremony?" Josiah asked.

"All I can say is, it's a good thing I did my homework. You told me there was nothing to worry about. What if I hadn't known all the Sages?"

Josiah shrugged. "Atum knew the information would come to you. Don't ask me why, but it always happens that way. No one has ever had trouble identifying Sages during an initiation. As long as you've read through the Chronicles, the rest takes care of itself."

"I'm just glad I didn't blow it in front of everyone."

"You certainly didn't."

We arrived at my door. Ten minutes were about up, and I figured Josiah would have to get back to the meeting, but I needed to put some perspective around all this. No one was more qualified to provide perspective than Josiah.

"What's your take on what Atum was saying? Did you know anything about my mission? About what's expected of me?"

He shook his head slowly. "None of us knew, Daniel. I don't even think Atum fully understood what Communion meant until recently. Apparently, he had another meeting with the spirits." He glanced over at me. "Look, don't get caught up in all that right now. I know it seems overwhelming, but things will fall into place. Trust me."

I tried to take his advice in stride, but my stomach filled with butterflies as I recalled Atum's speech. It was all way too much to deal with.

"I forgot to ask," he continued. "What was your overall impression of Atum and the other Sages?"

"I have to admit," I said reluctantly, "Atum looked much smaller than I expected. No less powerful though."

"That's a good observation. Anyone else make a particular impression on you?" He folded his arms and leaned against the wall outside my door.

"Everyone seemed very nice," I said, with my best poker face.

"Good enough." He started back down the hallway. "I'll catch up with you in the morning."

"Wait," I called out. "One more thing. Atum mentioned something about dark souls. Who was he referring to?"

Josiah's eyes shifted down to the floor and then back up at me. "You'll learn about them soon enough. Just get some rest. We'll catch up later." He shuffled off and disappeared around the corner.

I wasn't sure what to make of all this, but Josiah was right about one thing—I really was in need of rest. I still felt weak and even dizzy at times. I had a feeling we would be making the long journey back home in the very near future. Something told me, though, that life on the other side of the Atlantic would never be the same again.

CHAPTER 20

Breakfast at the castle was a pretty low-key affair. Everyone was gathered at the giant dining room table, except Atum, who had to catch an early morning flight to Romania. I strolled to the table, and Andrew, Atum's butler, pulled out a chair between Sumati and Josiah. I took a seat and listened to the tail end of one of Aydin's stories.

"So I said to the minister, 'But I wasn't referring to you at all, Sir Ellington. I was referring to your wife.'"

The room exploded with laughter. Darya laughed so hard, she snorted, which set off another round of hilarity. Even Josiah had to wipe tears from his eyes. I wished I'd been there for the start of his story.

"Look who's joined us," Sumati said. "Good morning, Mr. Holden."

I laughed quietly to myself. "You can call me Daniel, you know."

"Well then, Daniel it is." She placed her hand on my shoulder. "And how are you this fine morning?"

"Hungry," I replied.

"You're in luck." Balaam pointed from across the table to something behind me. I turned around and saw Andrew approaching with a covered silver platter. He set it down in front of me and removed the lid. Steak, eggs, and potatoes. These people apparently ate in style.

"Thank you." I nodded to him.

Nuha placed her hand on my arm. "So what did you think of the ceremony yesterday? Nerve-racking, isn't it?"

I shrugged. "A little, I guess."

"A little?" Aydin piped up. "You're a better man than me. I peed my toga during my initiation." The group burst out laughing again.

"Don't listen to him, Daniel," Nuha said. "Aydin still pees his toga."

I had the feeling I was going to like hanging around with the Sages.

I continued listening to story after fascinating story from this company of legends. The only Sage who kept to herself was Lucina. She barely said a word during the entire breakfast. This seemed out of place from the woman I remembered from my Roman and Viking lives. That angelic figure had been calm and gentle, but she didn't strike me as shy. I did my best not to look at her, an exercise in self-discipline for sure. At one point I turned to catch a glimpse, only to get caught in the act by the hazel-eyed angel herself. We shared a few seconds of silent tension until she finally broke it with that heavenly smile. I grinned back like an awkward schoolboy.

When I glanced at Josiah, his disapproval couldn't have been more obvious. In fact, he didn't say one word to me for the rest of the meal. What was his deal? Lucina was gorgeous, and I was smitten. Was that really such a stoning offense? It wasn't like we were sleeping together.

Eventually, Josiah spoke, although he wouldn't look me in the face. "Time to go. We've got a plane to catch."

We walked around the table and said good-bye to each Sage. When we came to Lucina, she stood and motioned toward the door.

"I can walk you out." She turned toward Josiah. "I'll call you tomorrow with my flight details."

"We'll have things ready for you," he replied. Their interaction couldn't have been more sterile and empty of emotion if they'd tried. Lucina reached out to shake his hand in a gesture that looked more like a peace offering between warring tribes. He shook it in return, without the slightest sign of emotion.

I did much better. The Italian goddess wrapped her arms around me, setting off another short burst of fireworks. "I'm looking forward to working with you, Daniel. Can't wait to get started." She turned to rejoin the rest of the Sages. I tried not to gawk as she walked away, but the sexy sway of that body was impossible to ignore. It took every ounce of discipline that I had to force my head in the other direction. Her effect on me was intoxicating. After the buzz died down, her words echoed in my brain.

"Wait a minute. What did she just say?" I asked, turning toward Josiah. "Am I missing something?"

He frowned, avoiding my stare. "I'll tell you at the airport. We'll talk in private."

Malcolm approached as we headed out the foyer. "The bags are loaded, and the motor's runnin'."

I sneaked one more glance at Lucina. She was chatting at the far end of the table with Sumati but turned and looked at me, midsentence, as if she'd felt my gaze. She waved again and returned to her conversation.

Malcolm did most of the talking on the way to the airport, which was a good thing, since Josiah stared out the window, silent. We made the trip in about twenty minutes, and afterward, Malcolm helped us unload the luggage.

"Good luck to ye, lad," Malcolm shouted as Josiah made his way toward me. "Don't be a stranger now."

I waved good-bye and grabbed my bags.

Josiah was already twenty steps ahead of me and moving at a ridiculously fast pace. We made it to our gate in half the time it would take a normal person. My mentor wasted no time burying himself in the "Life" section of a *USA Today* newspaper.

When we settled into our seats on the plane, I finally laid it out on the table. "So are you going to tell me what's going on now, or should I wait forever in suspense?"

He set his phone down and shifted his attention to me. "If you must know this instant."

"Sorry, but I'm dying to know what this is all about."

He looked out the window and then back at me. "Remember what we talked about on the trip over? Let's just say our discussion at Council last night didn't exactly turn out as we had hoped. Or perhaps I should say, as *I* had hoped."

"I'm not following you."

"I won't be mentoring you any longer, Daniel. The Master has decided Lucina is a better complement to your future training needs. At least that's how *he* sees it." He paused. "The two of you will work closely together for the foreseeable future."

Part of me was ready to burst with excitement, and the other part felt an immediate loss. I wondered what had driven Atum to make this decision. I wasn't sure what to say in a situation like this.

"Doesn't this go against tradition?" I asked.

"It's not the first time Atum's gone against protocol. Balaam's mentorship was atypical as well," he said.

"But you didn't have a problem with that, did you?"

Josiah shook his head. "I don't have a *problem* with this decision either. It's the choice of mentor I'm not comfortable with." Finally, he was starting to open up.

"I don't mean to be nosy, but what's up with the two of you?"

He looked over at me, surprised, and then stared at the seatback. "It's a long story that dates back many centuries. Let's just say Lucina and I don't see eye to eye. In the entire Sage family, she's the only one I find difficult. We're just not meant to work together, that's all."

"But you won't have to work together. She'll be working with me," I brilliantly reminded him. Was there more to this rift than he was letting on? Maybe he saw this whole arrangement as an embarrassment. After all, the mentoring of charges was one of the main responsibilities of a Master Guide. The only exception was with Balaam, who was also his charge. Atum assisted Josiah in her training.

"It's not that, Daniel. It's standard protocol that Lucina lives with us during this mentoring period. It would be an insult if I asked her to live anywhere else. This mentorship could take years. If I had the time, I'd build her a place of her own, but that's not going to happen in two days. And not in the dead of winter either."

"Two days? She's coming to stay with us in two days?" I practically shouted. A gray-haired lady two rows up turned around in her seat and shot me a dirty look. I ignored her.

"Two days and counting," he said with a sigh. "Can't wait."

"If it makes you feel any better, she could stay with me. I have plenty of room." I couldn't believe what was spewing out of my mouth. I found it hard to breathe just being in the same room with this woman. Now I was suggesting living with her?

Josiah stared at me, expressionless. "I don't know if that would be acceptable," he finally said.

"Acceptable to Lucina?" I asked.

"Acceptable to Atum. Lucina would have no problem with it. In fact, I'm quite sure she'd be thrilled at the prospect. It's Atum who might not approve." He contemplated this in silence for a second. "I'll think about it. Oh, and one more thing…" He reached behind his neck and removed the Celtic cross necklace. "I believe this should be in your possession from now on."

"What? No, Josiah, I couldn't. You keep that. It's yours."

"It was never mine. It was meant to be yours from the start. Besides, now that I'm out of the mentoring business, there's no point in hanging on to it. Just take good care of it." That was it. He pulled a SkyMall magazine from the seatback in front of him, hid behind it, and went back into his private world.

I was dying to know what had caused all this bad blood between him and Lucina. She didn't seem like the feuding type.

So what was the deal?

CHAPTER 21

We had exactly two days to prepare a room for our guest from across the ocean. The question was, would she be staying with Josiah or with me? I received my answer the next morning. Halfway through brushing my teeth, I heard a loud revving noise outside. I ran to the front door, mouth full of toothpaste, and opened it to find Josiah's pickup, piled high with furniture, backed up to my front porch.

I spit a white glob of toothpaste onto the snow as Josiah stepped out of the truck. "Been hitting the garage sales again?" I joked.

Josiah walked to the back of the truck and unhitched the tailgate. "Not quite. But I wish I'd thought of that. Could have saved some money." He climbed into the back of the truck. "I'll need some help lowering this dresser."

"Hang on a minute," I said. "Lucina's moving in with me? I thought you were going to ask me to move in with you, so she could stay in my cabin."

He tossed me a pair of soft leather gloves. "The thought crossed my mind. I'm pretty set in my ways, though. I don't do well with housemates. Nothing personal, of course."

"Of course," I said, slipping my gloves on.

"I'll slide this to the edge, and you grab ahold of the legs," he said matter-of-factly.

I held my gloved hand up. "Can we take a step back for a second here? When did you decide this? Did you run it by Atum?"

Josiah tightened his gloves. "You ask a lot of questions, young man. If you must know, I made my decision last night. And no, I did not run this by Atum. This is my call."

"It's okay by me."

"I'll bet it is," he mumbled to himself.

"What's that supposed to mean?"

Josiah pointed to the lowered tailgate. "Question-and-answer time is over. We'll start with this dresser. You just focus on using your back and legs. Wouldn't want to see you laid up when our lady friend arrives."

The big day arrived in a hurry, and the wait at the airport seemed to take forever. I thumbed through an old newspaper for at least thirty minutes, trying to occupy my restless mind.

"Here we go," Josiah announced dryly, looking past the crowd.

I followed his gaze. The stunning beauty was coming down the escalator. Lucina had the kind of presence that made everyone else fade into the background. She didn't try to hog the spotlight; it just followed her wherever she went. She noticed us right away and immediately lit up with that amazing smile. Goose bumps spread across my body like a heat rash as my heart kicked into full throttle.

I was halfway to the escalator when I realized I'd left Josiah behind. I turned around, but he was still seated, reading his newspaper.

I reached for Lucina's carry-on bags. "Let me help you with those."

She put her bags down and wrapped me in a warm embrace. "Daniel, it's so good to see you again."

She smelled like a lilac bush in full bloom. Her touch sent shivers through my body. We headed toward Josiah, who still hadn't risen from his seat. I pretended not to be annoyed.

"Everything go okay with your flight?" I asked, not knowing what else to say.

"We were held up a bit in Rome, but we made up most of the time in the air. I can't tell you how excited I am to be working with you," she gushed, energizing me with her wide-eyed enthusiasm.

"I was a little surprised when I heard… you know… about the mentoring," I stammered. "Definitely not disappointed though." I wasn't sure if this was the right thing to say, but I was running on pure adrenaline and couldn't be held accountable for anything coming out of my mouth.

Lucina lowered her voice, even though we were still a good forty feet from the slouching Master Guide. "I hope *he's* okay with it."

"Hard to say what he's thinking," I whispered back. "Tough one to read."

"I'm glad we'll be staying in the same house," she said. "I haven't had a roommate in eons."

When we got within five feet of Josiah, he finally stood and extended his hand for another dry, businesslike greeting. We made small talk at baggage claim and chatted more during the ride home. Or more like Lucina and I chatted. Josiah sat silent behind the wheel.

When we pulled up Josiah's driveway, Randall was there, waiting for us. Sure enough, he charged forward when Lucina stepped out of the Cutlass.

She jumped back in horror and grabbed my arm. "Oh my God! Daniel!" She moved behind me for protection. Mimicking Josiah, I held up my hand, and the ferocious beast fell into submission. Even though I was just taming an already trained house pet, it felt empowering to come to Lucina's aid. The fact that she called out for *me* was the best ego boost I'd had in a long time. Randall sniffed around at our guest's heels.

"It's okay." I scratched the frightening beast behind its ears. "This is Randall. He won't bite. He's just a big puppy dog."

Lucina let go of my arm and offered up a cautious hand to Randall, who licked it like a gravy-covered biscuit. Josiah was too busy getting bags out of the trunk to notice.

"I can honestly say, this is the biggest dog I've seen in over twenty centuries," she said. Something about her comment stuck with me. Maybe it was finally hitting home that I had fallen hard for a woman who was not only older than my adoptive mother, but older than my mother's most-distant ancestors. Not that it mattered. I wouldn't have cared if she'd been cruising around since the Stone Age. She looked about twenty-five, tops, and was the most irresistible package of feminine perfection I'd ever laid eyes on.

Josiah set the bags at our feet. "Would you care to come in for a drink?" he asked in a strange display of social etiquette.

Lucina held her hand up. "Oh, I'm fine, really. But thank you. I could use some help lugging all this stuff to my new quarters though, if it's not too much trouble."

"No trouble," Josiah and I both said in unison.

Lucina chuckled in response.

Josiah's expression was blank, as usual, but he did help with the bags. He started to walk back to the car but stopped midstride. "By the way. I'm cooking a special dinner tonight to kick off this next phase of Daniel's training. Why don't you stop by around six o'clock?"

Lucina and I looked at each other. She nodded.

"Sounds great, but you didn't have to do this, you know," I said.

"Of course I know. But I want to. Six o'clock, then?"

"We'll be there," Lucina replied.

Josiah headed back to the car to grab Lucina's bags.

After getting Lucina's things in place, we ended up in the family room with a couple hours to kill before dinner.

I plopped down on the couch, and to my surprise Lucina plopped down right next to me. Her flowery scent and spellbinding eyes had my stomach doing cartwheels. I had dreamed about being alone with her like this, but I had never counted on being so nervous. I couldn't just sit there staring at her. I had to say something.

"I just realized I never offered you a drink."

She waved me off. "Thank you, but I'm fine."

"How was your trip? Oh, wait… I already asked you that at the airport." I'd always known my ability to make small talk was weak, but this was pathetic.

She leaned back into the couch cushions. "It's okay. I don't mind. My trip was fine—even though I hate being cramped up on planes. I had a window seat, though, so at least I had some scenery during the flight."

"How about something to drink?" I asked.

"Didn't you just ask me that?"

I nodded. "Unfortunately, yes."

"Is everything okay, Daniel? You seem tense."

"I'm just a lousy host. And I'm horrible at small talk."

She patted me on the shoulder. "I don't think you're a lousy host. You know what? I think I will take that drink after all."

I pulled out what was left of Josiah's Christmas wine.

Lucina stretched out on the couch as I approached with her drink. "I was a little surprised by the dinner invitation tonight."

"Surprised? How's that?" I asked, knowing damn well what she meant.

"I'm sure you've noticed by now that Josiah isn't exactly thrilled with the new mentoring situation. I was relieved that I'd be staying with you."

"I did pick up on that," I said, dropping the understatement of the year. "I think this arrangement will work out best for all of us." I handed Lucina her wine.

She took a sip and set it down on the coffee table. "I certainly hope so. Anyway, it's nice of him to make us dinner and all. I'll give him that much. One thing I know about Josiah is that he's a fantastic cook. Do you cook, Daniel?"

"I try, but most of my creations are more suitable for Randall than for humans."

She laughed again. "Well, I'm not very picky, so I'm sure your creations will go over just fine."

"Can I ask you something?"

"Of course," she said.

"Do you always go by Lucina?"

She leaned back and spread out her arms. "Funny you should ask. Only Josiah and Atum call me by my formal name. I'm not sure why, but they always have. All the other Sages call me Lucy. You know, like in the song."

"What song?"

"'Lucy in the Sky with Diamonds,'" she said, scanning my face for some sign of recognition. "Sorry, that's probably a little before your time."

I laughed. "Are you kidding? I love the Beatles. My parents played them all the time around the house. I'm more surprised that *you* know who they were."

"Just because I'm older than dirt doesn't mean I haven't kept up with current music."

I let out a quick laugh. "I wouldn't exactly call them *current*."

Lucy's expression of mock horror quickly gave way to her adorable smile. "Well, young Sage, once you've clocked a few hundred years, you might think differently. Anything that's happened in the last century is pretty current to me."

"Point taken." I pretended not to notice the way she twirled her hair around her finger as she looked at me. One of the guys in my tenth-grade gym class told me that if a girl plays with her hair while you're talking to her, she's into you. The guy who said it was probably the biggest chick magnet ever, so I never doubted him. Though right now, it was probably wishful thinking on my part.

Talking to her was as easy as breathing. I couldn't think of anywhere else I'd rather be or anyone else I'd rather be with. This woman had been around since the Roman Empire, but it felt as if she was only a few years older than I was. I would have spent the next six hours staring into those glorious eyes if I could have. A Master Guide was expecting us, though, and we needed to head to his place for dinner.

Lucy stopped talking the minute we left to go to dinner. It was as if someone flipped a switch and shut down her personality.

Josiah welcomed us in and offered drinks. After a few minutes, we settled down for an amazing dinner, expertly prepared by the gourmet chef himself. Josiah's culinary skills were no secret to me, but on this night he really outdid himself. Roasted duck, seasoned potatoes, fruit salad, vegetable medley, and three plates of hors d'oeuvres I'd never even seen before and definitely couldn't pronounce. When did he have time to pull all this together?

Dinner tasted even better than it looked. Everything seemed to be going pretty well until Josiah excused himself and returned from the basement with another bottle of wine. He placed it next to Lucy and went into the kitchen to get the corkscrew. I waved to get Lucy's attention, but she was fixated on that bottle. Any front she'd been putting up for the sake of the occasion was completely gone now, and she couldn't have looked more uncomfortable if she'd been sitting on broken glass. Josiah seemed oblivious.

The bottle had a weird shape to it, round and fat on the bottom, with a tall, skinny neck and ultra-fancy Italian writing carved into the glass. When he offered another drink, Lucy declined. She closed her eyes, as if trying to keep her emotions contained.

"I'd like to make a toast," Josiah announced. "This bottle was purchased during our convergence in Rome. The year was 1501, to be exact. You remember, don't you, Lucina?"

Lucy stared down at her plate, not responding.

"Well, it was a time to remember, Daniel, that's for sure. I guess you had to be there," he slurred, obviously feeling the effects of all that wine. "Anyway, raise your glasses with me, whatever you're drinking, for a toast to the newest Sage. Daniel, I wish you a successful mentorship and a fruitful mission in years to come. You're a wonderful addition to our family."

Josiah and I clinked glasses. Lucy sat motionless, expressionless.

"Did I ever tell you about the night I had dinner with Michelangelo?" Josiah asked.

"I would have remembered that," I said.

He gazed off into the distance as he attempted to recall the details. "I believe the year was 1499. Michelangelo had just completed what I consider to be one of his greatest masterpieces, the *Pietà*."

Lucy pushed back her chair and stood. "If you'll excuse me for a minute."

"Are you okay?" I asked.

"I just need to use the ladies' room." She walked to the bathroom and shut the door.

After about ten minutes, Lucy still hadn't returned. I was getting ready to go and check on her when the door opened. She walked back to the table and sat down.

Josiah was getting to the end of his story. "He was so drunk by the third course, I had to practically carry him back to his house."

I laughed. He could be very amusing if the mood struck him. Lucy was not amused, though. She glanced at me and motioned her head toward the door when Josiah wasn't looking. Before I could thank him and bring the evening to a close, he handed me the ancient bottle.

"Pass that down to Lucina, if you don't mind," he slurred.

I handed her the bottle. I could see her pupils dilate from three feet away as she stared a hole through Josiah. The temperature in the room went up about ten degrees in two seconds flat. Josiah was oblivious.

"Lucina, I think it's only right and salutary that you uncork this very special bottle," he said with a smirk. "After all, it was meant to be consumed over five centuries ago."

Lucy pushed herself away from the table and stood. "Of all the dirty tricks. You planned this all along, didn't you?"

Josiah threw up his hands. "I think you're overreacting."

She glared at him, eyes burning with anger. "Overreacting would be smashing your *special* bottle against the wall. That would be stooping to your level, though."

"I hardly think—"

"Daniel," she interrupted, "feel free to stay and make merry with our host. I've had enough merriment for one night." She squinted her eyes at Josiah and stormed toward the front door. I got up to chase after her, but she was out on the porch before I made it to my feet. I thanked Josiah for dinner and ran after her.

When we got back to the cabin, Lucy headed straight for her room and slammed the door behind her. A minute later she emerged and sat down on the couch. She patted the cushion seat next to her, an offer I'd never turn down.

"I'm sorry you had to be exposed to that." Tears hovered in her eyes. "I'm trying not to let him get to me, but I can see that this is going to be difficult."

"You don't need to apologize," I assured her. "I'm not sure what this is all about, but I guess it's none of my business anyway."

"No, Daniel, it *is* your business. If we're going to be working together, we shouldn't have secrets between us. It's time you knew the truth. That bottle of wine was no coincidence. I can't believe he's resorted to this."

"Sorry, but I don't understand."

"It's a long story." She rearranged herself on the couch. "But here goes. Josiah and I had worked together here and there since the initial convergence of Sages in Galilee. We'd always enjoyed a nice working relationship, until the Sages converged again in Rome during the Renaissance. Something was different about him. I sensed it after our first few days together. He was the perfect gentleman, but he seemed unusually focused on me. Josiah, if you haven't noticed, is an extremely powerful Sage."

She shrugged. "What can I say? He was a Master Guide, and he was interested in me. I have to admit, I was flattered—all the attention, the flirting."

"Lucy, really, you don't need to—"

"It wasn't long before we became lovers," she said, looking down at her hands. "For the first few months, it was wonderful. He swept me up in a whirlwind of love and affection." Her face reddened. "When you've spent nearly fifteen centuries alone, it's almost therapeutic to become romantically involved with someone. Our relationship was forbidden, of course, so we kept it a secret, sneaking off together whenever the opportunity presented itself. I guess that made it all the more exciting, but it didn't last." Her voice trailed off.

I felt obligated to say something, anything, to break the silence. "I'm sorry things didn't work out for the two of you."

"We never stood a chance," she said. "Josiah's dark side started to come through after a while. He just changed... so possessive, untrusting. He started treating me like his property."

Another silence followed. I broke it with the first thing that came to mind. "So what's the story with the wine?"

She rolled her eyes. "Apparently, he bought it in Rimini, my hometown, and brought it back to Rome. It was part of an elaborate dinner he prepared for me one evening. He went on and on about how beautiful I was and how perfect we were together. The wine came out before things got really uncomfortable. Josiah took my hand and proposed." She closed her eyes, shaking her head as if still in disbelief. "Well, as much as that type of thing is even possible with our kind. It was the thought that counted. He was pledging himself to me, and only me, forever."

"What did you say to him?"

"I didn't know what to say. I was flattered, I guess. Probably more shocked than anything else. He was a Master Guide. What *could* I say? I told him I didn't think it was appropriate for two people who work together to marry—or whatever we'd end up calling it." Her eyes settled directly on mine. "That wasn't the real issue, of course. I mean, we all know how Atum feels about this sort of thing, but even he wasn't my biggest concern."

"What was it then?" I asked.

"I couldn't see us together for the long haul. To be honest with you, I've always been a bit unnerved by him, even back then. I think he's spent too much time casting out demons and hunting down the dark ones. It's affected him. He comes across as downright creepy sometimes." She shuddered and glanced toward Josiah's house. "I guess it took me a while to get past my initial infatuation and wake up to that reality."

"So I take it your dinner in Rome didn't go over so well after all?"

"That's putting it mildly. He wouldn't take no for an answer. He started manipulating, using his eyes on me. I knew, by then, how to avoid his hypnotic stare." She shook her head again, as if remembering a terrible nightmare. "Then he started getting loud. I don't know if he was drunk or just insulted. I tried to leave, but he grabbed me by the arm. I pulled away and stormed out. I looked back before I left, and he was slumped down, staring at me. I'll never forget the look on his face, that hateful intensity. I can't even describe it. I felt... scared," she said. "That was the last time I saw him, until the next convergence. We've more or less worked around each other ever since."

"I'm so sorry. I don't know what to say."

"It's okay." She patted me on the knee. "You don't need to say a word. I should have known better. I was hoping things had changed for the better between us. Pretty naïve of me, huh? I'm sure my appointment as your mentor didn't help matters, either. No one at my level has ever been asked to mentor before. Is it any wonder he feels slighted? How could I have thought he'd be anything other than bitter?"

"If Atum chose you, then I'm confident you're the best person to teach me," I said. "I know you'll do a great job, and I know that you've got my back."

She stood and gazed toward the window. "I'll stick by you—that you can count on. And as long as I keep my distance from the Prince of Darkness next door, I'm sure I'll be able to keep the focus entirely on your training. I hope you don't mind, Daniel, but we're going to be spending an awful lot of time together in the months ahead."

I didn't mind. Not in the least.

CHAPTER 22

My first morning of training started with a walk through the snow-covered trails that snaked through Josiah's property. I didn't get the point of it, but I didn't complain. I was with Lucy, and that was good enough for me. She seemed to be in her element outside, taking every opportunity to point out and name each animal, plant, and tree that we came across. Eventually, the conversation turned to my training. The plan was to start with something called the *foundational skills*. Most of it went right over my head.

We'd been walking for about thirty minutes or so when we stopped to rest on a fallen tree. Lucy pulled a pair of gloves out of her pocket and put them on. "I hope I'm not boring you," she said.

"Not at all." I traced the triquetra symbol in the newly fallen snow with my boot. "Can I ask you something?"

"Ask me anything. I'm game."

"What exactly do Sages do? I mean, I get that we all have these missions, but what do you do all day when you're not working on your mission?"

Lucy laughed. "We're always working on our missions, Daniel. Right now, my focus is mentoring you. If I weren't doing this, I'd be busy transitioning souls into and out of their human bodies. Believe me, with over 150,000 people passing on each day around the world, I have more than enough to keep me occupied. There's three times as many being born each day."

I stood to get the blood circulating in my legs. "So you pretty much transition these souls day and night?"

She shook her head. "Not exactly. Only certain souls require my assistance—a very small percentage, but still enough to keep my plate full. When I'm not transitioning, I work with people who have damaged auras."

"Josiah told me about that. You can see auras too?"

"We all can. You will too... in due time." She shifted gears. "I can't wait to teach you how to meditate. It's the cornerstone of your training. Perhaps we can get started today. Just the basics."

I couldn't get over how enthusiastic she was about our work. I could have sat there and listened to her until the sun went down, but the snow was falling hard, and we needed to either start moving or risk getting frozen to that log.

The next three weeks followed the same basic pattern. An early morning walk on the trails and an afternoon training session on advanced meditation. Sitting in front of a fireplace in total silence for close to an hour at a time would normally be my definition of torture, but with Lucy, I looked forward to these sessions. They placed me in such a state of tranquility, I felt like I was floating.

Once Lucy was satisfied with what I'd accomplished, she said I was ready to dive into the first foundational skill, *implanting*. According to her, I was progressing through these meditation sessions at an incredible rate. What she based this on, I had no idea. To me, it seemed like the same routine over and over again, day after day. I didn't get the sense that I was moving forward at all. Either way, it was time to test the waters with a new challenge.

Implanting was a common technique used by all Sages to subconsciously influence humans. Lucy described the process as planting a "seed of thought" into a person's mind, cultivating it, and allowing it to grow. How well that seed blossomed depended on the mental and emotional state of the person, along with the strength of his or her free will.

One thing every Sage needed in order to pull this off was physical contact with the host. Usually, a handshake or a casual hand on the shoulder did the trick. This initial contact, I learned, allowed the Sage to tune in to the energy vibrations of the host and synch up his or her own vibrations. The next step involved peering deep into the host's eyes while maintaining physical contact. The eyes, she explained, are the doors to the subconscious, doors that can be pried open just long enough to implant a thought. The entire process, if done correctly, should take no more than five seconds, sometimes even less for an experienced Sage.

Lucy stood by patiently for days as I tried over and over again to read her vibratory patterns and synch up my frequency with hers. We practiced relaxation, frame-of-mind exercises, and every other technique she could think of, but it went nowhere. I did everything she told me, but I didn't even come close to connecting. After one particularly futile session, she finally voiced her frustration.

She craned her neck back and let out a sigh. "I'm so sorry, Daniel."

"Sorry? Sorry for what? I'm the one who's not getting it."

She looked at me and then at the floor. "I'm not so sure about that. I've never mentored before. I should be able to get you through this, but I'm failing miserably."

"You're not failing, Lucy. I am."

She placed her hand on my shoulder. "Don't be so hard on yourself. You've picked up everything else way ahead of schedule. I guess we shouldn't expect everything to come so easily. We'll figure out what the problem is. I'm sure of it."

I knew exactly what the problem was, but I couldn't bring myself to tell her. Holding her soft, delicate hands and staring back at that beautiful face put me in a completely different state altogether. With every breath, her chest heaved. Every blink of her eyelids revealed the sparkling hazel gems beneath. The soft, wet curves of the most kissable lips I'd ever seen threatened to pull me in like a powerful magnet. If I was going to learn how to implant anytime soon, we were going to need an entirely different approach.

CHAPTER 23

Within a few short weeks, Lucy and I had become inseparable. From the time she arrived in Geneseo, I could hardly remember spending a waking moment without her. Normally, this would have been way too much smothering for me, but with Lucy it was different. I had to admit she'd grown on me to the point that I couldn't imagine my life without her.

By this time, we'd pretty much given up on implanting and, instead, spent our time focusing on reaching deeper states of meditation. Apparently, I had to master this ability before we could work on the next set of fundamentals. This was nowhere near as enjoyable as the implanting exercises, mainly because I had to keep my eyes closed for hours at a time and couldn't see Lucy's adorable face. That might also explain why I picked it up so quickly. Lucy basically hypnotized me and talked me through deeper and deeper levels of the trance state. We worked our way back into my childhood, and soon I was remembering things from as far back as my infant years. Uncovering these hidden memories reminded me an awful lot of my mind-bending experience with Josiah's magic plate. The only difference was that the magic came from within me. Soon, Lucy predicted, I'd be able to tap into these memories without assistance.

One Friday afternoon, my mentor decided to cap off a long day of mediation training with a trip into town. She wanted to see the college and walk the campus. We grabbed a quick bite to eat on Main Street and then toured the campus. After hours of touring every square inch of the campus, we stopped at the gazebo next to the College Union, just in time to catch a brilliant orange sunset.

Lucy hopped up on the edge of the gazebo and hung her legs down. "Sometimes I wish I could have gone to college," she said.

"I'm guessing that type of thing wasn't exactly encouraged back in ancient Rome?"

She kept her eyes on the sunset. "Not exactly."

"Well, I think you'd make an amazing student. You might even get recruited into a sorority."

She laughed. "Can you imagine?"

We headed home after hitting a few stores on Main Street. Lucy called me into her room to help her hang a picture she'd bought uptown. I sat on the edge of her bed, doing more watching than helping.

"When do you think I'll be ready to start on the next foundational skill?" I asked.

She turned away from the picture. "Come again?"

"You mentioned it last week… *exploring* or something."

"*Viewing,*" she corrected. "It's called viewing, and Sages don't learn this during the mentoring period."

"Why not?" I asked.

"There's really no point at this stage. We don't develop the ability to go that deep into the subconscious mind until much later in life."

I looked down at the ring on my finger and held my tongue. I always hated it when someone told me I couldn't do something. It felt like a direct challenge. Lucy probably didn't mean anything by it, but I still couldn't help feeling a little insulted.

"Please don't take it personally, Daniel," she said. "You're progressing really well with the deeper meditations, but viewing is a whole different level of self-reflection. It'll be years before you're ready to go down that road."

"How long did it take you?" I asked.

"I was the youngest to view, aside from Atum, of course. I took my first past-life journey about thirty-five years or so after I was revealed. I don't think any of the others were able to do it in less than a hundred."

"Josiah said that no one's *ever* done it in less than a hundred," I said.

"Oh really?" She crossed her arms, looking me up and down. "So you've already discussed viewing with Josiah? And no one bothered to tell me?"

"It's not like that," I said, coming to Josiah's defense. "I kind of walked in on his meditation session one night, and he explained it to me the next day. He didn't go into specifics or anything. I never even knew what it was called."

"He told you no one ever viewed in under a hundred years?" she asked, tapping her finger against her arm.

I nodded, wishing I'd never opened my big mouth.

"He knows damn well I was the youngest. He's just jealous. So typical."

"Maybe I could do it even sooner," I suggested with a wink.

Lucy's expression softened. "Sorry, I didn't mean to come off so defensive. I'm not trying to write you off, either. But do you honestly think you can achieve something that even Atum couldn't at your age?"

"Josiah said I've done other things ahead of schedule."

"This just gets better by the minute," she said, finger still tapping. "And would you mind sharing some of these *things* with me?"

Now I'd really done it. I should've quit while I was behind. It was too late; there was no getting out of this one.

"I, ahh, had some dreams," I muttered. "More like memories, actually."

"What kind of dreams?"

"The kind where you see segments of past lives." I paused to check her expression. "I've had several, actually, but none since I returned from Scotland."

Lucy pursed her lips. She strolled over to the bedroom window and stared out into the yard. I didn't dare mention it, but she reminded me of Josiah at that moment.

"I can't believe he didn't tell me this. He *wants* me to fail. This proves it." She walked over and sat down next to me on the edge of her bed. "I'm sorry, Daniel. This isn't your fault. I shouldn't mix you up in my issues with that man. I've pulled you in more than enough already."

"It's okay. I don't mind." I placed my hand on her knee.

Lucy looked down. I took my hand off her.

In one quick motion, she grabbed my hand and returned it to her knee. "It's all right, Daniel," she said in a quiet, soothing tone. "You can touch me. I trust you."

I wasn't sure what she was suggesting, but my heart pounded wildly as we looked into each other's eyes. Everything else faded away. The flowery aroma of her hair intoxicated me. Her smooth, delicate lips promised soft kisses of unimaginable joy. Those few seconds of unspoken intimacy went by like minutes, intensified by her touch and amplified by the silence of the moment.

My future flashed before me. The right move would open the door to an amazing life with this beautiful woman by my side. The wrong move would ruin everything.

Lucy responded with a gentle kiss to the cheek, causing a near short circuiting of my central nervous system. Her silky lips moved toward my own. The soft caress of her fingertips along my wrist pushed me to the outer edge of anticipation. I closed my eyes, held my breath, and waited. But no kiss came. When I opened them again, Lucy stood before me, blushing, scanning the room.

"I think I'd better get ready for bed now," she said.

I nodded, not knowing how else to respond. She headed toward the bathroom.

I lay back for a second, staring at the ceiling in disbelief. What had just happened? Could I really have been that close to kissing the woman of my dreams? What did this all mean? Even with the excitement of the last few minutes, I couldn't stop my eyes from shutting. I'm not sure how long I was out, but I did sense lights turning off and, to my surprise, Lucy's warm body next to mine in the bed. I didn't dare speak or shift my weight. If a move were to be made, it would have to come from her.

None did.

CHAPTER 24

Morning greeted me with a rude blast of daylight, shining in through the blinds. I rolled away but nudged up against something. Lucy's smiling face stared back at me.

I recoiled. "Lucy, I'm so sorry. I don't remember—"

"Shhh." She placed her finger over my lips. "You don't need to say anything. I'm the one that should apologize. This is my bed, after all."

"You? Why would you—?"

"I felt you put your arm around me during the night." She looked away for a second, biting her lower lip. "I knew you were asleep but didn't want to wake you. It's been so long since I've felt the warmth of a man in the night. I have to admit, it felt nice." She covered her eyes with her hand and sighed. "A more seasoned mentor would never have allowed this to happen. This is so unprofessional of me. My God, if Atum ever found out—"

"Lucy, don't." I propped myself up on an elbow. "I'm the one to blame. I've had feelings for you since the first time I saw you, two thousand years ago." The words slipped out before I even realized what I'd said.

Lucy sat up in the bed and looked me square in the face. "What do you mean, two thousand years ago?"

My careless tongue had tripped me up again. "I shouldn't have said that. Look, I haven't been completely open with you. I know you'll hate me for this, but I didn't know how to tell you. Remember those memories I mentioned yesterday?"

"You mean the past-life memories you shared with Josiah, but neither one of you bothered telling me about?"

I lowered my gaze to the bedsheets. I felt terrible for keeping this from her. "Yeah, *those* memories. Well, anyway, I saw myself lying on the floor of a huge coliseum in Rome, gored and left to die in this horrible room with the dead and wounded. You appeared out of nowhere and touched my face. You told me everything was going to be okay... that I was going to a peaceful place. I know it was you, Lucy. I'm positive. You were the last thing I saw before closing my eyes for good."

Lucy's face went white. "I see," she whispered.

"I'm sorry. I should've told you. But that's not all. There were other memories. I saw you again in ninth-century Ireland. I was part of a Viking clan that had raided a small town and killed off the resistance. I remember searching through a home for valuables. There was this old man, and then I found myself looking into your eyes, mesmerized. I didn't see anything beyond that. God, curse me if I hurt you in any way."

Lucy's eyes widened. She sat straight up on the bed. "Not at all. I remember. The Viking put down his weapon and walked out the door. I watched from the window. He was powerful—a barbarian—but he walked away. The rest of his clan raped and plundered, but he continued walking toward the water. That was the last I saw of him."

I reached out and touched her face. "I'm in love with you," I blurted. "I've tried to keep this to myself, but I don't want secrets between us. You're the only thing that matters to me. I know I'm not supposed to say this, but I can't keep this to myself anymore."

I stroked her cheek with the back of my hand, knowing her reaction would define the rest of my life. She placed her hand over mine and held it there. Then she took me off guard, throwing her arms around me and pressing her body close to mine. Our lips came together. Euphoria. The last piece of the puzzle was in place, and I felt complete for the first time in my life. I didn't want to spend another day without this woman by my side.

When we released each other, Lucy held both of my hands and gazed deep into my eyes. "Everything will be different from now on," she said quietly. "Everything already is."

"I hope I didn't just mess things up between us."

Her grip tightened on my hands. "You didn't mess up anything, Daniel. You only solidified what was already there. I knew there was something special about you when we met at your initiation. I tried to shake it off, but there was this strange mix of déjà vu and attraction I've never felt with anyone else. The more time we've spent together, the more I've come to realize you're the one I've been waiting for all along." She let go of my hands and swiveled to the edge of the bed. "This new information about your past lives puts things into an entirely different perspective. Of all the people I've tended to over the years, what are the chances that our paths would have crossed even once, let alone three times? And those are just the lives we know about." She shook her head. "I can't write this off to chance anymore. I was chosen to mentor you for reasons that are beyond me. I'm sure of it now."

"And what are we going to do about Atum?" I asked. "You've said it yourself—he doesn't approve of this type of thing."

"No, he doesn't, and I'll bet he wouldn't approve of a mentor sharing a bed with her protégé either." She put her face in her hands. "God, what am I going to do?"

"I didn't mean to put you in such a bad spot, but I had to tell you. I couldn't keep this from you anymore."

"You did the right thing." She pulled her hands away from her face. "But I'm going to need some time alone—to process. I need to figure out how to move forward." She stood and moved toward the door, but stopped and turned toward me. "One more thing—since we're in the spirit of openness. There's something you should know about me. I don't want this to be a surprise later on. I have nothing to hide anymore either."

She turned her back to me and pulled her nightshirt up over her head in one swift motion, revealing her naked body in all its glory. My eyes practically jumped out of my head. This woman was the perfect blend of sexuality and delicate feminine beauty. Her skin was like the purest, finest marble, except for one spot. A dark purple mark stretched from the middle of her back to the top of her right calf. It looked like she'd been burned or scalded at one time, creating the only blotch on an otherwise perfect canvas.

Lucy pulled her nightshirt back on and faced me again. She looked me in the eyes for a brief second and then looked away as if embarrassed. "I was injured in France during the Second World War. We were setting up a trauma unit with the Red Cross when bombs started raining down. So many died." She closed her eyes for a few seconds. "I obviously survived, but I came away with this little beauty mark. I just thought you should know. I hope it doesn't change things between us."

I'd never felt a more powerful emotion than the love I felt for her at that moment. If I was reading this right, the most perfect woman on earth was worried she wouldn't be acceptable in my eyes. Could this really be happening? Overwhelmed by emotion, I wrapped her up in a passionate embrace once again.

"We can't." She pulled away. "Not now. Not yet. I have to spend some time by myself, Daniel. Things are moving way too fast. I need to sort this out… get my head together."

"Sorry. I couldn't hold back anymore. I really do love you."

"I know you do, but I can't let this get in the way of your mission." Her voice cracked, and her eyes filled with tears. "God, I'm so confused. What have I done?" The pool of tears spilled over and ran down her cheeks.

I reached out to wipe them away, but she pulled back. "I really need to spend some time alone. Please understand. Can I take your car?"

I nodded.

Lucy walked into the kitchen and grabbed my car keys. The door shut behind her, and the Civic roared to life.

I couldn't believe this turn of events. Just when I thought I'd reached the peak of happiness, I was thrown back down to the ground. Lucy was slipping through my hands. I had to do something. But what?

CHAPTER 25

The next week was one big blur. Lucy was typically gone when I woke up and didn't return until bedtime. It was the first time in months we'd been apart, and it seemed strange not having her around. I was dying to know what she was doing with herself all day, and how long she'd go on like this, but I left it alone. I managed to pass some of the time visiting old friends in Geneseo and hanging out with Josiah and Randall.

My routine was out of sync since Lucy went on sabbatical. Even my sleep was affected. The dreams had returned. These weren't the full-blown dream-memories I had had before initiation, though. Random images flashed in and out of my slumbering mind each night, leaving me frustrated and confused in the morning. None of it made any sense, and the things I *could* remember seemed meaningless. I was searching for something— anything—that could shed more light on my relationship with Lucy or this all-important mission everyone kept talking about. The only common thread I came up with was that most of these images took place in a desert.

I finally mentioned this to Lucy one night as she made another beeline for the bedroom. "I had the dreams again."

Lucy stopped short of her bedroom door. "How long has this been going on?"

"Last couple days," I said.

She walked into the living room with a new sense of urgency and sat down on the couch. She motioned me to join her. "I'd love to hear about it."

"There isn't much to share. The images come and go, and none of it makes any sense. The only common theme is the desert. All my memories now are taking place in a desert."

"Do you know which desert? Any concept of geography or time period?" she asked.

I shrugged. "Don't know. All I see are sand dunes, and camels and a river." I nodded to myself. "I always see that river, now that I mention it."

Lucy stroked her bottom lip with her thumb and forefinger. "Interesting."

"What's interesting? That I'm having the memories again?" I asked.

She shook her head. "What you described aren't memories; they're images, flashes. The Viking episode–that was a memory."

"But I was having full memories. Now back to the images again? Sounds like I'm regressing."

"I wouldn't say that. It's hard to judge with you. Your progress is so atypical. Even the images you're having are a hundred years ahead of schedule. Why you'd go from images to memories, and then back to images again, is anyone's guess."

It was one big puzzle to her, but she seemed motivated to work through it. I was just thrilled she was ready to work with me again. Before long, we discussed the possibility of exploring the viewing technique. Apparently, her soul-searching had come full circle.

The next morning got off to an unexpected start. I picked up on Lucy's energy before I even made it to the coffee machine.

"Get a good night's sleep?" she asked from her seat at the kitchen table.

"Pretty good. No memories or images, though, if that's what you're driving at."

She stood and walked toward the stove. "Let me fix you something."

I stepped away from the coffee machine. "Really? What's going on? You look like you've been up for hours."

She grabbed a frying pan from the cupboard, eggs from the fridge, and a loaf of bread from the counter before I finished stirring my coffee. I'd never seen anyone move so fast that early in the morning. "I *have* been up for hours."

"Couldn't sleep, I take it?"

She cracked an egg. "Just figuring out how I'm going to ease you into your viewing exercises today."

"Today? We're starting today? I know we discussed it, but I didn't realize you wanted to jump right into it."

She glanced over at me. "Why wait?"

"No complaints on this end. I wish I had a better understanding of what this technique is all about, though."

"The concept is simple," she said, moving the eggs around the pan with her spatula. "Viewing is a way to seek personal growth. We use the technique to explore our inner selves. Think of it as a way to unlock long-forgotten past-life memories. You also get to see things through a different set of eyes, which helps provide perspective." She turned and faced me. "We can hold off on the training if you think it's too soon."

"No way. I'm definitely up for this."

"I thought you might say that. But I have to warn you—don't get your hopes up. No one anywhere near your age has ever attempted viewing before. It might take weeks, months, perhaps years before you finally get it. I just don't want you to get discouraged."

"I'll keep that in mind," I said.

The following morning, we picked up where we left off. Lucy took me through the familiar deep breathing and controlled heart rate exercises. Once I'd gotten my breathing and pulse synchronized with Lucy's, the next step was something she called *whitewashing*, a complete blanking out of all thought. This was the most difficult step, she warned, and I wouldn't be able to tap into the superconscious state until I could demonstrate the ability to blank out all conscious thought for at least one full minute. True whitewashing was impossible for mere mortals and extremely challenging for developing Sages.

The other challenge was finding the right medium. All Sages, I learned, use some form of natural medium as their own personal gateway to the superconscious mind. For Lucy, this medium was as simple as being out in nature. Josiah used fire to reach the trance state, while Atum preferred large bodies of still water. Asha, I was told, needed the warmth of the sun to view, and Sumati used a full moon. Darya was the only Sage, other than Atum, who could view by using multiple mediums, but a cold, snowy environment was her preference. My challenge would be to discover what worked for me, assuming I was even ready to do this in the first place.

Whitewashing was actually pretty simple in theory but not so easy to pull off. Sitting across from each other, we closed our eyes and focused on maintaining a clear mind. The first time a thought entered either one of our minds, we had to say, "noise," and start all over. We practiced this for about two hours straight, Lucy outlasting me every time. The experience was humbling, but my *intervals*, or periods of time when I was clear, were increasing, and this was a sign of improvement.

After another two days of practice, I outlasted Lucy for the first time. My intervals increased dramatically, and I showed no sign of stopping. After another three days of practice, I outlasted my mentor almost every time. Part of my improvement was tied to a discovery I made on my own. I learned I could focus on an imaginary point of light in the distance and block out all incoming thoughts, or noise. For whatever reason, this technique worked, and whitewashing became more than just a possibility. I was doing it on a regular basis.

Whitewashing had gone better than expected, but there was only so much I could take. I needed something more challenging, but I didn't know how to say this to Lucy without sending the wrong message. Lucy put things on a different track during dinner one night.

"Good progress today. You've come a long way," she said, between mouthfuls of soup.

"Yeah, I wanted to talk to you about that."

She took a sip of her water. "I'm listening."

"Whitewashing is great, but—"

"You're ready for the next step," she finished my sentence.

"How'd you know I was gonna say that?"

"Woman's intuition," she said.

"More like Sage intuition. Don't you think?"

She raised her eyebrows. "Perhaps. If you want to know the truth, though, I've taken you as far as I can. The next step is for you to find your own medium, and that can only be accomplished through your own experimentation."

I nodded. "I'll give it my best shot. Any suggestions as far as getting started?"

Lucy put down her spoon and crossed her hands in front of her. Before she could say a word, her phone rang. She answered it.

"Who is it?" I whispered.

Lucy pointed toward Josiah's house. He was the last person I expected to hear from. She closed her eyes and squeezed the bridge of her nose. Apparently, the news was not pleasant.

I walked to the living room and sat down on the couch. Lucy followed me.

"I'll be there," she said into her phone as she sat next to me. "Any particular time? Okay, see you tomorrow." She clicked her phone off.

"What was all that about?" I asked.

"Apparently, it's time for a coaching session." She rolled her eyes and slumped in the seat.

"Are you kidding?"

"I wish. Josiah is apparently required to meet with me every so often to make sure we're on the right track with your training. It's odd, though. Atum had always delegated the training of charges to the Master Guides in the past. Your training is different. Atum's not only involved, he's deciding what you should learn and when. It's like he wants to control every aspect of your training. Your program has been the most unorthodox I've ever seen." She shrugged. "I guess I have to trust the Master knows what he's doing."

"I certainly hope so," I said.

The corners of her mouth turned up. "Wait 'til they hear how much progress you've made. They probably won't believe me at first."

"So you're meeting with Josiah tomorrow?"

"Tomorrow at ten," she said, without an ounce of enthusiasm. "I'm not sure how long these coaching sessions last, though. This is all new to me."

"Sounds like the perfect opportunity for me to work on my viewing experiment," I said.

She nodded in agreement. "Sounds like a plan. Remember what I told you, though. Don't expect too much. These things take time."

"Aye-aye, Captain," I joked.

Lucy walked over and sat on the arm of the couch. "Seriously, Daniel, I don't want to see you getting down on yourself." Her sweet scent wafted over me, and I squirmed. I wanted to reach out and touch that perfect silky skin. Being this close to her was like getting invited to a gourmet feast when you're starving and then being told not to eat. I would have given my left arm for so much as a kiss, but her warning to take things slow rang painfully in my ears.

"Good-night." Just like that, she was off to her bedroom.

I considered taking a cold shower. Instead, I shuffled off to bed and called it a night.

When I woke the next morning, I tried to remember my dreams, but the only things I could recall were another desert landscape, a roaring river, and an elaborate palace. What was up with this? My images and memories used to be all over the board. Now my sleeping mind was obsessed with desert scenes. The hardest part was not being able to do anything about it.

"You're up early," I said to Lucy on my way to the fridge.

She was sitting at the kitchen table, holding the newspaper open in front of her. Without looking at me she said, "Not really, Sleeping Beauty. You logged about eleven hours last night according to my watch. I guess all that whitewashing wore you out."

"Guess so." I let out a yawn. "Or maybe it was those annoying images fluttering around in my head all night long."

She laid the paper down on the table and gave me her full attention. "Anything worth mentioning?"

"Just more deserts and palaces. At least I'm getting consistent themes. That's a good sign, isn't it?"

Lucy stood and walked toward me. She leaned against the counter, arms crossed. "I'm not sure." Her brow wrinkled. "You've got a strong connection to a past life in a desert region. That's pretty obvious. Why you went from sporadic images to consistent themes, though, is anyone's guess."

"Maybe that's where Josiah comes in," I suggested. "Maybe he'll have some ideas."

Lucy scowled. "Oh, he'll have plenty to say, I'm sure. I'm not keeping my hopes up. I haven't had a positive interaction with that man for over five hundred years. Why should today be any different?"

I opened a new bottle of maple syrup. "Give him a chance. Maybe he'll surprise you."

"That's what I'm afraid of," she said, marching off to the bathroom.

I scanned through the newspaper while she showered. The headlines were the same predictable heap of bad news. Thirty minutes later, she was ready for her review with Josiah.

"You'll do great," I said, hoping to boost her confidence.

She rolled her eyes. "I wouldn't bet on it."

"Don't worry. Everything will work out in the end. Just don't read too much into what he says."

Lucy stared at me like she couldn't believe what I'd said. "You know, sometimes I wonder if it's your age or if you're really that naïve."

I stepped back. "What? Where the hell did that come from? I'm just trying to be supportive."

Her eyes narrowed. "You might want to think about whom you're being supportive of, because it sounds like you're giving that man a whole lot more credit than he deserves."

I threw my hands up. "Forget it! Forget I said anything. Go to your goddamn review. I hope you have a hell of a time." I stormed off to my room and slammed the door.

Lucy knocked on my door. "Daniel, I'm sorry. Can I come in?"

"No," I snapped.

I heard the front door close. Randall's familiar greeting echoed across the yard, and then all was quiet.

CHAPTER 26

I sat on the edge of my bed, steeped in regret. What had come over me? Lucy was obviously under a ton of stress. Did I really need to lay into her like that? That was the first time I'd ever lost my temper with her. I hoped it would be the last.

I decided to take my mind off what had happened and work on viewing. My experiment followed a script right out of Lucy's playbook—testing nature as a possible medium. I grabbed an old blanket from the trunk of the Civic and followed the trail we'd walked each morning. The perfect spot was about a quarter mile in, nestled between two maple trees. The forest was mostly still, with a slight breeze kicking up from time to time. It would have been nice if it was a little warmer, but I wasn't going to get picky in the dead of winter.

Within minutes, I was able to reach a steady breathing and pulse rhythm. Getting into a state of relaxation was second nature to me now, but whitewashing was a whole different story. The sounds of birds chirping, a squirrel leaping from branch to branch, the occasional gust of wind rattling through the frozen brush—I couldn't tune any of it out. I tried moving farther along the path but couldn't find a spot where I could concentrate. Finally, after one last frustrating attempt, I headed home.

I checked the time when I got back. According to my cell phone, I'd been out in the sticks for close to three hours. That explained why I couldn't feel the tips of my fingers. I was more surprised that Lucy hadn't returned from Josiah's. Something didn't feel right. Three hours to talk about my training? What if something was wrong? I had to put it out of my mind and trust that the two Sages, with over six thousand years of experience between them, could handle things. I decided to light a fire and warm my frozen skin.

My experiment had been an abysmal failure. I remembered Lucy's warning not to expect too much at first. Regardless, something told me I was close to figuring it out. Staring into the orange and yellow flames flickering away in the fireplace, I continued retracing. Then it hit me. The fireplace had been blazing every time Lucy and I had practiced whitewashing. Why didn't I think of that in the first place?

Sitting down in front of the fire, I mimicked the position I had found Josiah in the night I crashed his meditation session. I brought my breathing and heart rate into synch in no time. The next phase was the hard part. Eyes closed, I tried my old technique of focusing on a central point of imaginary light in the distance. This seemed to block out distractions, but nothing else happened. I decided to try something I'd never done before—meditating with my eyes open, like Josiah had done.

I focused again on the imaginary point of light over the tips of the flames. My eyes stung from not blinking, but I forced myself to keep them open. My vision blurred as tears formed. Soon, all I could see were colors of every kind swirling together with bright, wispy clouds. As the clouds faded, I found myself traveling backward at incredible speed through some sort of tunnel. My body became one with the bright colors, soothing me from the inside out. I closed my eyes as tunnel walls flashed by.

When I opened them again, the tunnel was gone and a bright sun beat down on my head. My jaw dropped. I knew this place. I was standing on a sand dune in Luxor, Egypt, with the Nile River flowing behind me. I was inside a new physical body, smaller and leaner than the one from my current life. It was all coming back now. My name was Seti. I was a twenty-one-year-old freeman living during the reign of the pharaoh Ramesses the Great. The year was 1252 BC.

I recognized the second home for Ramesses' queen, Nefertari, off in the distance. The structure had been in place for years but was often used as a getaway for the royal family. I'd been commissioned as a stonecutter to work on outfitting the palace with two new monuments dedicated to the goddess Isis, a gift from the pharaoh to his queen.

Just beyond the palace, a huge crew of slaves pulled enormous granite slabs across the desert sand. Every pull seemed perfectly choreographed as they pulled in unison. These massive blocks of stone would soon be positioned and erected. Then it would be up to me to carve the rough-cut outline that the highly skilled craftsmen would later sculpt to perfection. Work was scheduled to begin tomorrow.

I was confident in my own abilities, having been mentored since my early teens by some of the best stonecutters in the land. The job ahead was another chance for future opportunities within the kingdom. This was a time of great prosperity, and there were no shortage of projects, as Ramesses was one of the greatest builders in our history. Personal recognition from the pharaoh and his inner circle went a long way toward improving one's lot in life.

I had the ability to pull back and see my tanned, chiseled body from the perspective of Daniel, the invisible observer. As the desert sun stung the back of my neck, I became aware of an incredible thirst, but I wasn't allowed to leave until the inspector was satisfied with my progress. Hours later I walked to a spot where the riverbank was low, and I filled my pouch. As I crouched down in the reeds, I kept an eye out for crocodiles, which were never far off in these waters.

There was a shuffle behind me. I turned around and spotted a young lady approaching the river. Her garments identified her as part of the royal family, but she was walking alone, which was forbidden. The sun sat low in the sky, making it all the more unusual for this young woman of means to be out wandering the riverbanks alone. She glanced over her shoulder several times before wandering down to the riverbank.

I craned my neck around the reeds to get a better look. She was about my age and gorgeous. She kicked off her sandals and dangled her feet above the water from the edge of a steeper bank.

I was leaning over to get a better look when something large moved silently across the water. She must have seen it too, since she scrambled to stand, but she slipped off the edge into the water. A massive crocodile's head appeared above the surface as it accelerated into attack mode. Screaming, the young lady pulled herself onto the bank, but she slipped back in again.

I bolted out of the reeds and reached for the lady as she clawed desperately at the muddy riverbank. I grabbed her hand and yanked with all my might, straining from the pull of her weight. The crocodile lunged out of the water, snapping its massive jaws at her outstretched legs. With strength I never knew I had, I grabbed a hold with my other arm and heaved her over the edge as the beast grazed the back of her leg with its sharp teeth.

I helped the frightened maiden to her feet. Seeing her perfect features face-to-face, my heart rate accelerated. Her eyes, in particular, were wild with color and strangely unsettling. The more I looked into those eyes, the more familiar they appeared. She had the exact same eyes as Lucy. Wait! This beautiful woman *was* Lucy! There was no mistaking it. I stared longingly at her through Seti's eyes. She glanced away for a moment but returned my stare immediately. It was as if both of us were hypnotized by each other and couldn't break the spell of fascination.

Finally, she spoke. "You saved my life. Who are you? Where did you come from?"

I hesitated at first, still in the grasp of this exquisite beauty. "I am Seti, freeman and stonecutter. I've been commissioned to work on the queen's palace. I was down in the reeds getting water when you approached. I wished to make my presence known, but I didn't want to startle you. Then I saw the crocodile."

She continued staring at me with the same awestruck expression. "You saved my life. Clearly, you were sent by the gods to protect me." She shifted her gaze skyward. "I am forever in your debt."

"Might I ask who you are and why you're down here alone?" I looked around to make sure no one had spotted me alone with this beautiful young woman.

"I am Pakhet, daughter of the pharaoh. I am eighteen years old, but my family treats me like a child. They won't even let me out of the compound without court-appointed guards watching my every move. The guards are easy enough to get past," she said with a mischievous wink. "I've learned a few tricks over the years."

I sensed something dangerous about this situation. Smitten as I was, I knew it wasn't in my best interest to be caught alone with the pharaoh's daughter. It didn't matter that I had saved her life. There were strict expectations for social interaction between men and women, let alone common men and daughters of royalty. We weren't even allowed to look at the royal women for fear of immediate punishment.

"You're a princess," I said. "Much trouble would befall me if I were found in your presence."

"It is so, but life's greatest rewards are not without risk." She kissed me softly on the cheek and stepped back. "I must be on my way. Perhaps our paths will cross again." She took another step and then winced in pain.

"You're bleeding," I pointed out. Her wound wasn't much more than a deep scratch, but a streak of blood ran down the back of her leg.

"It is nothing, Seti. I'm a big girl, despite what my parents think. I can take care of it. Someday, I hope to repay you for saving me." She turned back and winked again before disappearing down the path.

I looked back at the riverbank, trying to digest what had just happened. I had saved a princess from certain death, and she seemed as fascinated with me as I was with her. What had I gotten myself into, though? She was royalty. I was working class. The royals would have my head if they knew I had touched one of their own. Still, the thought of her stunning beauty left me spinning.

A new scene emerged. It was nearly twilight, and I'd been working all day on the monuments. I came down to the river to wash off the sweat and stone dust from my weary body. I hadn't seen Pakhet at all during the day, but the memory of her face was still fresh in my mind. I stripped down to my loincloth and entered the cool river down by the reeds. As I emerged from the water, my heart leapt. Pakhet stood watching me, a grin on her face. "I thought I might find you here."

"The sun is low in the sky. Too low for a girl to be walking by the river alone."

Pakhet glanced around. "I see no *girls*. Whom were you referring to?"

"Sorry, your highness. I should address you as *lady,* of course."

"That won't be necessary, Seti," she said, looking me up and down.

"Then what should I call you?"

"Pakhet will do fine." She stood toe-to-toe with me. A flowery scent filled my nostrils as she moved closer. Teasing me. Torturing me. I swallowed hard, trying to keep my impulses under control. "Why do you look at me like that, Seti?"

"Look at... What do you... I mean—"

"Shh." She placed her finger on my lips. "You don't need to explain." Rising up on her toes, she kissed me gently on the cheek. It felt like suicide, but I couldn't resist. I pulled her lips to mine, savoring the sweet taste of her soft, wet tongue as our bodies swayed under a darkening sky.

"I don't ever want this moment to end," she whispered in my ear.

"You're not alone in your desire," I whispered back, glancing over my shoulder. "But I think you'd better get back before your people come looking for you."

"Meet me here again tomorrow night?" she suggested with a playful grin.

"I still say this is dangerous," I admitted. "Yet I can think of nothing that would please me more."

Pakhet's good-bye kiss lingered for several more minutes before she finally released me from her grasp. "Same time tomorrow night." She headed back down the path and disappeared out of sight.

We had many secret liaisons down by the river. Innocent flirting and tender kisses soon turned into passionate lovemaking under the moonlight. The thrill of raw passion coursed through my veins like a raging river as I explored every contour of Pakhet's voluptuous body night after night. I inhaled the unforgettable aroma of her flowery scent and savored the sweet aftertaste of her honeydew kisses.

Pakhet's ability to slip past her royal keepers was due, in large part, to her cousin's secret affair with the man who stood guard in the rear of the palace. Pakhet and the guard had a certain *understanding*, she explained, and she wasn't the least bit worried about getting caught. I wasn't quite as confident, but my love for her made it, as she pointed out, worth the risk.

Time flashed by until it reached autumn. My work on the monuments was complete, but I'd managed to find additional work on a nearby mausoleum under construction. Every evening, I made my way down to the river to meet my royal lover. I never felt more alive than when I held Pakhet in my arms and gazed into her glorious hazel eyes. I wanted these nights to go on forever.

More time passed. The sun dipped below the western sky much sooner these days. I found myself down by the river again, waiting for Pakhet. A full moon lit up a star-studded sky, while the calming flow of the Nile created the perfect backdrop for two young lovers. I should have been bursting with anticipation at the arrival of my princess. Instead, my stomach was in knots. Pakhet was late. Very late. Something must have kept her longer than expected, I told myself. Maybe her favorite guard was off duty and she couldn't meet me. Then again, what if something had happened to her on the way here? What if she was in trouble and needed my help? There was only one way to be sure.

I moved along her well-worn trail, calling her name in muted whispers.

No answer.

The moon guided my way to the palace's back gate. Mounted torches lined the entranceway, while two rows of human statues stood guard. I waited for Pakhet to emerge, but each passing minute made our reunion more and more unlikely. Something didn't feel right. Something didn't smell right. My nostrils widened as I breathed in a sweaty aroma that seemed somehow out of place in this quiet natural landscape. The last thing I heard was a grunt, followed by a sickening thud. A sharp pain ripped across the back of my skull; then all was dark.

CHAPTER 27

The stars moved across the sky like a thousand fireflies swarming overhead. It felt as if the world was moving below my feet.

It was.

Two muscular guards were carrying me toward the palace. Their faces were barely visible in the dim moonlight, but something in the way they related to one another told me they were brothers. There was something familiar about them. I felt a strange connection to them in my current life as Daniel. I knew them. But how? Then it came to me—the twins! I was being carried off by ancient incarnations of Kaiden and Argylle, Atum's faithful bodyguards.

The scene changed again, and I found myself facedown on the royal throne room floor. Looking up I saw the pharaoh, Pakhet sobbing beside him. Ramesses, cold as marble, glared at her and slid his finger across his lips. Pakhet struggled to muffle her sobs.

The brothers stood alongside another guard, who I guessed to be Pakhet's once trusted accomplice. He stood silent, like the others, staring straight ahead. I didn't blame him for his little charade. Considering the consequences, I wasn't sure I'd act any differently.

Ramesses rose from his throne and motioned me to stand. I did as commanded, head throbbing from the blow I had taken on the trail. How long could I stay upright before dizziness and nausea sent me crashing to the floor? The pharaoh was a slender man and several inches shorter than I was, but my legs trembled as he peered into my eyes.

"Do you know why you stand before me?" he asked.

I said nothing. Of course I knew, but I didn't know how to answer without damning myself.

"Answer me!" he shouted.

I blurted out the first thing I could come up with. "You weren't satisfied with the monuments I cut?"

The back of his hand crashed into my right cheekbone.

"How dare you insult me? You will tell me the truth. Now confess!"

Tears streamed down Pakhet's face. I glanced at her accomplice, wondering if it was he who had betrayed her. It didn't matter anymore. It was too late for me, but I had to do what I could to protect Pakhet. I still didn't know how much she'd told them.

I stared down at Pharaoh's sandals. "I'm aware of no offense."

"Liar!" He slapped my face, and my head snapped back. "Take the princess to her quarters," Ramesses ordered his guard. I looked at Pakhet's beautiful face for possibly the last time. I had committed a grievous sin with the Pharaoh's own flesh and blood. Sweat formed on my forehead as fear consumed me. My knees shook uncontrollably, and I found it difficult to breathe. My punishment would be severe. I closed my eyes, praying that the pharaoh would make it quick and painless.

"No! Don't hurt him!" she screamed. "Don't you touch him!" Another guard locked up her arms as she kicked and thrashed.

Ramesses moved in close. His eyelids narrowed, and his mouth curled downward in a sinister snarl. "The princess confessed to your little trysts by the river. What I need to know, though, is if she's still untarnished." His voice trembled with anger as he moved in closer to my face. "This, she refuses to confess."

I looked down at the floor again. "It's true." My voice cracked. "We did carry on for some time, but your daughter is still pure."

"Yet you cannot look me in the eye?" He was so close to my face, I could smell the stench of his wretched breath. "Look me in the eye and confess the truth!"

"She—she is still untouched," I stammered.

The pharaoh's shoulders hunched forward, and he shut his eyes. "Now I know that my daughter is no longer innocent," he said in a dry, emotionless voice. "Take him to the holding cell and chain him up. I want two guards on him at all times. We'll settle this matter tomorrow night." He stormed out of the room.

The brothers dragged me to a darkened chamber, complete with shackles and chains. The twin I knew as Kaiden threw me against the wall. They chained my wrists and stood guard at the chamber's entrance.

The smaller of the two, whom I knew to be Argylle, turned to me and taunted, "You played that one well, didn't you? The princess never confessed a thing." Both brothers chuckled.

"So tell us, lover," said Kaiden, sneering. "How does a lowly stonecutter get to sample the ripest fruit in the royal family?"

"Probably hung like an ox," the smaller one suggested. They both erupted in laughter.

A part of me remembered this ordeal. I just couldn't tap into the details. Regardless, I knew where this was heading. My heart raced, and my legs gave out. I hung by my shackles as fear turned to dread.

The scene shifted to the guards releasing me from my chains. I hadn't been able to put my arms down for an entire day, and the sudden rush of blood into my limbs felt like the sting of a thousand hornet bites. The larger brother tied my hands together behind my back and shoved me forward. I struggled to stay on my feet.

A bright moon beamed down as legions of stars lit up the evening sky. The pharaoh stood by the riverbank with a small entourage of witnesses. Pahket sobbed beside him, avoiding my eyes. With death all but certain now, I appealed silently to Amon-Re. If he heard my prayer, the ruler of all gods might be persuaded to exert his power and spare my life.

Amon-Re wasn't listening.

With a simple nod from the pharaoh, Argylle tied my legs together and prepared the sack. I knew what was coming next. I looked at my sweet Pakhet for the last time. Her radiant eyes, wet with tears, were the last image I saw before the sack encased me in darkness.

CHAPTER 28

In one swift motion, I was hoisted overhead and heaved into the unforgiving Nile. The frigid blast of rushing water shocked my sweat-covered skin. I struggled to break free from the ropes. Sinking, I strained to hold my breath. If I could just free my wrists… I thrashed and pulled on the ropes in desperation, but it was no use. My lungs were about to burst from the pressure. I couldn't hold my breath any longer. I heard the faint sound of bubbles as I ejected my last breath into the Nile. Water flooded in. Freezing. Choking. Pain. Darkness.

My spirit hovered above the river, looking down at the sinking sack below. Although I felt pity for Seti, he seemed somehow distant now, even separate from me. I was free from the bonds of the flesh. Free from the shackles of society and all the constraints and corruption that went with it. A bright light appeared above me, its pull impossible to resist. Moving through the tunnel again, I blasted forward with incredible speed. Chimes and a beautiful, almost musical voice sounded in my ears. Joyful anticipation filled my soul as I raced toward the inevitable union with this perfect light of warmth and love.

"Daniel," a soft voice called, soothing my spirit as I neared my destination. "Daniel," it chimed again as I entered into the light. I squinted at first, unable to focus. The world was a confusing blur of color. When my eyes finally adjusted, I was greeted by an unexpected sight: flames.

"Over here," the soft, familiar voice called. "Daniel, honey, are you okay?" I shifted my eyes from the fireplace toward the voice and saw my sweet Lucy smiling back at me.

"Look at me. Take slow, deep breaths."

Lucy's gentle voice eased me out of my stupor. I became aware of the immediate surroundings, and my heart rate returned to its normal rhythm. Keeping the focus on Lucy's eyes seemed to help with the adjustment, and soon I was completely at ease.

"How are you feeling?" she asked, dabbing my chin with a moist towel.

"Fine… I think. What's this? What's with the towel?"

Lucy ran her hand down the back of my head. "You've been drooling for the past twenty minutes, my dear, maybe longer."

I felt my face get flushed. "I've been out that long?"

At least. I've only been back for twenty minutes. I'm assuming you started viewing well before that.

I glanced outside into darkness. "My God, I've been out for hours! Is that normal?"

"Perfectly normal."

"And the slobber?" I asked, glancing at the drool cloth.

"Not so normal." She ran her hand down the back of my head, calming me further. "But it does happen from time to time. It just means you've had a very intense experience. Want to tell me about it?"

"I'm surprised you'd want to hear anything from me," I said. "I'm sorry I lost my temper earlier."

She tossed the cloth on the floor beside me. "It's not all your fault. I was pretty wound up myself. I say we put it behind us."

"I like the sound of that."

After a long silence, Lucy's eyebrows raised. "Well?"

"What?" I shrugged. "Am I forgetting something?"

"Your viewing experience. You were going to tell me all about it."

"Oh, that. I'm not sure you want to hear this. It doesn't have a happy ending."

She softened her tone. "I'm a big girl. I can handle it."

The hairs stood up on my arms as Pakhet's words flowed from Lucy's mouth. "All right. But keep an open mind." I walked Lucy through the beginning of the memory, including as many details as I could remember. As soon as I described how Seti pulled Pakhet out of the river, she straightened up, eyes wide with amazement.

"Are you okay?" I asked. "Do you want me to stop?"

"No, no, no," she said. "Go on."

I continued all the way through to Seti's death in the river. She'd been holding her hand over her mouth the entire time, but it was clear I'd finally struck a nerve. Tears ran down her face. We sat in silence for a long, uncomfortable minute. Lucy appeared to be in a state of shock.

"There's one more thing I need to tell you." I hesitated to go much further, but there was no point stopping now.

"Go on," she whimpered. She pulled her trembling hands away from her mouth.

"I recognized Pakhet from the first time I looked into her eyes. She wasn't just the daughter of Ramesses. She was you. And you were her. One and the same," I said, glancing over to check for a reaction. "I recognized the brothers who guarded the palace too. The twins, Kaiden and Argylle."

"Amazing," she finally said. "Absolutely amazing."

"What's amazing?"

"Where do I begin? None of us has ever had the ability to recognize people from our current life when viewing. I don't think even Atum can do that." Her brow wrinkled as she glanced away.

"What's wrong? You look concerned or something. Everything's fine."

"Everything is *not* fine. This confirms my worst fear. I saw some of what you described when I reviewed my life as Pakhet. I just never knew who Seti was beyond our life in Egypt. Don't you see, Daniel? We shouldn't be together. We can't be together, at least not *that* way."

"What are you talking about? What does something that happened over three thousand years ago have to do with us now?"

"Everything." Her expression sank along with her posture. "We weren't supposed to be together in Egypt, but we went ahead anyway… and look what happened. You died back then because of me."

"Hang on a minute. You can't possibly—"

"We're not supposed to be together now either, Daniel. Atum discourages this for a reason." She stood and ran her fingers through her hair. "Don't you understand? You have a mission. Someday, you'll lead the righteous souls of earth in the final battle against the dark souls. Nothing is more important than that. And nothing can distract you from this mission."

"I'm not buying this," I challenged. "I love you, and you love me. That's what's important. Who says we can't fight this battle together?"

She faced me. "It doesn't work like that. You know I love you. But I've been trusted to prepare you for your mission, not distract you from it. The memory you had is a warning to us. Asha taught me how to interpret memories from previous lives. This is absolutely a warning."

"This is absolutely nothing!" I pounded my fist down on the side of the coffee table, knocking an empty glass to the floor. "I won't let this come between us. I love you too much. Nothing is getting in the way of you and me."

Tears formed in Lucy's eyes again. I tried to put my arms around her, but she pulled away. "Please don't. Please. It only makes things that much harder."

If only I'd kept my mouth shut, we wouldn't be having this conversation. Lucy was slipping away. I wasn't going down without a fight, though.

"Lucy, please, hear me out. I *do* see the pattern, and it makes perfect sense. Atum selected you to be my mentor for a reason. I'll bet he doesn't even fully understand why. You and I are a team, always have been. Who knows how many other lives we've shared together? Who knows how many of those lives had happy endings? You're my mentor because we *belong* together. That's the message from my experience."

She looked up at me with eyes so full of pain it was all I could do to restrain myself from wrapping my arms around her and holding her close. Without warning, she ran into her room and shut the door. I stood there, helpless, hearing her muffled sobs through the bedroom door. I took my chances and knocked. The door opened, and Lucy motioned me to come in. She sat on the edge of the bed, head between her hands.

"Will you at least consider what I'm saying?" I pleaded.

"I am considering," she said through quiet sobs. "You may be right, but it doesn't matter. I'm obligated to share all of this with Josiah. It's expected. It's required."

"And what happens if you don't?" I suggested.

"It doesn't work like that. We have an obligation to be honest with each other. Even if I lie, Josiah will know. He's a Master Guide, Daniel. He has over a thousand years of development on me. The man has skills and abilities I haven't even begun to develop. I have to tell him, and when I do, he'll have me removed from this assignment, and you and I will be separated for good."

She stood and faced me. Her tear-filled eyes brought me back to the sight of Pakhet, standing on the bank of the Nile, moments before I took my last breath. As I had in Egypt, I craved nothing more than to feel her soft skin pressed against mine. I felt confident the feeling was mutual. I took a chance and put my arms around her.

To my surprise, she clung to me like it was our last good-bye. With her body pressed tightly to mine, I lifted her off the floor and felt her legs clamp tightly around me. Lucy tore open my shirt and ran her tongue up and down my neck. The warmth of her breath on my skin sent shivers through me. Our bodies descended to the bed. Cradled in her loving embrace, I discovered paradise. I never wanted to leave.

CHAPTER 29

A heavy thud jolted me out of a deep sleep. Lucy climbed over the top of me. As she rose from the bed, I was treated once again to the glorious site of naked feminine perfection. The only item she wore was the matching Celtic cross necklace I'd given her two days before. I hadn't bothered to explain the history behind it, only that it represented the bond between us.

Lucy threw on a robe and shuttled out the bedroom door before I could stop her. I'd gotten as far as the edge of the bed when I noticed her standing petrified in the hallway, staring straight ahead. I ran out wearing only boxers and came face-to-face with the last person I wanted to see. Josiah glared back.

"Josiah," I blurted. "I didn't know you were here."

He stood silent. Expressionless. "Well, well," he finally said. "This is an entirely novel approach to mentoring. Wouldn't you agree, Lucina?"

"I was going to tell you." Lucy pulled the top of her robe closed. "It wasn't—"

"Don't bother." His nostrils flared, and his jaw tightened into an angry scowl. "I knew you were unfit for this responsibility, but I had no idea how much so."

He glanced at her neck and then turned his angry eyes toward me. "You gave the *cross* to her? After all I've done for you, and you give your cross away like some recycled gift?"

Lucy stared back at Josiah with a blank expression. "This?" She reached behind her head to remove the necklace.

Josiah raised his hand. "No, leave it on. The two of you appear to have quite a bond here. I wouldn't want to come between two lovers." He flashed another disgusted look my way and stormed out without another word, slamming the door behind him. Lucy wandered into the kitchen, staring at the floor. She held on to the refrigerator's handle like it was the only thing holding her up.

For the first time since we'd met, I felt guilty about our relationship. She was in deep trouble with the Sage hierarchy, and it was my fault. "Don't worry," I said. "He'll get over it. He just needs a little time."

"You obviously don't know him very well." She looked up from the floor. "He won't let this go. He never lets anything go. He's going straight to Atum, and nothing can stop him." She held the cross out from her chest. "Why didn't you tell me this came from Josiah?"

"It didn't come from Josiah. It came from me. He gave it to me after my initiation. The one around my neck he gave to my mother before I was born."

"You told me this represented the bond between us." She shook her head, eyes downcast.

I held my own cross between my fingers. "This cross is the only bond I have with my birth mother, a mother I never knew. The cross you're wearing represents my bond with you. A bond

I'd die for. The fact that it was given to me by Josiah shouldn't matter."

Lucy sank into a kitchen chair. "It doesn't matter anymore. Josiah won't let up until he's destroyed that bond anyway. This is war. Nothing can stop him now."

"That's it." I started toward the door. "I'm going over there to straighten this out right now."

"No!" She sprang from the chair. "You *cannot* go over there now. You don't understand, Daniel. It's not safe. Not when he's like this."

"Don't worry. I'm not afraid of him. He'll listen to me."

She threw her arms around me. "No. I won't let you. Stay here with me, and let him cool off. Please, for me." She stepped back, zoning in with a hypnotic stare. My willpower evaporated on the spot, leaving me stunned and defenseless. It was a dirty trick, but it worked.

"Okay. Okay." I looked away as my senses cleared. "But I really think you're overreacting. Josiah would never do anything to hurt me."

Lucy sighed. "I wish that were true. He's dark, Daniel, and there's no telling what he's capable of. He's the only person I've ever met that can actually scare me. I've seen him when he's got an ax to grind, and believe me, it isn't pretty. This just became personal."

Lucy's warning made me think back to the day on the icy bridge when I'd looked into his eyes and felt raw fear. There was a mysterious darkness in those eyes that was unforgettable. Still, he was my friend and my original mentor. I couldn't have him believe that I'd gone behind his back.

"All right, fine. But tomorrow I'm going over there, no arguments."

Lucy's mouth hung open.

"What's wrong?" I asked.

"What's wrong? Well, let's see. My boss hates me and has for the last five hundred years. I got a terrible review yesterday, which you never even bothered to ask me about, by the way. Oh, and to top it off, I just got caught sleeping with my student. What could *possibly* be wrong?"

"I'm sorry I didn't ask you about your meeting yesterday. I guess I've been a little distracted."

"I didn't want to talk about it anyway. But it wouldn't have killed you to show some support." She placed a hand to her forehead. "I'm sorry, Daniel. I didn't mean to take this out on you. I can't believe things have gotten so convoluted. I knew this assignment was going to be a challenge, but I never imagined things would get so mixed up."

Lucy was stressed, and I had no clue how to help her. Nothing I said would bring her any comfort. I wanted to tell her things would work out in the end, but I wasn't sure of it myself. Now that we'd managed to piss off Josiah, nothing was certain.

"You didn't screw anything up," I finally said. "Josiah's just jealous. My training is going great, and we're way ahead of schedule. And then there's the matter of our relationship. He's just going to have to learn to accept that you and I are a team now and nothing, not even him, can stop it."

Lucy sighed. "He's not going to accept anything. You don't know him like I do. Josiah's always been the warrior soul for the entire Sage family. The man's not wired like the rest of us. When he sees something he deems wrong or unjust, he strikes back with fury. He's very powerful, and in our world, he's feared. I know what he's capable of. I've seen some of his dirty work firsthand."

"What dirty work?" I asked. "What does that even mean?"

Lucy cringed. "Oh God, what have I done now?"

I knew there was something more to Josiah's role in the Sage order than his sphere of influence. I'd picked up on it when I saw how Malcolm and the twins treated him. They didn't just respect him. They feared him. That kind of clout isn't earned by promoting spiritual enlightenment. "What are you keeping from me?"

Lucy tried to look away. She looked back at me nervously. "Josiah was right. I am unfit for this assignment. Atum should never have given this to me."

"Please." I grabbed her hands. "I need to know what you're talking about."

She groaned. "Why not? What *else* have I got to lose at this point? Look, there's something you haven't heard much about yet, but it's not an issue of trust. It's more like an issue of readiness. It's not standard protocol to talk about this until training is complete. Then again, your training has been anything but standard."

"Go on," I prodded.

"There are dark forces among us, Daniel. They've been walking the planet since time immemorial. Mathias, their leader, has been around as long as Atum. Maybe longer. They're known as the *Goths*."

"Goths?" I repeated.

Lucy's eyebrows arched. "You've never heard of the Goths?"

I shrugged. "I remember something from world history about a barbarian tribe that sacked Europe."

"Close enough," she said. "They wreaked havoc across most of the Roman Empire. The legend is that some of their leaders were direct descendants of Mathias... his children, if you will. I don't know if it's true or not, but Atum started referring to them as Goths around the fourth century, and the name stuck. Before that, we referred to them as the dark ones, or the dark souls. Some of us still do." She went silent, tapping her foot rapidly on the floor.

"What's wrong?" I asked.

She stood and paced back and forth in front of me. "I shouldn't be telling you this."

"Lucy, please. I can handle it. Besides, how am I supposed to save the world if I don't even know what I'm up against?" I scanned her face for a reaction, but found none.

"Why not?" she asked as if speaking to herself. "You'll find out on your own anyway." She sat back down and placed her hand on my knee. "Goths are like Sages in many ways. They're mortal, but like us, they can live for thousands of years. They exert great influence over humans, but while we've spent our lives inspiring and coaching civilization to seek the greater good, these souls have done the opposite. Their mission is to lead humans down a path to self-destruction. They used to outnumber us almost ten to one."

"Are these demonic spirits or something?" I asked.

"Their bodies are human, but their souls…" She took a deep breath. "No one can say for sure. I only know that their intentions are pure evil, and they're extremely clever at keeping their true nature hidden. You'll find them in the shadows, promoting every kind of evil and sin imaginable. I must admit, despite all our efforts, they've made great strides in recent years. Drugs, human slavery, terrorism, genocide—they've had a hand in all of them. The sins aren't new, only the methods used to promote them."

"I'm confused," I said. "I don't understand what any of this has to do with Josiah."

Lucy headed to the window and peered at Josiah's house. "Josiah is, and always has been, our primary defense against the Goths. He knows them better than any of us, and he has the strongest ability to sense their presence. His greatest pleasure is tracking them down and…" She turned toward me. "He's slaughtered scores of them over the centuries, Daniel. Atum estimates there are only about twenty left, including Mathias. With modern technology, though, they're able to reach more people now than ever before."

"So that explains what Josiah meant by 'know thy enemy,'" I said.

She rolled her eyes. "He knows his enemy, all right. Too well, if you ask me."

"What do you mean? Are you suggesting he's one of them?" I asked.

"I think he's danced with the devil so many times, he doesn't recognize evil for what it is anymore," she said. "We have a duty to purge humanity of these filthy souls, but Josiah takes things too far. He spends so much time hunting, killing, and poring through his little black books that he's lost sight of his true calling. He's the Master Guide over all human spiritual development. Dare I say civilization hasn't exactly made the greatest strides in this area?"

Despite Josiah's outburst, I felt the need to defend him. "Maybe he feels he has to rid the planet of these dark souls before he can move his mission forward."

"He's lost his way, Daniel, and I don't trust him. He's been wallowing in the darkness too long. There's no telling what effect it's had on him."

I had a hard time swallowing this. Josiah had a dark side. That much I knew. But the man had saved my life, built a home for me, and filled me with hope and purpose. How could he be this heartless assassin?

"I'm still going to see him tomorrow. I've seen the good side of this man, and I'm not giving up on him. I can reach him."

Lucy closed her eyes in frustration. "If you don't mind, I'd like to take your car and go for a ride by myself. I really need to get out of here. It feels like the walls are closing in."

"Of course you can take my car. Are you sure there isn't something I can do to help you?"

She shook her head. "I need to be alone now."

I wanted to help her, but I knew she needed her own space. After she left, the fading sound of tires on crushed stone echoed from the driveway.

CHAPTER 30

As I fumbled around with the coffeemaker in my semiconscious state the next morning, I couldn't shake the feeling something was wrong. Then it hit me. I hadn't heard Lucy come home last night. Her bedroom door was shut. A good sign. I peeked out the window. My car was parked in its usual spot. Another good sign. From my post, I could see into Josiah's kitchen. There didn't appear to be any lights on, so I wasn't sure if he was home. I knew Lucy was dead set against my talking to him, but I couldn't pass up this opportunity. With any luck, I'd be back before she woke up.

I trudged through what was left of an early spring snowstorm, soaking my jeans to the knees in the wet, slushy slop. It was early April, but the cold morning wind made it feel more like February. Strangely, I hadn't heard Randall's ferocious howl yet. I knocked on the door, but no one responded. I tried again, louder this time.

Nothing.

Josiah's Cutlass wasn't around either, but that didn't mean anything. He typically kept his cars locked up in the garage. I walked around the porch and peered in a window, but the house seemed empty. So much for the big confrontation.

On the way back to my cabin, I heard my cell phone's ring coming from the kitchen table. I had to get it before it woke Lucy. I whipped open the front door and grabbed it before the voice mail kicked in.

It was Josiah.

"Josiah, I wasn't expecting you," I said between huffs. "I was just over at your—"

"Bad news," he interrupted. A long pause followed, and I was starting to wonder if my phone had dropped the call. But then his voice came back. "There's been another tragedy."

My heart accelerated. What if he was talking about Lucy? I glanced over at her door.

"I'm sorry if this isn't the best time, but you must be made aware," he said. "Atum just told me the news. Asha is dead. Murdered."

I stood there, speechless. Thank God he wasn't talking about Lucy. My guilty conscience kicked in. How could I be so insensitive, so self-centered? Next to the Master, Asha was the most senior of all Sages. My thoughts went back to initiation, when I saw her sparkling hair and beautiful glow for the first time. Lucy would be devastated. Asha was the closest thing to a mother she had ever known.

Josiah continued, "Sumati and I are contacting the rest of the Sages. Atum is arranging to have the body flown to Scotland from Morocco, where she died. The funeral will be at Atum's castle. Do you think you can make it to Stonehaven by Saturday?"

"Ah, Saturday. Yeah, I guess," I mumbled. What had I just agreed to? I wasn't even sure what day it was.

"All right, I'll reserve tickets for you and Lucina. The funeral is Saturday afternoon. I'll pick you up at the airport when you get in."

The reality of what he'd just told me was still sinking in. "Josiah," I called out, "does anyone know what happened? Or who did this?"

"Atum sent Malcolm ahead to look into the matter. We'll get to the bottom of it; don't worry."

"Where are you right now?" I asked.

"Buffalo. I was on my way to catch a flight to Scotland when Atum called and broke the news. I'd planned to call you later and let you know I wouldn't be around for a few days. Anyway, I'll be there to pick you up on Saturday when you get in," he repeated. "One more thing, Daniel. I think it would be best if *you* broke the news to Lucina."

"Me?" I squeezed my eyes shut. The last thing I wanted to be right now was the bearer of bad news. I'd caused her enough pain already.

"I think it would be best," Josiah said. "We're not exactly on good terms right now. I'm not even sure if she trusts me. Besides, she'll need a shoulder to lean on. She and Asha were very close."

"All right. I'll tell her."

"Good. I'll call you again when I have your flight information. Oh... and Daniel? Keep your cell phone with you. We need to stay connected at times like this."

"Got it. Talk to you soon." I ended the call and stared out the kitchen window at my footprints in the dirty, slushy snow.

"Daniel?" a voice said from behind me.

I spun around, startled, to see Lucy.

"Lucy," I gasped. "I didn't know you were up."

"You'll tell me what?"

"I think you should sit down." I hesitated for a second to try to find the right words. There weren't any. "There's been a terrible tragedy. Asha is dead. They think she was murdered. I'm so sorry."

She stared at me.

"Did you hear what I said?" She appeared almost catatonic, not responding, not even moving. Slowly, tears formed, spilling over and down her cheeks. I held her as she sobbed into my shirt. Then she pulled back.

"Where's Josiah?" she asked, pale-faced.

"He's in Buffalo. He was catching a flight to Scotland when he received Atum's news."

"Oh my God! Oh my God!"

"What? Lucy, what is it?"

"Don't you see? Josiah's lost it. He's completely dark now. He murdered Asha to get back at me." She covered her mouth with her hand as she paced the floor.

"Lucy!" I steadied my hands on her shoulders. "C'mon, sweetheart, you're getting carried away. Josiah's a lot of things, but I really don't think he's a murderer. Besides, he's on the other side of the ocean from Asha. He couldn't have harmed her."

She stepped away from me. "You don't know where he is right now. If he's really in Buffalo, he's probably on his way *back* from Morocco."

I put my hands up. "All right, let's just calm down. I think there's a—"

"Remember what I told you about the Goths? Who do you think is responsible for all those deaths? He's a skilled assassin, Daniel. He's murdered more times than you can imagine."

I didn't want to upset her any more than she already was, but I felt obligated to stand up for Josiah. "He's *supposed* to kill Goths. You told me yourself. Part of our job is to rid the world of the dark souls."

Lucy scowled and narrowed her eyes. "He's done his duty; I'll give him that. But he takes it too far. Most of us have never killed a soul, Goth or otherwise. Among the Sages, Josiah is the angel of death. There's more, though. He's... he's different from the rest of us. I've heard he can project his consciousness into other living things and see through their eyes. You know, animals and the like. Why can't any of us do that?"

I shrugged.

"He's different. I've spent the last five hundred years dreading the day when he'd turn those strange powers on his own kind. I'm afraid that day has arrived."

I stepped in front of her. "You're wrong about this. I've spent a lot of time with the man, and I *know* he wouldn't murder his own."

"No one's questioning your insight, Daniel, but you don't know him like I do. Josiah seeks justice in the world like the rest of us, but we were given limits, and he ignores them. Some of the Goths he killed were tortured. Atum does not condone this, and Josiah's been warned on more than one occasion. I don't feel safe around him, and now I'm afraid for you."

"For me? Why would you be afraid for me?"

Lucy sat down at the kitchen table, her tone much softer. "You trust him. You don't see the danger."

Josiah had been acting weird lately, weirder than usual, and his cold detachment had always been something of a mystery to me. Still, my gut told me Lucy was overreacting.

"There's no point in debating this now," I said.

"Asha," Lucy whispered. "It can't believe it. Not Asha." She walked back into her room and shut the door.

I didn't go after her.

CHAPTER 31

The flight to Scotland went without a hitch, and, just as promised, Josiah, Malcolm, and the twins greeted us outside Aberdeen Airport. It was as if we'd been assigned our own team of bodyguards. I guessed Atum wasn't taking any chances. We headed back to the castle in two separate vehicles. It felt like a mini–presidential motorcade.

The funeral was set to begin at twilight, according to custom. Lucy and I stayed inside the castle for the next couple hours, hanging out and making small talk with the other Sages. The whole crew was there, but everyone was having a hard time coming to grips with the tragedy at hand, and there was more than a hint of fear in the air. None of us saw Asha's death as a random act of violence. Something more was at play here, and we all felt it. It was as if something, or someone, was watching over us, stalking us, waiting for the best time to strike.

As daylight faded, Atum finally appeared. Josiah passed out robes, and Atum led us to the underground chambers of the castle. The great Master trudged on slower than usual, and I wondered if all this stress was taking a toll on the old man.

The light of Atum's candle was all we had to guide us down the steep, narrow steps. As beautiful and well kept as the castle was, the underground chambers had the feel of a medieval dungeon. They were cold and dark, with a dampness that penetrated to the bone. As soon as we reached the bottom of the stairs, Asha's body came into view. Muffled whimpers penetrated the silence from time to time as everyone struggled to keep their emotions in check.

Sumati handed each of us a candle. One by one we lit them from the Master's flame. At Atum's command, Josiah and Sumati motioned the rest of us to form a circle around the casket. Lucy nudged me into position, since I was lost on what to do. This was all new to me, but it didn't take long to figure out how the group was organized. Immediately to Atum's right was Sumati, followed by Josiah, Balaam, Darya, Nuha, Lucy, Aydin, and me. We were arranged in order of birth, another tradition that had Atum written all over it. Through tears and long periods of silence, Atum delivered a moving eulogy to our fallen friend. Afterward, he instructed us to place our candles on the floor at our feet.

I couldn't help but notice how beautiful and lifelike Asha looked, even in death. If it weren't for the absence of the perpetual glow that had surrounded her in life, you'd never know she was gone. It was as if she'd settled down to an early evening nap.

"Let us now commence with the *bonds of ascension* and greet our newly risen sister," Atum said. He grasped my right hand while Aydin clutched my left. Everyone's eyes started closing, so I followed along. Another ritual was about to begin. My hands became cold, really cold, and both Aydin's and Atum's hands became icier with each passing second.

Finally, Atum broke the silence. "It has begun."

I opened my eyes to see what he was talking about, but everyone was still standing in place, eyes shut. My palms and lower wrists had numbed to the point of discomfort. Looking around, I noticed everyone had tilted their heads back. I tilted my own head back, closed my eyes, and waited for whatever was supposed to happen next.

An ice-cold sensation shot through the veins of my right arm and traveled down to my feet. Atum's hand felt like an icicle, with not the slightest hint of warmth. The bone-chilling numbness worked its way up from my feet, through my legs, and out through my left hand. I was frozen from the waist down. The deep freeze advanced through my lower abdomen, and I felt like I was being pulled upward. This pulling sensation intensified, and I was losing all feeling in my body. I wanted to cry out for help, but I knew I had to keep my mouth shut. What would happen if my heart and lungs seized up? Was this supposed to happen, or had something gone terribly wrong? Why hadn't anyone told me about this?

My heartbeat slowed to an occasional thud. I had to do something. I couldn't just stand there and freeze to death. With great effort I tried to force out a cry for help. I only managed a whimper. My mission would be over before it ever had a chance to begin.

I prepared to take my last breath, drawing in as much air as my crippled lungs would allow. Exhaling slowly, I closed my eyes and prepared to die. When I exhaled, a jolt shot through my body, sweeping me into a vortex of swirling energy. It flowed through me, filling me with a sense of peace and freeing me from the chains of the body. A feeling of weightlessness came over me, and I embraced it like a long-lost friend.

The next thing I knew, I was looking down at my physical body below. Lucy's spirit shadowed me to the left. She cast off the same soothing light I remembered from my deathbed vision in ancient Rome.

I felt connected with all the other Sages as an endless river of eternal knowledge flowed through each of us. A musical vibration massaged my entire soul as a whirlpool of energy formed before us. Then everything was still.

Atum gave a nod, and everyone moved back from the center of the whirlpool. Four spirits materialized in front of us, their bodies shimmering with a heavenly light. Asha was the first spirit to materialize, followed by Jian, Cyrus, and Marius. I recognized the latter Sages even though they had passed on centuries before my birth. The spirits transmitted telepathic images of hope and encouragement—except for Asha. She shared images of blood, chains, forests, and gravestones, an ominous vision of things to come.

Asha's eyes settled on me. Her mouth remained closed, but she *spoke* to me directly. "Your trials will be many, for destiny deems it so. But fear not, my brother. You are the rock that completes the foundation. You are the chosen one. Let nothing come between you and your mission." As she retreated back to the center of the vortex, all four Sage spirits shimmered with increasing intensity. Then, one by one, they faded into the light and disappeared.

Instantly, I was back in my freezing-cold body, still clinging to Atum's and Aydin's hands. Warmth returned, slowly releasing me from the icy shackles. When I opened my eyes, I saw tears streaking down the faces of Lucy, Darya, and Aydin.

"It is complete," Atum announced. "Let us now proceed with our collective mission, and assure that our beloved Asha did not die in vain." With that, everyone released hands and blew out their candles.

Malcolm and the twins arrived to carry Asha's casket to its final resting place in the Valley of the Righteous, a small graveyard about a quarter mile from Atum's castle. We followed the body in a candlelit procession and circled the open grave where they planned to place Asha's casket. After a few final prayers, our sister was lowered into the earth.

Atum threw a shovelful of dirt on the casket, and each Sage followed his lead. When Aydin handed the shovel to me, I shivered. Looking down at the casket, I heard Asha's words echo in my brain. What if I wasn't this rock she spoke of? What if I failed in my mission? I glanced at all the other Sages encircling the grave as the crushing weight of responsibility bore down on me.

Later that evening, I sat on my bed, alone and in the dark. I wanted to put this whole experience behind me, but I couldn't focus on anything other than Asha's haunting message. She was trying to prepare me for something. But what? As usual, I had no answers, only questions.

CHAPTER 32

I wasn't sure how I got there, but I could barely see five feet in front of me. The air was stale and dry with the stench of death. Where the hell was I? Skeletons and well-clothed corpses lying in bunk beds carved from stone lined the walls. Catacombs! My footsteps echoed through the tunnels like falling rocks in a canyon. I tripped on uneven ground and stumbled forward, bashing my shoulder against the wall. Someone tapped on the back of my neck. I jumped back and shrieked. An arm and hand, stripped of flesh, dangled where I stood. I had to get out of this place.

Something was behind me. I could hear it breathing, heaving, keeping a steady pace. The corridor stretched into infinity, a straight shot into the unknown. There were no windows, no doors, no crossways—just countless corpses in various states of decay lining the walls and keeping quiet company.

No matter how hard I strained my legs, I couldn't move any faster than a quick walk. My pursuer was gaining on me. The breathing grew heavier, louder. A faint tapping sound echoed in the distance, morphing into a deep thud, drawing closer with each strike.

"Daniel," a voice echoed off the catacomb walls. I turned around but saw no one.

"Daniel, can you hear me?" The voice grew louder, more desperate. How did they know my name? "They're waiting for you, Daniel!"

I shot up in bed and looked around the room.

Just a dream.

What a relief. It was morning, but I had no clue what time it was. The tapping noise was real. It came from the hall. Stumbling out of bed, I tripped over my own shoes and nearly broke an ankle on the way to the door. I opened it to see Lucy staring back at me.

"Sleeping in, are we? Love the hair, by the way," she teased. "I think that style really suits you."

"Very funny," I said through a huge yawn. "What time is it anyway?"

"Time to get dressed and come to breakfast. The others are heading for the airport soon, and they'd like to see you before they leave."

"Wait up. I'll just be a minute." I wiped the sleep from my eyes and scrounged for some clean clothes to put on - all the while thinking about that bizarre dream. What did it mean?

Breakfast was a laid-back affair. Most of us were still coming to grips with our recent loss, and there was a general lack of energy. I talked mostly with Lucy—partly because I was hopelessly infatuated with her, and partly because Josiah was a mere six feet away. I knew she couldn't even look at him without tying her stomach up in knots.

Josiah checked his watch and stood. "You'll have to excuse us, Atum, but we have a flight to catch." That was my cue to get ready to leave.

Atum rose to his feet, silencing the room in the process. Josiah promptly sat back down and glanced at his watch again, frowning.

"I suppose it's time to get this out on the table, so to speak," Atum said, a fleeting smile on his lips. "Friends, I have reason to believe that each and every one of us is in grave danger. As you know, Asha's death was no accident. Moving forward, we must be vigilant. This is especially true for our newest member. If the Goths have knowledge of Daniel's existence or his whereabouts, they'll launch an all-out war upon us. He is the last piece of the puzzle, and his initiation brings us one step closer to achieving our collective mission. I don't think I need to remind you that the very definition of our mission is the complete obliteration of our enemies. Mathias and his minions are all too aware of this." Atum scanned the table slowly with laserlike eyes. "From here on out, no one is to be alone. Aydin, Nuha—you'll be staying with Sumati. Daniel and Lucy will return to the States under Josiah's protection." He glanced at Malcolm waiting by the front foyer. "I'm sending Malcolm back to Melbourne with Balaam and Darya." He motioned toward the ladies. "He'll stay with you until further notice. Be alert, my children. Rely only on each other. We've known for centuries this day would come. We will prevail." Atum patted Josiah on the shoulder, and the two of them exited the room.

Before we could leave for the airport, Atum motioned to Lucy and me, waving us into a side room I'd never been in. A round marble table with thirteen marble stools sat in the center. Josiah was already seated at the table. We sat down beside him.

Atum placed his grandfatherly hand on my shoulder. "It is time, my son, for the next phase of your training."

"Yes, Master," I said, looking to Lucy for insight. She glanced at Atum and then back at me, clearly unaware of whatever the senior Sages had in mind.

Atum handed me a stack of file folders. "Wait until you get back to the States. Then I want you to memorize this material. Your mentors can answer any questions you might have." He nodded toward Lucy before returning his attention to me. "Be safe, my son. Stay with the family at all times, and keep up the great progress you've been making." He patted my back again. "Everything will work out in the end."

If only I could be that confident.

CHAPTER 33

We hadn't been back in the States more than twelve hours before Josiah called us to a meeting. Lucy sat on the couch, head tilted back with eyes closed.

"Ready to go?" I asked.

"God, give me the strength to deal with that man," she said, opening her eyes.

"You're making too much of this." I grabbed her coat from the front closet and tossed it to her. "It's just a meeting."

She rolled her eyes. "Can't wait."

Josiah got right down to business the minute we arrived and laid three pictures on the table. All three looked as if they'd been taken with a telephoto lens. A tall menacing guy with long dark hair and a beard appeared in the first two photos. The third picture, a close-up shot, looked like the same guy, but clean-shaven and with short blond hair.

Josiah hovered over me. "Do you know who this is?"

I shook my head.

"By now, I'm sure you've heard of the Goths. This is their leader."

"Mathias," I said. "I've heard of him."

"I see." Josiah shot Lucy a scowling look. "Normally, a Sage with your level of experience wouldn't be privy to this type of information. On the other hand, you have shown an unusual aptitude for learning." He spread the remaining folders across the table. "Besides, we're on the cusp of a paradigm shift. The world as we know it is changing, and we need to be prepared." He pointed at me. "You, more than any of us."

Lucy chimed in, "I probably shouldn't have, but I've given Daniel a brief primer on our enemies. After Asha died, I felt it was necessary." She looked down at the floor and bit her lower lip.

Josiah shrugged. "Asha's murder was the work of the Goths. There's no doubt in my mind. It's time Daniel learned the full story." He zeroed in on me with intensity in his eyes. "The day will come when this information will be useful to you."

Lucy continued staring at the floor, motionless.

Josiah pushed the third picture of Mathias in front of me. "Assuming you've got a handle on basic Goth history, let's focus on the present threat. Mathias has been around at least as long as Atum. We've learned precious little about his early life, but we do know he's an extremely charismatic figure, both feared and revered by his followers. He's also a master of disguise," he said, arranging two of the photos side by side. "You can always tell a Goth, though, by the color of their eyes. Take a good look at this close-up."

I saw right away what he was talking about. The eyes were impossible to miss. A strange shade of ice-cold, crystal blue, they projected a complete absence of warmth or feeling. Even from a photo, those eyes projected the very essence of evil. I could only imagine the effect in person.

"Their souls are as empty as their eyes," Josiah said, rummaging through another file of photos. "This man is one of the last remaining princes," he said with a look of disgust. The man in the photo had horrible skin, peppered with pockmarks and scars. His bald head was offset by a dark goatee and cold, steely blue eyes. He couldn't have looked more evil if he'd had horns coming out of his head.

"Did you say *princes?*" I asked.

Josiah nodded. "Mathias is their so-called *king*. He refers to his first seven charges as princes. They are to the Goths what Master Guides are to the Sages. We like to refer to them as the *Princes of Darkness*. They control vast geographic areas throughout the world and wield enormous power within their territories. Only four of the original seven remain, though. The other three were killed off by each other... and by us." He shot an uneasy glance at Lucy, who immediately looked away.

Josiah pulled out another picture. "This lovely mug shot belongs to Calisto, also known as *El Diablo* throughout Central and South America. He's one of only two remaining princes in the Western Hemisphere. He keeps to the southern regions, where he all but owns the drug cartels, enslaving human souls using chemicals. Calisto's not limited to the drug trade, though. He also has his dirty little paws in prostitution, gambling, executions for hire... you name it. None of the Goths are specialists anymore. Their numbers are too diminished now, so they have to branch out. These days, they're relying more and more on technology and human assistance. Calisto has upwards of a thousand foot soldiers at his beck and call throughout the Western Hemisphere. At least three of his lieutenants are Goths."

I needed to put the picture down. This Calisto was so hideous, his image turned my stomach.

"Handsome little devil, isn't he?" Lucy said.

"His twin isn't much better." Josiah laid down another photo. "This is Donato, the other prince of the west. Not an identical twin, but you can see the resemblance."

I glanced down at the photo and saw right away what Josiah was talking about. This guy wasn't quite as ugly as his brother, but every bit as evil looking. He had the same bad skin, too.

Josiah took a seat next to me. "From what we can tell, Donato spends most of his time between Mexico and the southeastern United States. He helps his brother move drugs from time to time, but his real focus is the sex trade. He has prostitution rings from Central America all the way up through Canada. Brothels, strip clubs, escort services… all part of his empire. We hear he's involved in the Internet as well." Josiah pushed the photo away in disgust. "One can only wonder how many souls this scum has enslaved through the centuries."

"What about the other princes?" I asked.

"We have no photos of the others, but we do have evidence." Josiah pulled out another folder. Inside was a sheet of faded yellow-brown paper with statistics written in Code. "Prince Vladimir," he began. "I last tracked him in Poland during the Second World War. He disappeared off the radar in the spring of '45. He had very close ties to the Nazi party and was in tight with the upper brass. He was especially close with Heinrich Himmler. Rumor has it, that old Vlad here was the true architect of the Final Solution. Amongst the Goths, though, Vladimir is closest to Mathias. Between them, they control all of Europe, Africa, and Russia."

He took another paper out of the folder. "And last, but not least, our dear friend Prince Azar. This little monster controls everything from the Middle East to the Pacific Rim and has the largest army of any Goth. I've been tracking him for centuries."

He crossed his arms and stared down at the paper as if challenged by the name staring back at him. "One of the rare Goths I've yet to lay eyes upon. He can't elude me forever, though." Josiah stopped midstream. "You have something you want to ask me, don't you?"

"If you don't mind," I said, wondering how he knew this.

"Never hesitate to ask, Daniel. Anything, anytime. This is how we learn."

"I just wanted to know if these Goths can, you know, multiply."

Lucy's jaw dropped.

Josiah paused for a moment. "They can multiply, but only with their own kind. They've had about a dozen females through the centuries whom they used as breeders. This is why they've outnumbered us for so long. There's only one female left that we know of, and she's heavily guarded. Her name is Isa, and she's the sole property of Mathias. He refers to her as his queen."

"So what happened to the other female Goths?" I asked.

Josiah glanced over at Lucy, who was now squirming in her seat. He continued, "We set about targeting the females as a top priority a few hundred years ago. We tracked them down one by one and eliminated them. All but Isa, that is. We've never been able to break through the shield of Goths surrounding her, protecting her."

I looked at Lucy, but she refused to make eye contact. Josiah also avoided my eyes. "It's a necessary measure, Daniel. Unavoidable. The Goths multiplied so fast, the entire balance had shifted in their favor. If something hadn't been done, they would have taken over. Humankind would have suffered an intolerable trial of ignorance, violence, and hatred. As bad as things are in the world, they'd be much worse if it weren't for our cleansing."

"And Sages?" I asked. "Why can't we multiply and tip the balance in our favor?"

Josiah straightened in his seat. He opened his mouth as if to say something but stopped himself. He dropped his hands down on the table and looked me in the face. "We simply cannot reproduce. We weren't put here on this planet to breed like cattle. We have distinct missions to accomplish, and tending to families is a distraction we cannot afford."

I wasn't satisfied with his answer. "With all due respect, Josiah, how do you know we can't reproduce? Is it written somewhere? I didn't see that in the Chronicles anywhere."

He repositioned himself in his seat. "The Chronicles were meant to be an archival account of our lineage, Daniel, not a handbook for interacting with the rest of the human race. I know this answer doesn't satisfy you, and it shouldn't. You seek the principles behind the explanation, and that's the mark of a true Sage."

Josiah's compliment did little to ease my curiosity, and it must have shown in my expression. Lucy flashed her eyes at me again, a clear sign it was time to put this subject to rest.

"Look, there's never been a case of a Sage bearing children; this much I know," he assured me. "Over the years, Sages have engaged with mortals more times than we'd like to admit, and Atum has never interfered. He's always respected our right to exercise our own free will. It would be a great disappointment, though, if any of our kind did reproduce. Such carelessness would demonstrate a clear lack of focus and a propensity for the desires of the flesh. Our focus should be on the higher objectives."

Josiah's explanations only added to my frustration. He was a hypocrite. And why did he assume that Sages could only couple with mortals? He never even mentioned the possibility of two Sages together, probably because Lucy was sitting across the table.

Josiah pulled out two more folders. He laid down a photo of a woman with two children at her side. The woman wore a leather biker vest and had boyishly short spiked hair. Her face was made up with a heavy dose of dark eyeliner and red lipstick. Still, you couldn't help but notice the telltale ice-blue eyes. The boy looked to be about seven or eight, and the girl was a few years older. They had the same ice-blue eyes.

"Isa?" I asked.

He nodded. "The Goth queen herself. I took this photo about ten years ago in Romania."

"I thought you said all the female Goths were eliminated except the queen. What about this little girl?" I asked.

Josiah and Lucy exchanged uneasy glances. After a long pause, he said in a quiet voice, "The girl was eliminated shortly after this picture was taken." He placed his hand on my shoulder. His eyes grew watery. "This is not our typical way, Daniel. We're here to promote virtue, brotherhood, and unity for all God's creatures. But evil knows no mercy, and evil receives no mercy. We do what's necessary for the greater good."

I couldn't take my eyes off this little girl. She didn't come across as dangerous or evil, just a kid standing next to her mom. Would I be able to kill like this if it came down to it? The thought of it made me shutter.

"Why haven't they gone on the offensive?" I asked. "It seems they'd be more than motivated to pursue and eliminate every one of us."

"They *have* pursued us, Daniel. But they rarely get far." He leaned in closer. "We have a tremendous advantage over them. We can sense their presence from miles away. Lucina can attest to this." He nodded toward Lucy. "Still, one can never be too careful. This is why Atum hired Malcolm and the twins. The older he gets, the more vulnerable he feels."

"No one will ever harm the Master," Lucy added with confidence.

"Don't be so sure," Josiah warned. "Overconfidence is our greatest vulnerability."

Lucy sank down in her seat and looked away.

"I hope you found this helpful, my friend." He handed me a stack of folders. "Here's a list of names, descriptions, and general whereabouts. Take these to your room, and study them. Bring them back when you're done."

"Will do," I said.

Lucy and I made our way toward the door. My head was spinning from this new information. Why hadn't I been made aware of the Goths sooner? I was being groomed to lead an army into battle, yet until now, I had no knowledge of the enemy. It was frustrating, to say the least, but I kept my emotions in check.

"One more thing," he called out. "We need to stay close. Let me know if you need to go anywhere. It's not safe for us to travel alone anymore."

CHAPTER 34

Saturday morning started off on a positive note. The sun beamed down for the first time in days, and I felt unusually upbeat for someone who'd just rolled out of bed. I walked out onto the porch to check the weather, morning coffee in hand. The temperature couldn't have been more than forty degrees, but the air was so still, I felt comfortable in just a short-sleeve shirt. I hadn't been outside for two minutes when the sun did a disappearing act behind a heavy curtain of clouds. Then a light breeze whistled through the trees, and the temperature dropped at least ten degrees in a matter of seconds. So much for the nice spring day.

I stepped inside and shut the door behind me. A muffled groan sounded like it came from Lucy's room. I stood still, expecting to hear it again. Silence. I looked at the kitchen clock. Ten minutes after nine. Something was definitely wrong. She never slept in past six.

"Close," I heard her mumble.

I knocked on her door. No answer. I let myself in. Still asleep, Lucy rolled over on her side, exposing huge sweat blotches down the sides and back of her nightshirt.

I placed my palm to her forehead. She was blazing hot to the touch. "Lucy. Lucy, wake up." I nudged her.

"Getting closer," she mumbled, still half-asleep. "Closer."

"What's getting closer? C'mon, sweetie, wake up."

She opened her eyes and jolted back. "Daniel?"

"I'm here, baby; it's just me. You're having a bad dream, and you're burning up with a fever." I'd never felt skin that hot before. She had to be running at least a 105 temp. "I'm taking you to the hospital."

"No. No hospital," she grumbled. "I'll be okay."

I grabbed my keys and wallet off the dresser. "No way, you need to get to a hospital. Now."

"No, Daniel, we don't do that." She sat up, eyes wide.

"What do you mean, 'We don't do that'? You could die. You're burning up, for Chrissake."

"Daniel, I'm fine. Besides, Sages don't go to hospitals. If I get to the point where I need a hospital, trust me, you're better off calling a morgue."

"Really? We don't get sick, but you're burning up with a fever. Tell me how that makes sense."

"I'm not saying that exactly. I've been sick before, but I've never needed more than a few hours to get over it." She struggled to her feet and made her way to the bedroom window. She peered out. "The most I've ever needed was a little painkiller."

I rushed to the bathroom, rummaging through the medicine cabinet for aspirin. "Damn it!" I yelled in frustration. "The only thing in here is peroxide and a few Band-Aids."

"Don't bother," Lucy called from the bedroom. "Really. I don't need medicine."

"I'm not listening to this. I'll call Josiah. Maybe he has something you can take to bring down the fever." I returned to the bedroom. Lucy was lying back down again, white as a sheet. I placed my hand on her sweltering forehead again and pulled back from the intense heat.

"Oh my God! I think it's getting worse. Honey, please let me take you to the hospital."

She shook her head defiantly. "Can't do it. Josiah would never allow it. We don't register our identities unless it's absolutely necessary."

I slammed my fist down on the nightstand. "This *is* absolutely necessary! The hell with Josiah!"

"Daniel, I'm not going, and that's final."

"Then I'm going to the store to get you some goddamn medicine," I said.

"We're not supposed to go out alone," she reminded me in a pathetically strained voice. "It's too dangerous. Besides, I'm not so sure this is a fever."

"The more you talk, the less sense you make. I'm going to the pharmacy." I stormed out of the cabin.

"Daniel, no! You don't understand!" Lucy wheezed from the bedroom. "Daniel, please don't—"

I slammed the door behind me. I didn't even care if Josiah was watching. I hopped into the Civic and tore off down the driveway. Dwyer's Pharmacy was a few miles away in the center of town. I could be back in fifteen, twenty minutes, tops. I made it into town in record time and found a parking spot about twenty yards down from The Palace, a faded brick building with an old-fashioned marquee out front. I'd heard the building had been a popular bar for college students until it closed down back in the nineties. Judging by the crew of workers scurrying around the scaffolding, I got the impression it was being prepped for some sort of big reopening. They were just climbing down to the sidewalk as I got out of my car, probably on their way to an early morning break.

Then I felt it. A dull, nauseous feeling came over me. "Perfect," I grumbled. "Now both of us will be down for the count." I headed toward Dwyer's but stopped short. A tall dark figure in sunglasses stared at me from across the street. I looked up at the dark storm clouds looming overhead. Really? Sunglasses? Something about the way he stared at me so perfectly still gave me the creeps.

I tried to shake it off as I opened the door to the pharmacy. I'd gotten about two steps inside when another intense wave of nausea hit. The old man behind the counter doubled back as I clutched my stomach, trying not to hurl. Sweat streamed down my forehead.

"You all right, buddy?" the old man asked. "You don't look so good."

I covered my mouth and made a mad dash for the exit. Bracing myself against a street sign in front of the store, I tossed my cookies all over the sidewalk. Feeling better, I returned to the store. Lucy still needed medicine, and I wasn't going home empty-handed.

The old man's eyebrows wrinkled as he stood behind the counter, arms crossed. I grabbed a box of flu medicine and a bottle of aspirin and headed for the register. The druggist handled my ten-dollar bill as if it was covered in anthrax. The pharmacy felt like a sauna as I took my receipt. My stomach gurgled. Fresh air. I needed fresh air. Grabbing my bag of medicine, I practically sprinted out the door.

I stopped in front of The Palace and took a deep breath. My stomach churned again. Then, out of nowhere, a nails-on-the-chalkboard screech came from above. I looked up and saw something from the sky coming right at me. I reeled back as a sheet of glass slid down the scaffold onto the spot where I'd been standing.

The crash sent shards of glass in every direction. A few small pieces pierced my jeans and coat, but, other than that, I was unharmed. Glancing up again, I saw someone step off the scaffolding into an opening in the building's top floor. My sickness gave way to a full-blown adrenaline rush. Without hesitation, I bolted down the back alley toward the rear of the building. Rounding the corner, I looked in every direction. Not a soul in sight. Whoever ducked into that building was still in there.

My phone rang in my pocket. I fumbled for it and saw it was Lucy calling. "Lucy, are you all right?" I asked, still trembling from the aftershock.

"I'm actually feeling a little better." She hesitated. "Daniel, what's wrong? You're out of breath. What happened?"

"I, uh, think I'm coming down with whatever you had. I just tossed last night's dinner all over the sidewalk." I scanned in every direction, watching for the next strike. My heart was racing so fast, I thought I might pass out on the spot.

"Oh my God! Daniel, listen to me. Get in the car right now, and come straight home. Do you hear me? I mean it. It's not safe for you to be out there alone. You should have never…"

"Lucy?" I looked down at my phone. The battery was toast. My stomach spasmed again. I had to get the hell out of there. I raced back to the street, jumped into the car, and jetted back home as fast as my Civic would take me.

My near decapitation would have to stay a secret, at least for now. I didn't want Lucy worrying when she was sick. Josiah, on the other hand, would need to be informed ASAP. He'd know exactly what to make of this.

CHAPTER 35

As luck would have it, Josiah was nowhere to be found. Worse yet, he wasn't answering his cell phone. This was the second time he'd vanished without a trace in less than a week. I could almost hear Lucy's "I told you so" ringing in my ears. I wasn't sure what to do, other than wait for his return.

A full day had passed since the fever had struck. I felt like my old self again. Lucy was back to normal too, at least as far as her health was concerned. Her behavior, however, was anything but normal. She was a whirlwind of nervous energy, pacing the floor and looking out windows every few minutes.

"Care to tell me what you're looking for?" I asked, catching her in the act again.

She stared, unseeing. "Nothing. It's nothing."

"Okay. You're pacing, fidgeting, and standing guard at the window for no reason? That sounds logical."

She turned and shot me a cold stare. "Are you really that clueless? Do I have to spell it out for you?"

I rolled my eyes. "Let me guess. You think Josiah is stalking us."

She put her hand to her forehead and squeezed her eyes shut. "Oh, Daniel. What am I going to do with you?"

"I know. You think I'm too trusting. Well, let me just tell you—"

"Daniel!" She stomped her foot. "Wake up. I'm not talking about Josiah. I'm still not convinced he wasn't involved in Asha's death, but right now he's not my main concern."

"Goths," I said, finally putting the pieces together.

She threw up her hands. "Hallelujah!"

The sickness. The dark figure on the corner. The falling glass. It all pointed to the Goths, and I suppose some part of me had known this all along. Still, I couldn't bring myself to tell Lucy about the incident on Main Street. I couldn't risk sending her into a panic.

"I suppose that makes sense," I said.

Lucy put her arms around me. "I'm sorry I've been so short with you. It's not your fault."

I stroked the gentle curve of her lower back. "It's okay. I should have picked up on this." I stepped back from her. "I don't feel sick anymore. Does that mean we're safe now?"

She sighed. "We're never really safe. Goths are always a threat. This feels different, though. More intense. It's like everything has been ratcheted up a notch since your initiation." She paused, examining her cuticles. "Just like Atum predicted."

My cell phone rang. I answered with a curt, "Hello."

"Something's come up," Josiah informed me. "I need to run a quick errand. I just wanted to let you know I won't be around for the next hour or so." A long pause followed. "I know we're supposed to stay together, but I think you'll be safer here than where I'm going."

"Dare I ask where?" I hesitated. "You know, in case there's a problem."

"You don't want to know. Besides, I'll have my cell phone if you need to contact me."

"Take your time. We'll be fine," I reassured him.

"I should be back within an hour or so. Are you sure you're all right with this?"

"Josiah, we're fine. I really don't think—"

"Atum would not approve of my leaving you alone, you know," he interrupted. "I have a good sense for these things, and, believe me, if any of us were in danger, I'd feel it."

"I'm sure you would. Go and do what you need to. We'll be here when you get back. Besides, there's something I need to talk to you about."

"You know you can always talk to me, Daniel. We'll connect when I get back," he said. The phone went silent.

"He's leaving us, isn't he?" Lucy asked. "I can't believe it. He's supposed to be guarding us, and—" Lucy clutched her stomach, heaving forward like she'd just been stabbed with an invisible knife.

"Lucy, what is it? You okay?" I headed toward her, but a searing pain tore through my midsection. It eased into a dull ache, but perspiration soaked my forehead. Lucy's normally golden Mediterranean skin was clammy and pale.

"I'm all right now, I think." She grabbed the arm of the rocking chair and pulled herself to her feet. I tried to do the same, but my head was spinning and I had to sit.

"We have to get out of here." She trembled and ran to the window for another look. I'd never seen her so afraid before.

"Get out of here? Why? I just told Josiah we'd stay until he came back."

"Do we have to go through this again?" she asked. "There's a Goth nearby. That's what we're feeling."

"But Josiah would have warned us."

"He already knows, Daniel," she said robotically, staring trancelike out the window. "His senses are much keener than ours. If we're feeling it, then he's feeling it tenfold and yet feels no obligation to protect us. Think that's a coincidence?" She faced me.

I had nothing to say in Josiah's defense.

How could this be happening? How could Josiah go through all the trouble to train and prepare me for this noble mission, and then leave me to die? It didn't make sense. There had to be an explanation. Right now, though, I didn't have time for questions.

"What do you suggest we do?" I asked.

"We follow him. There's a reason he's not protecting us, and we're going to find out what it is. Grab your keys." She pointed to the spot on the kitchen counter where I always left my keys.

"Are you sure about this?" I asked.

"The only thing I'm sure of is that we're sitting ducks in this cabin." She grabbed the keys from my hands. "As soon as he leaves the driveway, we're heading out. I'll do the driving."

"Won't he know he's being followed? You said his senses are sharp."

"If there's one thing I've developed over the years, it's an ability to lie low. Trust me, he'll never know we're on his trail."

I shrugged my shoulders. She had about two thousand years of experience on me, and I wasn't about to doubt her now.

The tires of the pickup truck crunched loudly on the driveway as Josiah drove away. It was time.

"Wait." I motioned to Lucy as I backpedaled to my room.

"Daniel, what are you doing? We've got to go now! We're going to lose him if he gets much farther ahead," she shouted from the porch.

I returned with the monocular Josiah had given me. Since I didn't own binoculars, I figured this would be the next best thing for lying low and spying from a distance. We sprinted to the car, and Lucy had the Civic in reverse before I'd even settled into my seat. She sped out of the driveway and doubled the speed limit within the first quarter mile. We came to a four-way stop. She turned left.

"Why left?" I asked.

"Trust me, he turned left here." She bit her lip.

"I'm not second-guessing you or anything, but how do you *know* he went left?"

"How do Sages know half the things we do?" she asked. "Who knows? Just go with it." Lucy's eyes were moving rapidly from side to side.

She finally looked over at me. "You'll develop this ability too. We all have it. For most of us, it developed slowly over decades. For you, probably next week."

We came to another intersection. Without hesitation, she turned right. This put us on a long straightaway, heading right into the sticks. Josiah's pickup truck came into view about a half mile in front of us and quickly disappeared around a curve. Lucy decelerated.

"Lying back for cover?" I asked.

"He's slowing down," she said, even though the pickup was nowhere to be seen. "I think he's about to turn off." He came into view about twenty seconds later and, sure enough, made a right turn into what looked like an empty field. Lucy stepped on the gas as we neared the turnoff, which was just an old dirt path cutting through the tall grass.

She pointed ahead. "He's up there."

I watched the pickup truck come to a stop in the distance. We approached an abandoned, run-down barn just off the right side of the path. The backside of the old wooden structure was gone, but it was exactly what we needed. Lucy eased the Civic inside what was left of the barn. It was the perfect hiding spot.

We jumped out of the car and crept along the path, low to the ground. Luckily, the grass and weeds stood chest high, providing decent cover. We'd made it to within a few hundred yards of Josiah's truck when we heard something coming up the path. As I crouched down in the brush, a fresh wave of nausea hit like sledgehammer to my stomach. I did my best to hold back the sickness. Judging by the look on Lucy's face, I could see she was nauseous too.

A black pickup truck was heading toward us. It slowed to a crawl within a few feet of our hiding spot. Then it stopped. I was sure we'd been spotted. The burning in my stomach was almost unbearable. But then the truck continued on down the path, leaving clouds of dust behind it. The sickness lessened.

We snuck behind one of the few trees in the area, about two hundred yards from Josiah's vehicle. We had a pretty good view of Josiah sitting on what appeared to be a gravestone. The black pickup rolled to a stop, and the driver's side door opened. Josiah stood. Through the monocular, I could see my old mentor shifting his weight from side to side, looking downright uncomfortable. I had a clear view of the stranger's profile from my vantage point. He was tall and extremely thin, his black hair pulled into a ponytail. The two talked for a minute and then appeared to hand something to each other. The stranger turned back toward his truck.

Lucy reached for the monocular. "Let me have a turn."

I passed her the monocular, and she looked through it and gasped.

"What is it?" I asked.

"I don't believe it. It's him. He's still alive."

"Who?" I asked, reaching for the monocular. Lucy wasn't giving it up, though.

"Absolon, a legendary Goth," she answered. "He was killed off over a century ago by Josiah. Or so we were told."

Lucy handed me the monocular. I peered through the lens, and my heart rate tripled the second I saw his face. This Absolon looked exactly like the shady character I had seen standing on the corner of Main Street just minutes before I was nearly decapitated. The only thing missing was the sunglasses.

"He's leaving now," she whispered. We waited as the black pickup made its way down the dirt path again. I focused the monocular on Josiah. He was seated on the gravestone again, a hand over his mouth. He stood, and then he bent over and placed both hands on his knees. Eventually, he hobbled over to a large maple tree on the cemetery's perimeter. Bracing himself against the trunk, he heaved on the grass.

I looked away in disgust. "Why do you think they chose to meet in a graveyard?" I asked.

"It's a place of death. Something they're both intimately familiar with." Lucy grimaced. "Besides, this place is well off the beaten path, and the likelihood of running into anyone here is slim to none. I'll bet this place hasn't been visited in half a century."

Josiah trudged back toward the pickup truck. We crouched down again as he drove past. He made a left turn onto the main road.

"Let's go," Lucy whispered.

We raced toward the decrepit old barn and hopped into the Civic. Lucy took the wheel and threw the car into reverse, only she was a little too heavy on the pedal. The car slammed into the back corner post, and the structure shifted.

"Hit the gas! Forward," I shouted.

Lucy floored it, and not a minute too soon. We'd just cleared the roofline when the entire structure came crashing down behind us. Lucy took a sharp U-turn on two wheels, and we were back on the dirt path again. The Civic rocketed forward, spewing dirt and leaving dust clouds behind us. We came to a fast stop where the path met the main road and searched for any sign of Josiah.

Nothing.

Lucy hit the pedal again, and we lurched forward. After about a mile, she took a sharp left onto a side road we'd passed on the way up.

"We didn't take this road coming up, you know," I reminded her.

She shot me a sideward glance. "You didn't think we were going to follow the same path home, did you?"

"I figured we're not really familiar with—"

"I've got it covered, Daniel," she snapped. "Just because I'm a girl doesn't mean I can't find my way home."

"I'm not saying that. I just can't figure out how the hell we're going to make it back home if neither of us knows these back roads."

Lucy softened her tone. "Sorry, I shouldn't get so defensive. But you have to trust that I know what I'm doing. Besides, we can't very well follow the path we took here. I'm sure that's exactly what Josiah is doing. We need to beat him home, and the only way we're going to do that is to go faster and cut the distance."

We took another sharp turn that put us on a long straightaway. I peeked at the speedometer. Lucy was going close to one hundred miles per hour. Before I realized it, we were back on Reservoir

Road heading up the hill toward Josiah's long driveway. To our relief, Josiah hadn't made it home yet. He probably hadn't felt the need to break the North American land speed record as Lucy had.

She parked the car in its regular spot, and we jumped out. Two minutes later, I heard the truck's wheels crunching on the driveway.

I watched him head straight into the house. We'd actually made it back in one piece *and* didn't get spotted. At least, I didn't think we'd been spotted. You never knew with Josiah. The real question was what to do now.

"You know we have to tell Atum," Lucy said, examining my face as if looking for a reaction.

"Not yet. I have some unfinished business with Josiah. Let me talk to him first. Then we can see about talking to Atum."

Lucy glared at me. "Please tell me you're joking. You cannot seriously be thinking of telling him what we just saw."

"No, no, no," I corrected. "I just need to feel him out about something that's been bothering me. I want to get his perspective."

"I'm your mentor now, Daniel. You should feel *me* out."

There was no holding back the smirk on my face from that comment.

Lucy's expression remained serious.

"You know what I mean." She crossed her arms and stared at me like she was expecting something. Her mouth turned slightly down, a sure sign her feelings were hurt, but I still didn't feel comfortable telling her about my experience on Main Street. I knew how she jumped to conclusions when it came to Josiah, and I didn't want to add any more fuel to the fire. Given what I now knew about Absolon, I wanted to see where Josiah stood with all of this. I still wasn't willing to write him off as some secret accomplice to evil. There had to be an explanation.

Lucy looked down at the floor. "I can't believe it," she said. "I can't believe you want to speak to that man after what we just saw. Daniel, the man is a traitor to our kind. He's in league with the Goths. Why, in God's name, would you consider anything other than turning him in and letting Atum sort out his punishment?"

"We don't know he's a traitor yet. There might be more to this than we understand," I said.

"What more is there to understand?" She threw her hands up in frustration. "You saw it as well as I did."

"Saw what? What, exactly, did we see? Two guys exchanging something in a cemetery. We don't know what that was all about. Look, I hear what you're saying. I know Josiah has his issues. But a traitor? I'm not sure I'm ready to make that leap."

Lucy gazed off into the distance. Finally, she let out a long sigh and gently stroked my face. "Daniel, you know I love you, so please don't take this the wrong way. I have to make this call. I don't like to pull rank, but I have a duty to fulfill, and so do you. We *will* report this to Atum. It's the right thing to do."

I cringed. The consequences would be huge. My friendship with Josiah would be over, but that was the least of my problems. What would become of him? How would Atum deal with treason… if that's what this really was? I couldn't change what had happened, but I needed to talk to him. I felt compelled to tell him about my previous life in Egypt with Lucy. If only he understood our history together, he might be able to view our current relationship in a different light. I also needed to feel him out about what had happened on Main Street. If nothing else, I wanted to look into his eyes and see the truth—or the lies— written on his face.

I placed my hand over Lucy's. "Look, I understand it's the right thing to do, and I won't try to stop you. I just have two things to ask. First, give Atum only the facts, no opinions. Second, let me talk to Josiah about our past life together. I swear I won't say a word about what we saw today in the cemetery. You'll just have to trust me."

Lucy closed her eyes, tilted her head back, and sighed. I knew she wanted to get this over with, and I was only delaying things. She paused for a few seconds and then sat in the rocking chair.

"You know I trust you, Daniel, but this needs to be done soon, and I mean very soon. You do what you need to do. In the morning, I'm calling Atum."

"Fair enough," I said.

Lucy stood and started to walk away, but then she stopped in front of me. She touched my cheek, and I wrapped my arms around her. I knew she was scared.

She wasn't the only one.

CHAPTER 36

This latest turn of events left both of us exhausted, emotionally and physically. After a light dinner, Lucy went straight to bed, but I had too much on my mind to even attempt to sleep. I sat on the couch and went over what I needed to say to Josiah. I wanted to help my friend before Lucy pulled the rug out from under him. I couldn't blame her. He knew interacting with Goths was forbidden. Still, I refused to believe that he could have had anything to do with Asha's death. He may have been dark and secretive, but he'd never kill his own family. He'd fought for millennia to keep us safe. Why turn on us now? The stress from this whole situation made me sick. Literally.

I headed out into the kitchen. A glass of milk usually worked to soothe my stomach. I'd pulled the milk out of the fridge and was going to grab a glass from the cupboard when I noticed a dim light still flickering in Josiah's window. Good. I needed to get this business with Josiah over and done with so I could set my mind at ease. I left a note on the kitchen table for Lucy. I didn't want her waking and thinking I'd been abducted.

The air was frigid as I strode across the lawn, hands in pockets, breath trailing off behind me. I hopped up on Josiah's porch and rapped on the door, expecting Randall's bark.

Silence.

I knocked a little louder.

Not a sound.

It felt strange snooping around on his porch in the middle of the night, but I knew he was up, and I didn't want to put this off any longer. I tested the doorknob and found it unlocked, just like the last time.

I peered inside and spotted where the light was coming from. A few dying embers in the fireplace radiated a soft glow in an otherwise dark room. Josiah sat motionless in front of the fire, while Randall sprawled in his usual position on the floor. The scene was eerily familiar.

Bad timing. I started backing out of the room when I noticed Josiah wasn't sitting in his typical upright, cross-legged position. He was leaning back against the couch. It also seemed strange that the fire was out. He'd told me on more than one occasion that he always began his viewing sessions with a full stack of logs and a blazing fire. How long could he possibly have been in this trance? I moved in for a closer look.

Grace and agility have never been my strong points. I was reminded of this as I slammed my foot into the side table near the front door. It slid against the wooden floor with an obnoxious squeal.

No one budged.

I moved around to face him. Something seemed off. His eyes were wide open, but he wasn't vibrating like the last time. I mustered up the courage to touch his hand.

Ice-cold.

Randall was perfectly still on the floor, and it didn't even look like he was breathing. I bent down to figure out why. His head was twisted in an unnatural position, and his tongue was hanging out.

"Okay, okay. Get it together. Think. Think." I closed my eyes, hoping for a flash of insight to set me on the right course, to tell me what to do. No such brilliance appeared.

I turned back to Josiah. Maybe I was overreacting. Maybe he was in a really deep trance. There wasn't a drop of blood on him, and there was no sign of a struggle. I put my finger to his neck, hoping for a pulse. Nothing. It was as if a black cloud had passed through the room, killing everything in its path, leaving no trace behind. It didn't make sense. Then I remembered Asha's neck had been broken. I tilted his head back for a closer look. Nothing unusual. Then again, I wasn't really sure what to look for in the first place.

I stepped back to gather my thoughts. How could this have happened? I clenched my hands into tight fists, tightening and releasing them. My breathing accelerated into quick, shallow breaths. I paced the floor, waiting for someone or something to come in and make this all go away. Ever since we met, Josiah had been a guiding force in my life. No matter what his faults were, I always knew he had my back. Now that safety net was gone forever. My friend was gone. The tears started to flow as this new, shocking reality set in. I wondered how Lucy would react when she found out.

Lucy! I'd left her alone in the cabin. I had to get over there and check on her.

A dull thud echoed off the porch, altering my plans. I wasn't alone. I grabbed one of the swords mounted above the fireplace. Slow, calculating footsteps tapped quietly against the wooden floorboards of the porch outside. I rushed over and positioned myself behind the door. The footsteps stopped. Silence.

My sweaty palms gripped and regripped the sword handle. If the killer wanted to play games, I'd play right along with him. Being in a waiting position behind the door gave me a definite advantage. I held my breath. The door opened an inch. Then two. Then it stopped. A few seconds of silence dragged on like minutes.

The door creaked forward again, and fingertips appeared around its edge. I was ready to swing for the head with everything I had. The fingers slid upward along the door's edge ever so slightly. Another creak, another few inches. Suddenly, the door swung all the way open. I stepped forward, pulling my arms back into striking position.

"Daniel? Are you in here?" Lucy called out, stepping through the doorway.

"Lucy!" I exhaled.

She spun around to face me and let out a scream that could have shattered glass. Stumbling back, she smacked hard into the kitchen table behind her. I flipped on the light switch as fast as I could get to it.

"Oh my God! You scared the hell out of me!" she said, her eyes wide with shock. "What in the world are you doing? Where's Jo—" She stopped midsentence as her eyes settled in on the seated figure across the room. She started toward him.

"I wouldn't go over there if I were you," I warned.

Lucy stopped short of Randall and put her hand over her mouth. "Oh no. Oh God, no, not again." She stepped backward, stumbling into me. "Ahh!" she let out another ear-piercing shriek.

"It's just me." I pulled her into my arms. "Shh… It's okay. We're going to be okay."

Lucy pulled back. "It's not okay, Daniel. We have to get out of here. Now!"

Lucy was right. We weren't safe. It had been stupid of me to come over in the middle of the night, if for no other reason than because I'd left Lucy alone in that cabin.

Josiah's keys and wallet were on the table along with his cell phone and a piece of paper. I picked up the paper and studied it.

"Daniel, didn't you hear what I said? This is no time for snooping around. We have to leave. Now!"

I could hear the desperation in her voice, but I couldn't take my eyes off this paper. Unfamiliar names were scribbled down the left side of the page. I didn't recognize any of them, so I handed the paper to Lucy.

"Can you make any sense of this?" I asked.

Lucy looked at me like she was in complete awe of my stupidity. Grudgingly, she looked down at the paper. A gleam of recognition appeared in her eyes. She read out loud, "Vasily—St. Petersburg; Ozgur—Minsk; Dalibor—Lisbon; Botros—Amsterdam; Kell—Portland." She looked up at me. "I recognize some of these names. These are Goth lieutenants, Mathias's men."

"And the cities?" I asked.

"Their current locations, maybe? I'm not sure." She flipped the paper over and then back again.

"I'll bet anything, this is the piece of paper we saw Absolon pass to Josiah in the graveyard this afternoon," I said. "Or was it the other way around?"

"You had the monocular. You tell me. What did you see?" she asked.

"To me, it looked like Josiah was handing Absolon a wad of cash. Whatever Absolon handed back was hard to see. Something folded."

Lucy ran her finger along the vertical and horizontal creases in the paper. "Something like this?"

"Cash for information. It makes perfect sense," I said.

Lucy wrinkled her brow. I could tell she wasn't ready to let Josiah off the hook so easily. "We don't know that for sure," she reminded me. "Besides, why would Absolon sell out his own people?"

"Atum told me the Goths were notorious for stabbing each other in the back, selling each other out. Who knows? Maybe this Absolon is making a move. If he wanted to take down other Goths, who better to team up with than Josiah? The most feared Goth killer of all."

"I don't know." Lucy placed her hands over her face. "But I do know that we can't stand here pondering all night. We have to get out of here and call Atum."

I looked over at Josiah and Randall, still frozen in place exactly as I'd found them. "We can't just leave them here like this," I said. "We have to notify someone. The police. Someone."

Lucy pulled her cell phone out of her back pocket and called Atum. Her voice trembled as she broke the tragic news. I headed back to Josiah. I needed to see him again before we left, since I knew I'd never lay eyes on him again. If only I'd come over a little earlier in the evening, he might have decided not to meditate, leaving himself so vulnerable. Now I'd never get the chance to set things straight with him... never get the chance to tell him how grateful I was for his guidance and support.

She put the phone to her chest and whispered, "Atum is making flight arrangements for us. We'll drive to Toronto and catch the first flight out to Scotland. He thinks we're in great danger, and he wants us to get in the car immediately—grab a few essentials and go." She returned to the phone and said good-bye to Atum.

"So we're supposed to just leave Josiah here like this?" I asked.

She pointed to Josiah's phone on the table. "Not exactly. Atum suggested dialing 911 on Josiah's phone right before we leave."

It was better than nothing, but it still didn't sit well with me.

We made our way back to the cabin as quickly and quietly as possible. Lucy must have scanned the entire yard fifty times before we were even halfway across the lawn. Once inside, we did a clean sweep, but everything seemed just as we'd left it. We had thrown our bags together and were headed for the door when I noticed Lucy's hand on her stomach. A dull ache worked its way through my gut. Lucy let out a gasp and grabbed my shoulder to brace herself. A searing pain ripped through my abdomen, dropping me to my knees, Lucy along with me.

The pain lessened for a brief moment. "Is this what I think it is?" I asked.

"Goth," she wheezed, trying to catch her breath. "Close. Really close."

I stood and helped Lucy to her feet. We ran to the car and jumped in. I started the engine. But then I remembered what I'd forgotten to do.

"What are you doing?" she yelled. "Floor it!"

"We never made the call. We never called 911. Wait right here." I jumped out of the car.

"Oh my God!" Lucy shouted. "Forget the call, and get back here. Are you out of your mind?"

"I'm not leaving him like that. Not a chance."

"Daniel, wait," she cried. "Daniel!"

I raced back to Josiah's house and dialed 911 from his phone. The dispatcher's voice came through: "911 operator. What's your emergency?"

I placed the phone on the table, as the operator continued chirping, and ran out the door. As I approached the car, I noticed an empty front seat. Lucy! Where was she? I was looking in every direction when something tore through my midsection. My knees buckled, and I fell face-first into the grass. Lifting my head, I searched for Lucy again before another sharp pain sliced through me.

"Grab ahold," a desperate voice whispered.

Looking up, I saw Lucy's outstretched hand and grasped it. She helped me to my feet, and we both stumbled back to the car.

I attempted to climb in, but, instead, projectile vomited all over the back window. Lucy coughed and gagged from the passenger's side.

I'd straightened up to catch a breath of air when I spotted something on the peak of Josiah's garage in the dim light of the moon. A large black crow sat perfectly still, peering down at me. It tilted its head to the side and then flew off. I followed it with my eyes until it disappeared into the darkness of the evening sky.

"Do you want me to drive?" Lucy asked, climbing into her seat.

"No." I jumped in. "I think it's over. Let's get out of here before the next wave hits."

CHAPTER 37

We rolled into Toronto just before six in the morning. The airport was already bustling with people, and I scanned continuously for any suspicious, Goth-looking characters. There were plenty of characters to be found, but judging by my stomach, the place was Goth free.

Halfway through the airline attendant's preflight demonstration, my eyelids started getting heavy. All the pent-up energy from the last several hours seemed to drain from my body at once. I didn't open my eyes again until we hit turbulence on the way into Scotland. The next thing I knew, we were grabbing our luggage and heading into the airport terminal.

Atum's black Cadillac Escalade pulled up, and Argylle jumped out to help us with our bags. Kaiden stayed behind the wheel. It was hard not see them as the Egyptian bodyguards from my past life, but I reminded myself that they had no knowledge of that life and couldn't be held accountable for something that had happened thousands of years ago. Just knowing they were Atum's bodyguards made me feel relaxed, protected. I hadn't experienced that feeling since I last left the safety of the Master Sage's castle.

"No worries, Kaiden. I've got it covered," Argylle shouted sarcastically to his brother in the front seat. "Afeared o' gettin' wet, the little lassie," he grumbled, tossing our bags into the trunk. As usual, I caught about half of what he said.

Argylle opened the back door for Lucy, who climbed in quickly to get out of the downpour. The terminal roof provided us some cover, but the rain was blowing in sideways. It was next to impossible to stay dry. Kaiden jumped out and swung open the front passenger door for me.

"I can sit in the back with Lucy," I said.

"I wouldn't hear o' it. Anyway, Argylle wants to talk to ye."

Now, that was a new one. Argylle was about as talkative as a pissed-off grizzly bear. I hopped into the front seat as we made our way out of the terminal.

Argylle looked me over with his typical menacing glare. After sizing me up for a few long seconds, he set his eyes back on the road. "Atum's afearin' for ye. Both of ye. But ye in particular." He nodded toward me. I nodded back.

"Yer gonna be stayin' close from now on, ye hear?"

"Understood," I said with another nod.

Argylle nodded back and then turned his eyes toward the road again. That was the extent of our heart-to-heart. Still, it was the first time he'd ever put more than two whole sentences together for me since we'd met.

Lucy and Kaiden stayed quiet in the backseat until Kaiden piped up, "Rumor has it the Goths are closin' in on the mainland."

"They'll be in Stonehaven afore ye know it," Argylle said. He glanced over at me. "We'll be ready for 'em, won't we, Daniel?"

I nodded again in agreement.

The trip to Atum's was supposed to be a short ride, but the rain came down so hard we could barely see five feet in front of us. It reminded me of a good old-fashioned northeastern blizzard, minus the snow. Traffic was backed up as we approached Stonehaven, and Kaiden seemed more impatient with each passing second. "Get goin' another way, ye bloody fool," Kaiden barked at his brother from the backseat. "We'll be 'ere all friggin' day."

"Keep a lid on it back there. I'll do the drivin'," Argylle growled back.

I tried my best to keep a straight face. The sound of two brothers jawing back and forth was funny enough as it was. Throw in a couple stone-faced silent types, and it was all I could do not to bust out laughing, even with a case of fried-out nerves.

Traffic was backed up to the point where Argylle was forced to take his brother's advice. He steered off on a side road and headed into a heavily wooded area. The old country road twisted and turned so many times, it felt like an amusement park ride. Argylle navigated the winding road as if he could drive it in his sleep. Soon, we were so far into the sticks, I couldn't see another car or truck anywhere. The continuing silence was downright uncomfortable, and I was beginning to think that the twins had used up their monthly quota of dialogue in the last fifteen minutes.

"It's a pity about yer master. Josiah was a good man," Argylle said, proving me wrong once again.

"The best," Kaiden chimed in. "Still can't believe the bloody Goths got the best o' him."

"He was meditating," I said. "Never saw it coming. They didn't have the balls to attack him head-on."

"Nobody would," Argylle added. "Nobody with any sense about 'em."

Lucy was silent in the back. She rarely had anything good to say about Josiah, but that wasn't what was keeping her so quiet.

After Asha's funeral she'd confided that she didn't care for any of Atum's castle crew. She thought Malcolm was shifty, and the twins just plain gave her the creeps. She'd liked it much better when Atum's crew had consisted of just Andrew, the trusty butler, cook, and personal aide to the Master.

If Kaiden was aware of her attitude toward him, he didn't show it. In fact, he didn't pay one bit of attention to her. Part of it was the chauvinistic attitude the brothers had. Malcolm had it too. They didn't pay much attention to any of the lady Sages. They practically worshipped the male Sages, though, especially Josiah. In Malcolm's eyes, Josiah was one step removed from Atum, which to him was one step removed from God.

"Ye've got to be jokin'. In the name o' Christ," Argylle growled.

"What happened?" I asked. "Is something wrong?"

"We blew out a friggin' tire, that's what's wrong." He slammed his fist into the steering wheel.

"Of all the idiot maneuvers. And in this weather to boot," Kaiden complained from the backseat.

"Shut yer hole, and get yer fat arse out 'ere. Help me change the bloody thing," Argylle shot back as he pulled over to the side of the road. "Daniel, Lucina, ye'll need to get out for a bit. Sorry for the bother."

We stepped out of the vehicle into the pouring rain. Lucy opened an umbrella that was too small to cover more than one person. Argylle crouched beside the front driver's side wheel. All of us but Lucy were soaked to the bone inside of two seconds.

Argylle grasped the crowbar Kaiden had tossed to him and motioned me over. "Daniel, take a look at this. Tell me what ye think."

I ran around the front of the vehicle to meet him on the other side. The rain was coming down in buckets, and I nearly lost my footing on a patch of slick muck. Kaiden stood behind the vehicle next to Lucy like a protective watchdog. Why wasn't he helping his brother with the tire? *He'd be more help than I would.*

I peered over Argylle's shoulder. "Doesn't look flat to me. What's the problem? It's fully inflated."

"Now!" a voice shouted from behind the truck, followed by a high-pitched scream.

A flicker of movement came from my right. I pulled back as the crowbar grazed my right ear, shattering the driver's side window. With a grunt, Argylle attempted to pull the bar back into striking position, but I kicked him square in the groin. Argylle groaned and dropped to the ground.

I turned toward Lucy but felt something clasp my ankle. Argylle had me in his grasp. Lucy fought to break free from Kaiden, but his giant slab of an arm was draped across her neck, and he held a gun to her head. All I heard was her whimpered pleas for mercy.

Argylle soon had a death grip on my other ankle. He pulled me down to the wet grass with one yank and climbed on top of me. Pushing my face into the wet muck, he bore down on my back with the full weight of his massive torso.

Lucy's scream pierced the air, followed by a muffled gunshot. I pulled my face from the muck. "No!" I screamed.

Argylle pulled my head back by the hair. "Say g'bye to yer lady friend."

Kaiden was lying on top of Lucy, but he wasn't moving. A pool of blood advanced from underneath them and flowed out to where grass met pavement.

"Lucy!" I called out.

Lucy clawed at the grass, managing to free herself.

Kaiden rolled toward the gun lying next to him. A massive ring of blood stained his shirt just under the rib cage.

"Kaiden," Argylle shouted. "Yer bleedin'."

The injured twin was clearly in shock but still managed to grasp the gun. In a last-ditch effort, he tossed the weapon to his brother and then fell back motionless.

Lucy rolled into the high grass just as Argylle fired off a round of shots.

I screamed, "Run, Lucy! Run!"

Hot metal pressed against the back of my head as I thrashed wildly, trying to break free. "Get off me. Let me go!"

Argylle pulled my head back again and growled in my ear, "Yer gonna pay for this."

All I could see was a blur of bushes and shrubs through a veil of raindrops. Lucy was lying low and hopefully scampering off to safety. I continued kicking and clawing until Argylle planted his knee into the center of my back, squeezing the air out of me.

The gun pressed harder into the base of my skull as I closed my eyes, conjuring up an image of Lucy in my mind. I wanted my last thoughts to be of her. It was strangely comforting to know that I would exit this world the same way I had before, so many centuries ago. Lucy's beautiful face would be my last conscious image before I returned to the bliss of the eternal light.

"Ye bloody bastard. I should murder ye right now," Argylle roared. "But not yet," I heard him say, before a blunt object crashed into the back of my skull and all went dark.

CHAPTER 38

Pain. Throbbing. Where was I? My head pounded with the agonizing pain of a thousand migraine headaches. Everything looked blurry at first, but I managed to focus in on what looked like a huge wooden door off in the distance. Something about that door looked familiar. Where had I seen it? Wait. Atum's castle. I was in one of the underground chambers of Atum's castle. I'd never been in this room before, but that door looked like another I'd seen during Asha's funeral. I wasn't sure, but I thought I heard voices.

With consciousness came more misery. Each breath broadcast pain across my upper body. Chains shackled my wrists and ankles, making movement of any kind excruciating. Leaning my head back gently against the stone wall, I felt a lump the size of a golf ball, courtesy of my recent pistol-whipping. The pressure of the shackles numbed my hands. I desperately needed to straighten up and get the blood flowing again. Voices outside the door changed my plans midthought. I played possum.

"Hurl it higher. Yer breakin' mah friggin' back," someone complained. If I didn't know any better, I'd swear it was Malcolm.

That couldn't be, though, since he was in Australia watching over Balaam and Darya.

"We're carrying a lassie, for Chrissake. Ye must be gettin' old." There was no mistaking that voice, especially since it was the last sound I had heard before blacking out. I pried open my left eye and spotted Malcolm and Argylle carrying what looked like a coffin through the wooden doorway, heading straight toward me.

Who was this *lassie* they were talking about? What if Argylle *had* caught up with Lucy? Every muscle in my body tensed up at once. If Lucy was in that coffin, I was done. I'd beg them to kill me, since there would be no point in living without her.

"Looks like our lad's still down for th' count," Malcolm said, sounding half-winded.

"He should be down for good by now… and he would be if I had anything to say about it," Argylle said.

"Ye did yer job well, Argylle. But we need our mouse alive if we're goin' to catch th' kitty."

Catch the kitty? Lucy! They were talking about Lucy. She was still alive!

They set down the coffin with a heavy thud and headed back out of the room.

Twenty feet in front of me stood several raised stone platforms, similar to ancient mortuary tables. On one slab, a white sheet was draped over what looked like a hulking body. It didn't take a rocket scientist to realize that was my dear friend Kaiden. The other tables held four coffins. Two were open, but I couldn't see inside. I closed my eyes, trying to hold back tears. Asha's death wasn't an isolated incident. Malcolm and the twins had been going behind Atum's back and were working with the Goths all along. They'd probably been planted by the Goths in the first place. And now our predators had succeeded in hunting down their prey. Unless my instincts were wrong, only a few Sages remained.

Three more empty coffins lay open against the side wall of the basement. I had to believe these were waiting for whoever was still alive. An image of Atum materialized in my mind, and I tried to imagine how someone in such a weakened state could possibly survive this assault. I hated to admit it, but chances were that the father of all Sages was already dead and lying in one of those boxes in front of me. My stomach went sour at the thought of it.

Footsteps echoed through the cellar once again as the predators made their way down the basement steps. Malcolm continued barking orders at Argylle. As usual, I couldn't understand most of it.

"To th' right. Th' right, I said. *Yer* friggin' right, ye bloody moron," Malcolm snapped.

Argylle grunted as they made their way through the narrow door frame. "I know mah bloody right from mah left."

I cracked my eyes open just enough to see what the two of them were up to. I caught a glimpse of them maneuvering another coffin. How many Sages had these traitors murdered?

A cell phone rang. I knew that ring tone. It was my ring tone for Lucy. I watched, painfully, as Argylle pulled my phone from his back pocket.

"Give it "ere," Malcolm ordered. Argylle tossed the phone in the air.

Malcolm answered it with an ugly grin. "Aye, me lady. I'm afeart yer laddie is a bit tied up at the moment." He smirked, looking over at his accomplice. Argylle responded with one of his moronic chuckles. "If ye wish to see 'em alive again, ye better get yer sweet arse over 'ere, and quickly. I'm givin' ye to sunset, little lassie. If yer not 'ere by then, yer little pal 'ere will join the others. Don't let us down now."

He had her right where he wanted her. I knew my Lucy, and there was nothing and no one that could stop her from trying to save me. She was only doing what I'd do if she was the one chained to a wall. I had to warn her. They'd kill her just as sure as they were planning on killing me.

"Lucy, don't do it. It's a trap," I screamed.

Malcolm held the phone up with his finger on the End button, smiling ear to ear. "Good try, laddie, but yer a bit too late." He stuffed the phone into his coat pocket and looked over at Argylle. "Looks like our kitty's comin' home after all."

"What do we do now?" Argylle asked.

Malcolm walked over and propped my head up by the chin. "Ye keep a watch on 'em. I've got a lady Sage to greet." He started walking away, but then he stopped. "And Argylle..." He waved his finger as if to warn him. "Keep yer distance. I don't trust 'em. These Sages kin meddle with yer mind."

Malcolm strutted through the narrow doorway and back up the stairs. Argylle sat with his back planted against the wall, hands folded in front of him. I was struck with an overwhelming sense of déjà vu. Here we were, some three thousand years later, and history was repeating itself.

I continued staring at Argylle in the hope that the living statue would look my way. No go. He seemed content staring off into the distance. Then it dawned on me. Reaching Argylle was my only chance at breaking these chains, and my only shot at getting to Lucy before Malcolm did. The question was how. Argylle didn't trust me; this much I knew. If I could just find a way to lure him, I might be able to penetrate his simple mind.

He'd continue ignoring me if I pleaded with him, so that left me only one option: I'd have to taunt him.

I thought about what to say to cut through the dense fog that clouded his primitive brain. I glanced at the massive slab in front of me. "It's too bad about your brother, there." My voice pierced the silent dungeon like a sharp knife.

Argylle jerked back as if startled out of a trance. I could see he was struggling to resist the temptation to respond. He was following Malcolm's orders like the obedient foot soldier he was.

"What a terrible way to die. Don't you think, Kaiden?" I intentionally mixed up the brothers' names. He wasn't taking the bait. "I mean, Argylle here couldn't have been more than what, twenty-seven, twenty-eight? Too young, far too young." I watched closely for any sign of life. Still, no reaction.

I pressed on. "That must be so hard, losing a brother—a twin brother. Really, I feel bad for you, bro. You must feel lost without him. Must feel like losing your other half."

"That'll be enough out o' ye!" he finally piped up.

A response. This was my chance to tap into his psyche!

"Look, Kaiden, no offense. I just feel bad for you, that's all. I mean, look at the poor bastard over there. He's got to be stiff as a board by now. I just hope they prep him for burial soon. I mean, they can't just leave him there to rot. Can you imagine the smell in another day or so?"

Argylle's clenched teeth revealed tight balls of muscle along the side of his jaw. He was approaching his breaking point.

"Do you think he suffered much before he died?" I continued my impish prodding. "I hear stomach wounds are really painful, unless you die right away, of course. But old Argylle here didn't go that quickly. Looked to me like he suffered a whole lot before—"

"Bastard!" Argylle shouted as he stormed toward me, his eyes lit up like the fires of hell.

"I told ye to shut yer hole!" He backhanded me across the face.

The taste of blood filled my mouth. Argylle pinned me up against the wall, his left forearm over my throat and his right hand on my arm. He peered into my eyes with an intensity that could melt iron. I couldn't breathe. I whipped my head from side to side, trying to draw air into my lungs, but Argylle didn't budge. My vision became cloudy, and I fell still for a brief moment. I did have eye contact, though, and that was a start. I stopped gasping for air and peered directly into those furious orbs with every ounce of mental focus I had. His pupils dilated almost immediately. I was reaching him. I was implanting for the first time.

Argylle was coming under my spell. If I could stay conscious for another thirty seconds, he was mine. Stars appeared in my line of sight as the pressure on my neck continued. If something didn't happen soon, I'd be out cold for sure.

I continued to stare into his eyes, my head about to explode like a water balloon stretched beyond capacity. I imagined his arm lifting up off my throat, directing the thought through his dilated pupils. All that remained in my line of sight were those burning eyes. Time was running out.

Argylle shook his head as he tried to fight off my trance, but his arm came off my throat, allowing my desperate lungs to inflate again. Vision returned, but I had to continue penetrating while we still had physical contact.

"Keep your hand right where it is, and listen closely," I wheezed through bruised vocal chords. "Malcolm will be returning soon with the girl. When he does, he'll ask you to shackle her. Once you've got her secured, he's going to kill you."

His head nodded slowly as he soaked up my warning like a thirsty sponge.

"Argylle, you must deal with Malcolm, or you'll join your brother here before the sun sets tonight."

His pupils began to constrict. My window of opportunity was closing.

"Argylle, you need to release me from these shackles. Argylle, release me from the shackles," I repeated.

"Malcolm has the keys," he said, releasing his grip from my arm. He shook his head as if trying to clear his confused mind.

He scanned the room in every direction, completely disoriented. The scanning stopped when his eyes settled on his brother's body. He marched over and lifted the sheet. Argylle looked down for a few seconds and stepped away, his hand over his mouth. The room fell silent. The only sound was the occasional gurgle as he swallowed back emotion. He returned the sheet to its original position and marched toward his guard post.

I knew my words were firmly implanted in his brain. What I didn't know, was how long the effect would last. He continued walking all the way out the door. Where was he going? Had the spell worn off already, or was he heading out to get the keys? This was definitely not part of the game plan. Now what?

CHAPTER 39

I leaned my head back against the wall. I'd finally learned to implant but, apparently, not well enough. Who knew where Argylle was heading? I would likely die here, chained to a wall in this stinking dungeon. I didn't even want to think about what they'd do to Lucy.

Heavy, plodding footsteps echoed in the stairwell. I looked up to see Argylle, holding a long dagger in one hand and some type of bludgeon in the other, undoubtedly plucked from the walls of the Gathering Room. He hadn't left after all. I'd reached him. Implanting had worked! Now I'd just need to wait for Malcolm's return and pray that my words were still fresh in Argylle's memory.

The wait was like Chinese water torture, and it seemed unending. Argylle set his weapons down and walked to the door, injecting a fresh dose of fear into me. I prayed he was still under my spell. He opened the door and poked his head out. He listened for a few seconds and then closed it and returned to his seat, weapons in hand again. Close call.

The monotony was broken with a loud crash outside. Argylle sprang to life and positioned himself directly behind the door. I'd never imagined it possible, but the man-mountain trembled as if overwhelmed with nervous anticipation. Malcolm barked out a muffled command, and the door swung open. Lucy marched in first, with Malcolm a few steps back. She closed her eyes and leaned back her head when she saw me, as if thanking God I was still alive. My hands tightened into fists, and I yanked at my chains as Argylle moved forward to strike.

"Lucy, look out," I hollered.

Argylle pulled back midswing. He made another attempt at Malcolm, but his cover was blown.

"What the bloody hell are ye doin'?" Malcolm cried out, tackling him to the ground. Lucy dashed over to me, searching for a way to undo my shackles.

Argylle growled and threw Malcolm off with ease. The warring bodyguards wrestled for position while Lucy yanked on the chains. It was pointless. We needed that key.

Malcolm sat atop Argylle, choking him into submission. "Break out of it. Break out of it, man. He's put a spell on ye. Listen to me, ye idiot!" Argylle kicked his legs up, knocking Malcolm off balance. The dagger swung wildly in his free arm, slicing Malcolm's wrist wide open. Blood spewed from his open veins with each accelerated heartbeat. Soon, both men were coated in blood.

"Oh my God." Lucy turned away.

"Don't look," I said. "Go. Run away now, while they're distracted."

She threw her arms around me. "I'll die before I leave you here with those animals."

"Lucy, please," I begged. "Save yourself."

She released her grip and tugged at the shackles again.

Malcolm's cut was severe. He tried to make a dash for the door, but Argylle pulled him back to the floor. Lurching forward with the dagger, he pierced Malcolm just below the knee. Malcolm howled and yanked the dagger from Argylle's hand.

Argylle tried to get up on his feet but slipped in the advancing puddle of blood. Malcolm pounced like a mountain lion, plunging the dagger deep into Argylle's chest.

The wounded twin groaned and then fell back, lifeless.

Malcolm removed the weapon from Argylle's body and moved toward us.

Lucy jumped in front of me.

"He's got a knife," I warned her. "For God's sake, Lucy. Run. Just run."

She stood her ground. "I won't let him hurt you."

Malcolm hobbled across the floor. He held the dagger tightly in his good hand, pressing his forearm against the open, gushing wound. "Yer gonna pay for this, ye bloody warlock," he said with an evil grimace.

His eyes were wide open, but he wobbled more and more with each step. He came to within five feet of us and raised the dagger over his head. His eyes shifted toward the ceiling as his body swayed. The dagger fell from his hand. Malcolm toppled over and hit the floor with a sickening thud.

"The keys," I remembered out loud. "Malcolm has the keys."

Lucy crouched down and searched Malcolm's pockets. After a few seconds of frustration, she hit pay dirt. The chain had about thirty keys on it, and Lucy tried them one after another with no success. Her hands trembled, and she dropped them to the floor.

"Take your time," I said. "Don't panic."

"We're out of time, Daniel. For all we know, there could be Goths swarming the castle. C'mon, one of these damn things has to work. C'mon, please work!" Click. The left shackle popped open.

"Oh, thank God," Lucy said, quickly positioning herself to open the other shackle.

Another click. Freedom at last. After the blood returned to my arms, I wrapped her in a tight embrace. We didn't have time to relax. I picked up the bloody dagger and handed it to Lucy. Then I set my sights on the bludgeon lying next to Argylle's lifeless body.

"And what am I supposed to do with this?" she asked, looking down at the weapon in disgust.

"You're supposed to protect yourself with it." I picked up the bludgeon.

"You think I've never handled a weapon before, don't you?" she asked.

"I just want to make sure we're both armed, that's all. Stay here for a second. I need to check on something."

"Daniel, we really need to—" She stopped when she saw me approach the mortuary tables.

My mind raced as the caskets came into view. Sumati and Aydin lay still before me. I opened another casket to find Nuha. Another held Balaam. Lucy paced the floor, biting her nails.

"Who is it?" Her voice crackled. "Daniel, who?"

I tried to answer, but the words wouldn't come out. I grasped the lid of the last casket with both hands and yanked, but it wouldn't budge. After another good thrust, the lid swung open, and I jolted back in surprise. Darya stared back at me. Her eyes were still open. I slid my hand over her ice-cold forehead and closed her beautiful eyes forever.

My knees buckled. I held on to the edge of the marble table to steady myself. I'd been laughing and dining with these people only days before. Now they were lifeless corpses, empty of the courageous souls that had watched over and guided humanity for centuries.

"Daniel? Sweetheart?" Lucy ran toward me.

"Don't," I warned. "Don't come over here." It was too late. Lucy stood next to me with her hand over her mouth. She broke down into muffled sobs. I threw my arms around her.

"What about Atum?" she gasped. "Daniel, we've got to find him. What if we're too late?"

We probably already were, but I'd never admit that to Lucy. "Let's get out of here."

I started for the door, but Lucy grabbed my arm. She placed her hands on my face and stared through me as only she could. "Whatever happens, know that I love you and will always be with you. Always."

"I'd follow you to hell and back." I kissed her forehead and held her close. "Let's find Atum."

I held Lucy's hand, and we headed up the stairs. All fear was gone now, and I was ready to protect what was left of my family. If they wanted to take us down, they weren't going to have an easy time of it. I wasn't about to go gently into that dark night.

CHAPTER 40

We peered into the candlelit corridor. In the few times I'd visited the castle it had been bustling with people and activity. On this night you could hear your own footsteps.

Lucy pointed toward the upper chambers. We slipped through the dark hallway and up the winding staircase that led to the bedrooms. Squinting through the murky darkness, I noticed a light beaming out from an open door in the center of the hallway. Atum's room was in the center of the hallway. Lucy glanced at me out of the corner of her eye, and I knew exactly what she was thinking. What if this really was Atum's room and they'd already gotten to him?

We approached slowly. The occasional flicker of light suggested movement inside. For all we knew, we might be walking into a death trap.

"Enter as you will," a weak, raspy voice called out.

We entered to find the father of all Sages lying in his bed with the covers pulled to his chest. Andrew, his trusted caretaker, was at his side. Relieved as I was to see him alive, if it hadn't been for the familiar hazel glow still burning dimly in his eyes, I would have barely recognized him. His temples were so sunken into his face that he looked skeletal. His skin, mottled with age spots, appeared as brittle as a dried leaf. He'd aged a thousand years since I last saw him.

Atum focused his tired eyes on the blood-stained weapons hanging at our sides. "Those will hardly be necessary," he wheezed, struggling to sit upright. Andrew helped him maneuver into position. "The fact that you're standing here tells me that Malcolm and the twins have failed. You have every right to pursue this to its rightful end." He motioned for Andrew to leave. Andrew refused at first, but one hypnotic glance from the Master and the caretaker was on his way out the door without a peep.

"Rightful end?" I repeated, glancing over at Lucy. She held her hand to her mouth. "What do you—"

"Why?" Lucy said, tightening her grip in mine.

Atum sighed. "I asked myself that same question around the time of Daniel's revelation. I never wanted it to come to this, but I didn't have much choice."

"I don't understand," Lucy said. "Why would you kill your own kind? Your own children? After all the love and nurturing over the years? It doesn't make sense."

Atum strained to position himself higher in the bed but fell back on his pillow. "This has been the most difficult, painful ordeal I've ever been through. It's torn me apart."

His words did little to numb the sting of this betrayal. "You feel torn up, do you?" I asked through a quivering voice. "My heart goes out to you." I tightened my grip on the bludgeon. "What could possibly motivate you to betray the only people who ever truly loved you?"

Atum looked out the bedroom window. Tears hovered in his eyes. "Nothing in this world could ever motivate me to bring harm unto my own." He sighed. "But you must understand, this was not motivated by anything of this world." He struggled to catch his breath. "This action was set in motion by a higher source. There is much I haven't told you, my children." He covered his mouth as a fit of violent coughing overtook him.

"We're not your children," I said through clenched teeth. "Not anymore. You need to answer for what you've done, Atum."

"That I must." He focused his still powerful eyes on me. "You're everything they said you'd be and more."

I reminded myself not to look directly into his eyes. Who knew if this master deceiver had any other tricks up his sleeve—even in this weakened state?

"I've nothing left to lose now. My plan has failed, and my journey in this body is nearing its end. I suppose you have a right to know what led us down this unfortunate path."

"Go on," I said.

He closed his eyes and became still. "Around the time of your revelation, I was called back to the spirit world. There, the Council revealed to me the final details of the mission." His face reddened as another round of hacking started up. Lucy let go of my hand and moved to the Master's side, comforting him as he struggled for air. I didn't budge.

"Whose mission, Master?" she asked.

"*The* mission." He pointed his finger at me. "It is good for you... both of you... to hear this. The Chronicles will need to be updated, and you will be the ones to write the next chapters. You need to understand everything that's been revealed." He struggled again for air. "You see, our mission has always been protective oversight and development. What the Elders revealed to me just prior your revelation, Daniel, was the final phase of this mission."

He wheezed and coughed. Then he cleared his throat. "It was foretold that upon completion of our lineage, a series of events would begin to unfold, setting the stage for the great confrontation. The warning signs will be clear. Natural disasters will strike with increasing intensity. Wars will rage as famine, pestilence, and death spread across our weary planet like wildfire. Financial systems will crumble. World powers will draw back into the isolationist platforms of the past." He paused, wheezing for air again. "These events have already been set in motion. They're mere birthing pains—confirmations of the *second birth*."

"You mean the second coming?" I asked.

Atum shook his head again. "No, my child, quite the opposite, I'm afraid. Lucifer has spawned again. His second-born walks among us this very day."

"*Second*-born?" Lucy repeated.

Atum nodded. "The world has barely recovered from the wrath of his first progeny." He set his eyes on Lucy. "I'm sure you remember, my dear, the wake of destruction. The Holocaust and all its horrors were his legacy." He paused, wheezing for air. "But a shadow of what is to come."

I was beginning to wonder if the old man's body wasn't the only thing failing him. "The Holocaust?" I asked. "Are you trying to tell me that Adolf Hitler was the son of Satan?"

"Something like that," he said, straining again to reposition himself. "Revelation 19:19 spelled out the coming of *the first beast,* only I failed to recognize it. The seven-headed creature was simply a metaphor for the rise of the Third Reich and the Nazi elite. Adolf was the heart and soul of the beast, but the officers of his inner circle completed the monstrosity. As it was written, the beast was duly defeated, but not before taking millions of innocent human lives down with it. The Good Book also prophesied the coming of a *second beast*—a demon far more powerful than its predecessor. As the Elders have warned, he walks among us today, already recruiting and building his army of the damned. This will not happen overnight, mind you. It may take decades, centuries even. The beast will take all the time it needs."

"How do you know he's with us now?" I asked, goose bumps forming on my arms.

"His name is Caiphas, and he is young, Daniel, like you." He fixed his stare on me. "His power and influence are already well established amongst the Goths. To them, he is the Prince of Darkness incarnate, and they fear him. Worship him."

"How do we know this?" Lucy piped up. "Has anyone actually seen this Caiphas?"

"Only Josiah. He stumbled upon him while tracking Mathias two years ago, and quite by chance." Atum reached for his tissues again, spewing bloody discharge. Regaining his composure, he continued. "Mathias kneeled before Caiphas. That was our first indication. The Elders have merely—" He gasped again, continuing his struggle for air. Lucy moved to his side and rubbed his back. "Merely confirmed it," he finished.

I felt no pity. I just wanted the truth, and Atum was either spinning a web of lies or revealing one of the most dramatic and horrifying prophecies in the history of the human race.

"How does any of this justify killing off the very people who can fight against this beast?"

Atum turned his head toward me with a look of quiet acceptance. "The death of the Sages was foretold by the Elders as well. In time, all but one will perish. It is not written in the Chronicles, but it is so."

"And you wanted to be the last Sage standing." I sneered, clenching my teeth again in anger.

Atum held his hand up. "You don't understand."

"Oh, I think I understand perfectly. What I don't get is what good it would do you. With so little time left, how could you possibly fight this battle on your own—and in this condition?"

Atum took exception to this. For a brief second, his eyes glimmered again as he propped himself higher in bed. "The Elders revealed to me that the last of our kind will be restored to full youthful vigor, absorbing the strength of all departed Sages. This lone warrior will lead an army of righteous soldiers against Caiphas in the great war of wars." He collapsed back into his pillow, clearly exhausted.

"So the last Sage standing gets a new lease on life. How convenient."

Atum motioned me to his side. I stayed put, still seething as the dying leader continued his pathetic defense. "It's not that simple. Strength alone will not be enough to defeat the Goths and all their minions. The last living Sage must possess great wisdom and experience to achieve victory, and that, my son, is one thing I possess beyond all other Sages." He paused briefly and then lapsed into another fit of coughing that turned his face purple as he gasped for air.

Lucy flashed her eyes and waved me to come over and join her at his side. I tried to rein in my anger, but the pain of betrayal was overwhelming.

"Caiphas will pursue you. Both of you," Atum warned. "He will not stop until he eliminates every last Sage."

"Is that why you had Josiah paying them off?" I asked.

He raised his eyebrows. Then a slight smile emerged. "You understand more than I gave you credit for. Our alliance with Absolon has been in existence for nearly two centuries. In secret, of course. He offered information on the whereabouts of specific

Goths, and Josiah, in turn, helped eliminate some of Absolon's internal enemies. We exploited this to our mutual advantage. It's been a critical leverage point for many years now." Atum pointed his bony finger at me. "Beware of Absolon, though. He's a Goth and cannot be trusted. He will betray you as he surely betrayed Josiah. It's in his nature."

An image of Josiah, dead on the floor, rushed into my consciousness. I willed it away. "You'd know something about that, wouldn't you, Atum?"

"Daniel, that's enough. Let him finish," Lucy pleaded. She returned to my side, grasping my hand in hers.

Atum pointed at us. "I'm not surprised the two of you came together this way. I wonder why Josiah never reported it to me. It's for the best, I suppose. Two will be stronger than one. You'll need all the strength and experience you can summon in order to withstand what lies ahead."

"We'd be that much stronger if our brothers and sisters could stand with us," Lucy said.

Atum looked down at the bedsheets. "I did what I thought was necessary." He wheezed again. "My body pays a heavy price each time another Sage falls. I've gotten progressively weaker over these last few weeks. I knew that today would mark either a new beginning or the end for me." He lapsed into another fit of coughing.

"Communion was *my* mission," I reminded him. "You wrote this yourself in the Chronicles. You had no right to push others aside... to push me aside."

"Rallying the righteous is your mission; this much we knew. What we didn't know was who would lead the righteous in the final battle. Simply too much..." He covered his mouth, trying to hold back the next wave of coughing. "Too much at stake. I couldn't risk dying and leaving this in the hands of a lesser Sage. If Caiphas prevails, this will all have been in vain."

Atum's skin became a sickly shade of pale. "This Caiphas... he must be stopped." The violent cough returned, and Lucy positioned herself on the edge of the bed, supporting his head with her hand. Atum grabbed ahold of her other arm for support. Peering down at the fading Master, my anger evaporated. I never thought I'd see the day when this icon of power would look so feeble, so helpless.

"I never wanted to harm any of you. Please understand this." He squeezed Lucy's hand, gasping for air. His entire body tensed and convulsed. It was only a matter of time now.

"You must hear the rest of the prophecy," he cried out. "You need to know..."

Atum's chest heaved. Stillness followed. He didn't appear to be breathing, but his eyes were focused intently on the ceiling. His mouth hung open, and he started to nod, as if communicating silently with someone or something. His left arm extended outward, as if trying to grab hold of an invisible hand. The corners of his mouth turned up slightly, and his faced relaxed. Finally, he lowered his arm to his side and exhaled one last time.

The father of all Sages was no more.

CHAPTER 41

A full moon lit up the star-filled sky above us. Lucy and I huddled outside the castle's entrance. We'd been betrayed and nearly murdered, yet here we were, exhausted and traumatized, but still breathing.

Our family was gone now, and the fate of the world rested on Lucy and me. Neither of us knew if we had the strength to shoulder that burden. Neither of us knew what this prophecy was that Atum was talking about before he took his last breath. As usual, there were no answers, only more questions.

What needed to be done in the short term was clear enough, though. There were twelve bodies in the castle. Only three were still breathing.

I turned to Lucy. "Now what?"

She stared ahead. "Now we bury the dead."

"Don't you think we should wait until morning?"

She turned and looked at me. "I didn't mean *right* now. Besides, I've already taken care of it."

"Taken care of it?" I asked. "How's that even possible? It's been less than an hour since Atum passed."

"I talked to Andrew. He agreed to stay on for a bit and help us prepare for the funeral."

I stared back, unable to let my guard down. "How do you know he can be trusted? He might have known about the killings all along."

She put her hand on my knee. "He said he knew nothing of the killings, and I believe him. I would have known if he was lying. I looked in his eyes. Besides, Atum never shared secrets with anyone other than Sages."

I raised my eyebrows. "Malcolm and the twins?"

"All right. That was an exception. But trust me, Andrew is innocent."

"If you say so."

Two days later, the time had come to say good-bye to our brothers and sisters. The sun was already fading deep into the western sky as we prepared to lay the last of our family to rest in the Valley of the Righteous. At Lucy's insistence, Malcolm and the twins had been given a proper burial earlier in the day about two hundred yards south of the valley. I ensured they were placed in unmarked graves.

After a small candlelight vigil, Lucy led us in prayer as Andrew and I lowered the fallen Sages, one by one, into the ground. The burials were over, but Lucy and I still had unfinished business. No Sage funeral would be complete without at least attempting ascension.

Andrew excused himself and made his way back up to the castle.

Neither of us knew if contact was even possible with only two Sages present, but we joined hands anyway, forming the ceremonial bonds. After a few minutes of silent meditation, I felt the familiar cold work its way into my hands and wrists. Soon Lucy and I were frozen together, a closed circuit of pulsating spiritual energy. And then we were pulled to the outer realm. Tiny sparkles of energy flashed around us like June bugs, swarming together into a cyclone of moving particles. The whirlwind of energy rotated faster as ten hazy forms appeared in the center. Stillness followed, and the spirits of our departed family came into focus.

The spirits were as recognizable to us as they had been in life. As if on cue, the eleventh spirit materialized. Atum came forward and joined the rest of the family. The anger I'd struggled with at his deathbed was gone. There was no judgment or condemnation, just an overwhelming sense of love and acceptance that washed over everyone like gentle waves on a beach.

Each departed Sage connected with us telepathically, projecting thoughts of love and support. Each interaction was as unique as the Sages themselves, but it was Josiah's spirit that left the strongest impression on me. My former friend and mentor spoke no words, but instead projected images of Lucy and me joined together in a host of different bodies and historical settings. Of all the images, I recognized only Pakhet and Seti, but the point was clear. He concluded by projecting a final image of two Celtic crosses coming together and merging: two souls, one love, forever. At last, closure.

As expected, the final communication came from the Master himself. Atum resembled the strong and vibrant soul I'd come to know and admire. He projected his confidence in our ability to carry out the mission he had once entrusted only to himself. Soon after, he pulled back and faded into the mist with the rest of his family. The vortex of energy spun rapidly again, and then it settled into complete stillness. Lucy and I were back in bodily form, still clutching each other's ice-cold hands.

The sun dipped below the horizon, its pink-orange afterglow suggesting a bright morning to follow. We began our quiet walk back to the ancient castle with heavy hearts. At the top of the hill, I felt an irresistible urge to turn around and drink in one last scenic view before pulling the curtain closed on this eventful day. The Valley of the Righteous lay below us. The last rays of light from the dying day shined brilliantly over the top of the headstones as darkness approached. To the casual observer, this was just another countryside graveyard. The inscriptions on the stones revealed nothing of the impact these souls had had on the course of human history. Each life was an anonymous gift to the human race, and now they rested in a simple stretch of land near the coast of Scotland.

I caressed the worn-out edges of the cross still hanging from my neck, an enduring reminder of my departed friend and mentor. It didn't seem right Josiah wasn't here with the rest of the Sage family. Bringing his body back to this valley would be my first order of business when I returned to the States. Josiah was my link to the past, and his memory would remain alive in my heart forever.

Lucy's grip tightened around my other hand. This living angel had been with me from the very start. Our souls were woven together like threads of a common fabric, several thousand years in the making. Neither of us knew what lay ahead, but whatever the future had in store for us, we knew we'd face it together.

Eleven Sages would be watching over us from now on, but they wouldn't be the only ones. I looked over both shoulders as we continued on our way back to the castle.

Some things never change.

#